## A WAT

He pointed to the ship, ~~...~~ Eerie. A death ship.

We started in. Harry took the lead. Inside was pitch-black. We were making our way deeper and deeper into the wreck. It was claustrophobic. It would be very easy to get disoriented, lost in the maze. The hall seemed to go on forever, the end somewhere in the darkness out of reach of our flashlight beam.

I spent a few minutes measuring the depth and water temperature and took a water sample. We'd been down about thirty minutes, and I'd seen enough. Time to head to the surface. Harry was right behind me with the light when it suddenly went out. I was enveloped in black. It was like being pushed into a coffin. . . .

∾

### Praise for *Swimming With the Dead*

"A likable, exuberant heroine, the fascinating world of scuba diving, and a fast-paced plot make *Swimming With the Dead* the kind of mystery that takes hold of you and doesn't let go until the last paragraph. A terrific debut for Kathy Brandt."
—Margaret Coel, *New York Times* bestselling author of *Killing Raven*

"An impressive debut sure to please the outdoor enthusiasts, *Swimming With the Dead* teems with captivating dive scenes, picture-perfect island settings, and a host of colorful characters. Dive in. The water's great. You won't regret taking the plunge!"
—Christine Goff, author of the Birdwatcher's mysteries

# Kathy Brandt

# Swimming with the Dead

## An Underwater Investigation

A SIGNET BOOK

SIGNET
Published by New American Library, a division of
Penguin Group (USA) Inc., 375 Hudson Street,
New York, New York 10014, U.S.A.
Penguin Books Ltd, 80 Strand,
London WC2R 0RL, England
Penguin Books Australia Ltd, 250 Camberwell Road,
Camberwell, Victoria 3124, Australia
Penguin Books Canada Ltd, 10 Alcorn Avenue,
Toronto, Ontario, Canada M4V 3B2
Penguin Books (N.Z.) Ltd, Cnr Rosedale and Airborne Roads,
Albany, Auckland 1310, New Zealand

Penguin Books Ltd, Registered Offices:
80 Strand, London WC2R 0RL, England

First published by Signet, an imprint of New American Library,
a division of Penguin Group (USA) Inc.

First Printing, October 2003
10  9  8  7  6  5  4  3  2  1

*For Jessi and Matthew,*
*with all my love*

# ACKNOWLEDGMENTS

Thanks to Jack Zaengle, Detective Supervisor, Underwater Criminal Investigations, for sharing his expertise about underwater forensics. To Trevor Aronson and Linda Meininger of Dive Rescue International; Lt. Tim Trujillo, Dive Team Leader, Denver Fire Department, Engine 3 and his crew (Robert O'Neill, Doug White, Josh Schauer); Rick Leivas, Dive Coordinator, Desert Hills Fire Department; and the members of the Mesa, Arizona, Fire Department Dive Team for sharing their knowledge about dive rescue and recovery. Any errors are mine.

Special thanks to my editor, Genny Ostertag, whose perceptive comments made this a better book, and to my agent, Jacky Sach, for making it happen. And thanks to my sisters, Diddy and Saranne, for their faith and enthusiasm.

Most important, my deepest gratitude and love to Ron, my partner in adventure, for his advice and support and for taking this journey with me.

# Prologue

*The British Virgin Islands*

On the last day that he would live, he sat on the bow of the *Lucky Lady*, legs dangling over the side. He'd left the marina early, in light still muted pastel. Now the sky was saturated with intensity. The horizon brilliant with reds, oranges, and yellows spread across the glassy surface up to the water beneath his feet.

He'd had no trouble locating the wreck and tying up to the mooring. After a year exploring the waters of the British Virgins, he knew them like the rooms of his childhood. Now he sat waiting and enjoying the fleeting solitude. The sea was silent except for the gentle splashing of the boat rocking in the water and an occasional bar jack breaking the surface as it darted after its prey.

Finally he rose. He'd waited long enough. He'd left word to meet him out at the site, an old ship resting at the bottom, right below his boat. Though not a reckless man, he was impatient. Ever since he was a kid he'd been a solver of riddles, determined to be the first to arrive at a logical and correct conclusion. He would dive the wreck, find what he came for, and be waiting on deck, prize in hand, when the others finally arrived.

For a moment he hesitated. Realized that if he were really smart, he'd keep his nose out of it. But it was too late now. Besides, he'd never been known to keep his nose out of anything.

He made his way to the back of the boat, where he struggled into his wet suit. He attached his air tank and breathing regulator to his dive vest and turned the valve to check the airflow. Good. His gauge indicated a full tank; 3,200 pounds of pressure.

He scanned the horizon. Still no one in sight. Just miles of dark, empty water. He didn't dive alone if he could help it, but conditions here were not difficult, maximum depth seventy feet, no current.

He knew that swimming into a wreck was dangerous, and that he would need to watch himself, avoid catching a hose and cutting it on jagged metal or getting lost in the maze of passageways. But he had dived the wreck dozens of times, even diving alone when he'd found no partner. He was more than a competent diver; he was an expert, having logged hundreds of hours under the water. He would make his way into the wreck, find what he was looking for, and get out. It would take less than forty-five minutes.

He hauled his equipment to the back of the boat, put on his fins, tank, and mask, took one more look around, and rolled into the water. He adjusted his face mask, pushed the valve that expelled air from his vest, and went under.

This was the world he loved—serene, slow-moving, mysterious. In moments he was surrounded by hundreds of fish, huge schools of cobia, amberjack, and yellow-tailed snapper. They brushed up against his fins and stayed just out of reach of his fingertips. Every once in a while he reached out and touched one. As he swam toward the wreck, they trailed behind, a stream of yellow, silver, and blue.

He could barely make out the shape of the old refrigeration ship in the distance. Visibility was poor after the wind and rain of the night before. As he approached, fear caught in his throat for an instant. Every time he dove a wreck, he sensed death hovering in the cavernous, skeletal remains. The hollow structure, black against the blue sea, lay tilted on its side. The crow's nest pointed an accusing finger out to sea, condemning whatever force destined the ship to this final resting place. Rigging lines, laden with barnacles, hung in eerie drapes from the mast, coming to rest on the sea floor.

The wreck was actually teeming with life, an entire ecosystem that had begun years before with just a few tiny larvae. Coral and sponges had transformed the ugly steel hull into a tapestry of color. Angelfish, sergeant majors, wrasse, and damselfish swam through portholes and around cables and beams.

Off the bow, a school of hammerheads suddenly appeared in the dim light. Their ghostly silhouettes with characteristic snouts seemed one of Mother Nature's bizarre jokes. But these sharks were no joke. He'd seen one consume a huge southern ray using its head as a weapon. The hammerheads were gone before he'd had a chance to react. They never gave him a second look.

He knew there was more to fear above the water than below, but he was nervous as he hovered at the entry to the black void. Then he heard the distant whine of a boat engine. Good, he thought, some of the tension easing, the others had made it and would be waiting when he surfaced.

He swam into the first compartment, a huge area that had been one of the refrigeration holds. It was like swimming into a bottle of indigo ink. He switched on his flashlight, illuminating a tunnel of yellow ahead of him. A turtle scurried across the beam and disappeared. Things moved in the shadows, recoiling, retracting, retreating. A moray eel slithered through the water into a hole. Anemones snapped shut as he brushed against them.

His light found the entryway. He checked his gauge. At seventy feet, he had enough air in his tank for at least another forty minutes. Plenty of time.

He knew the route that would take him to his destination in the deepest recesses of the ship. He'd memorized the maze of companionways, crew's quarters, and compartments from the old diagram. He swam to the opening and shone his light into the passageway. Empty and dark. He could not see to the end, but he knew that it led to another compartment some twenty feet ahead on the left; from there he would make his way farther into the interior of the ship. He knew exactly where to find what he was looking for. Another half hour and he'd be on his way back to the surface.

He was one of those divers who was completely in tune with his surroundings when he dove. He had just made his way into the next compartment when he felt it. Something out of sync. The slightest movement of water, then the flitting of a shape in the shadows. He turned and caught sight of a squirrel fish as it vanished into the gloom. Something had frightened it. He swam back into the passageway and knew immediately that another diver had entered the ship. He recognized the sound—raspy, bubbly breaths bouncing off the steel hull.

Then he saw the diver, coming down the passageway toward him. At first he thought it was someone sent down to help him. By the time he realized his mistake, it was too late.

Before he could get his dive knife from his ankle strap, the diver was on him, wrenching his regulator from his mouth and enveloping him in fish netting. He grabbed for his air supply. Without it, he didn't stand a chance of fighting off his attacker. He twisted, straining to reach the mouthpiece floating just beyond his grasp. Finally he managed to grab it. He had it in his mouth long enough to take one precious breath. Just one.

Then the other diver was back on him, pulling the net tighter, tangling him in a mass of rope. His attacker was strong and fast, even in dive gear. Again the diver ripped the regulator from his mouth.

The more he struggled, the more tangled he became, the netting caught on his tank and wrapped around his fins. He could see the air bubbling out of his regulator above his head, just out of reach. His chest was on fire. His lungs screamed for air. His body starved for oxygen. He was hopelessly trapped.

He could see the other diver, the eyes glinting behind the face mask. He knew who it was. They had actually dived together once, only once. He wasn't surprised as he watched his killer move off into the shadows, waiting for the inevitable.

It wouldn't be much longer. He could feel things

slipping away. His vision blurred, darkened around the edges. He damned himself for being so stupid. He had so much living yet to do. So many more sunrises. He tried to hold on. But reflexes took over. He inhaled, filling his lungs with salt water.

# Chapter 1

I'm Hannah Sampson, Denver Homicide. Once, seems like a lifetime ago, I'd studied women's literature at the University of Chicago. That ended the day I held a six-year-old kid as she bled to death on the sidewalk a block away from campus. After that, a degree in literature seemed a farce. I became a cop and never looked back. But every now and then I regret the fact that my life is not my own. Like now.

I was almost asleep, an orchestra playing behind me. Waves lapped the shore between notes. The distant call of gulls, the occasional song of a whale blended with violins, cellos, and flutes. I was naked under soft flannel, drifting on that warm sea.

I was into the body thing, feeling the hurt-so-good pain that Jenny inflicted with precision. Her steel fingers plied the cabled muscle in my injured shoulder as I lay on the massage table.

I'd been lucky. The bullet that had ripped through my flesh had caused no long-term damage. Except to my ego. Plain stupidity, a failure in judgment, had almost gotten me killed. Thank God Mack had been there to back me up. He'd put a bullet through the guy just as he was taking aim at a spot between my eyes.

"Jesus, Sampson," he'd said, "you oughta know, for chrissake. Never turn your back on an informer who happens to be hooked on heroin." Mack was scared, though. I could see it in his eyes as he held his hand over the hole in my shoulder, trying to stem the blood that was leaking all over my down parka. A piece of goose down was stuck right on the tip of Mack's nose. If it hadn't hurt so much, I would have laughed. The last thing I remembered was reaching up to brush it away.

After three months of Jenny's kneading and stretching, I was almost a hundred percent again. I kept my appointments religiously—every Friday at four o'clock. I threatened death to anyone who interfered. Mack was the only one who knew where I was. Which brings me back to why, at that moment, I regretted the career choice. My cell phone screamed at me.

"This had better be important, Mack!"

"Get up, Sampson. We got trouble at the commissioner's office. Pick you up out front. Two minutes."

"No way! Damn cell phones," I muttered, wrapping the sheets around me. The massage would have to wait.

Mack was sitting in the cruiser at the curb when I emerged, tucking my half-buttoned shirt into my jeans. Boot laces dragged behind me in the snow. He was trying not to laugh.

"You think it's funny?" I asked.

I had tied my dark hair into a haphazard knot and pushed it under my baseball cap. My face was a road map, lined from lying in the face cradle.

My mother says that I'm willowy. That means five-foot-eight, 125 pounds, long legs, no breasts. At thirty-seven, I've learned to live with it. She says I have classic good looks—high cheekbones, straight Roman nose, mysterious brown eyes. I'm not sure about the Roman nose but I like the mysterious eyes part. Nothing like a mother to put the right spin on things. At the moment she'd be calling me anything but classic.

"I thought I looked like hell after a massage," Mack said. "Compared to you I look like Mel Gibson."

"Mack, let me set you straight once and for all. You will never, ever look like Mel Gibson," I said. "So what's the big emergency?"

"Don't know nothin' excepting to get our asses down to the commissioner's office and get 'em there now," he said.

He put the bubble light on the top and screeched around the corner onto Speer Boulevard. By the time we got downtown, the light snow that had been falling all day had turned into a blizzard. Traffic was heavy, people making the weekend escape to the slopes. Tomorrow they'd be skiing on hills drenched with sunlight and deep powder. But they'd be courting frostbite. It hadn't made it above zero for a week. And that was in Denver. The high country would be at least twenty-five below, and with the wind chill, it would probably drop to minus forty.

We skidded to a halt in front of one of the highrises near Capitol Hill. Once the likes of Buffalo Bill Cody and Molly Brown had lived in this area. During the 1860s gold rush, Horace Greeley reported that more pistol fire echoed through the "queen city of the plains" than anywhere else on earth. Now, just down the street, the Denver Art Museum was advertising for an upcoming Matisse exhibit. Some things change. Some don't. There was still plenty of gunplay on the streets of Denver.

"It's cold enough to freeze the balls off a polar bear," Mack complained as he stepped out of the cruiser and pulled on his Rockies jacket. He'd been wearing the same jacket in rain and snow since I'd known him.

I was looking like the Pillsbury Dough Boy, a new down jacket, stocking cap, and mittens. I resisted the temptation to pull my snow pants out of the trunk. I hate being cold.

"Jesus, Sampson, you look like a marshmallow. Come on! We're just going across the street, for chrissake," Mack insisted.

We had just stepped in out of the cold when the coroner's car pulled up in front.

"Bad sign," Mack said.

Up on the third floor, we were intercepted by Tom Kane, the police commissioner's right-hand man. Tom was a dresser, garbed now in a camel-hair coat that was dying to be touched. He was an ambitious guy, scratching his way to the top. I'd actually dated him once for about a month.

He was doing a nervous monologue as he walked us to the office. He stopped short at the door. "I found her," he whispered. "Came back to the office for my notebook. Greta was always the last to leave on Fridays. Everyone else starts the weekend early. Man, I can't believe this. She was supposed to finish compiling some data for me this weekend." I remembered now why I had quit dating Kane.

The office was a mess. Papers carpeted the floor and spilled out of file cabinets. Desks had been ransacked, drawers dumped. Pens, paper clips, and rubber bands were scattered everywhere. In the middle of it all lay Greta, high heels askew. Pink. Pink damned high heels. The last time I'd seen pink, pointy heels they were attached to my niece's Barbie. I'd given my sister hell for reinforcing such stupidity. Admittedly the woman on the floor looked like an aging Barbie. Colored blond hair, strawlike and teased, a pink suit to match the heels. Clearly not an up-and-coming CEO of the female persuasion. No self-respecting woman pushing against the glass ceiling would be caught, even dead, wearing pink. Except maybe Hillary Clinton.

Red stained Greta's blouse. She had been shot once, point-blank in the chest, from five, maybe six feet away. Surprise and confusion marked her face. It looked like she had probably died quickly, but not quickly enough. She lay on her side, her fingers buried in the carpet. The red polished nail on her right index finger had snapped. A splotch of blood pooled at the tip.

We would be questioning Greta's family and coworkers, but it was pretty obvious that she had taken the intruder by surprise. She was positioned just past the doorway to the file room. File folders were strewn around her, and it looked as though she had walked in on the murderer.

I carefully stepped past the body and into the file room. Several cardboard boxes were opened, old photos, books, and papers littering the floor. I bent to examine one of the photographs distorted by the shattered glass in a broken frame. In it, a young man, maybe twenty-three, strikingly handsome and smiling, stood between two other people, arms around one another. I recognized Police Commissioner George Duvall and his wife. They were standing on a dock, rows of boats in the background, tropical flowers bursting from every visible tree and shrub. An idyllic place from the looks of it, surreal behind shards of glass.

"That's Michael." Duvall had come up behind me so quietly I had not heard him. The commissioner was a distinguished man of about sixty-five, gray hair, thinning on top, still attractive. Cops respected him. He was known to be honest. He backed his people and was tough on the bad guys. The man who stood in front of me now hardly looked tough.

"That picture was taken at Christmas," he said. "His mother and I spent the holidays with him in the Caribbean. A week later he was dead."

I didn't ask for details. I'd read about it in the papers. I was uncomfortable with his grief. What the hell could I say? Nothing. I handed him the picture, and we walked back into the front office.

"Commissioner," Mack said, "any ideas about why someone would break into your office or what they might be looking for?"

"No," said Duvall, shaking his head. "There's nothing of value in this particular office. Mostly statistical profiles, demographics about crime patterns."

"Anyone who could profit from these studies?" I asked. "Someone who might want a record erased?"

"Unlikely," he said. "None of this is classified information. Any John Q. Citizen can get access by asking, and it's all backed up on computer these days."

"What about Greta? Any problems there? Jealous

husband or boyfriend? Someone who knew she would be here alone on a Friday evening?" Mack asked.

"Greta? I seriously doubt it," Duvall said. "I'd find it very hard to believe that she and Carl were having any kind of marital problems. She was devoted to her family, baked for her grandkids every week. She was always tempting the office staff with her homemade brownies and peanut butter cookies. It looks like whoever broke in was searching for something. I wonder if they found it."

I was wondering the same thing.

"Would you ask your staff to do an inventory? See what might be missing?" I asked, though it could take weeks to determine whether a file or slip of paper was missing from this mess. Every inch appeared to have been gone through.

"What about all those boxes?" I asked.

"All Michael's belongings. After he died I went down to the islands and packed up his apartment, his research material, some of his personal effects. Gave a lot away. I had the rest shipped here to my office. My wife's just not ready to be confronted with it. She's devastated by his death and she'll be hurt to find that his possessions have been violated. And now Greta," he said, his voice trailing off to a whisper.

By the time Mack and I left, Greta had been taken to the morgue. Only the bloodstained carpet marked her place. The office was covered with fingerprint dust.

We'd talked with the few people who had been in the building between four o'clock and the time Kane returned around six-thirty. No one had heard the shot. The janitor reported seeing a man heading down the stairs in a big hurry around five-thirty. Said he looked like everyone else that worked in the building: suit, tie, briefcase. Tall, in his thirties, dark hair. He hadn't given the man a second look. Figured it was just another guy in a hurry to start his weekend.

"Old bag lady ran right into him when she came out of the women's rest room," he said. "I'd told her more than once that the bathroom was not for her private use. She would curse me up one side and down the other and keep using it. She ran right into that fella. He was sure mad. Both of 'em went out the door at the same time swearing at each other."

I gave him my card and told him to call if he thought of anything else.

Outside, it was cold, dark, and still snowing. "Let's head out," Mack said. "There's nothing else to find here." Everyone else had left. The street was deserted.

"Let's just take a quick look around the street. Maybe that bag lady's still around," I said.

"Jesus, Sampson, you're never ready to call it," Mack complained as he followed me into the alley.

We almost tripped over two guys leaning against the concrete wall, huddled in a blanket that reeked of vomit and alcohol. They were guzzling tequila from a bottle wrapped in a brown paper sack.

They weren't in the mood to talk. Didn't see anything. Didn't hear anything. Sure they knew the bag lady. She'd been hanging around the door at the front of the building panhandling all week. Probably went over to the shelter with this cold. Called herself Josephine.

We offered them a ride to the shelter. No way

they'd go. Just happy to stay where they were sipping the gold nectar. God knows how they'd manage to survive. I hoped they'd find an unlocked window, make their way inside for the night.

We'd have the cops check the shelter for Josephine and keep an eye out on the streets. Maybe she'd seen something. The janitor would be spending his Saturday looking through mug shots for the guy he saw on the stairs. Every one of the fifty-some employees in Duvall's building would be questioned. Someone had to have seen something. Someone always did.

It was almost midnight when Mack dropped me off back at my car at Jenny's office. God, I could use a massage now.

A layer of snow blanketed the streets, muffling sound. A dusty glow encircled streetlights. I loved this time of night after a snow. Tonight, though, the streets felt ghostly, haunted.

Once I would have headed straight to one of the singles bars to shake off the emptiness and numb the anger. Try to fill the hollow spot that Jake had left with alcohol and sex.

It never worked. Sleeping or awake, numbed by gin or a good lay, the vision remained. I saw Jake sinking into the icy water of Marston Reservoir. In dreams I swam after him, reached out, trying to grasp his outstretched hand. He just kept going down, down into the murky depth, then faded into the void.

With time, the vision had blurred. I'd eventually learned to like being alone. I'm one of those people who can be. Sometimes I worry about it—see that I'm isolated. That's when I turn to my dog. She greeted me as I walked in my front door.

"Sweet Sadie," I said, scratching her ears. "Sorry

I'm late." She couldn't decide whether she was more anxious to be petted, fed, or let outside to pee. She opted for a quick pat, then bounded out into the snow.

Sadie is an Irish setter–golden Lab mix, with the temperament of a teddy bear. At three she has finally advanced from the sheer recklessness and irresponsibility of a child to a more subdued adolescent. No longer does she rifle through my bedroom for anything soft and cuddly, strewing pillows across the floor and chewing my slippers to shreds. Now, like any respectable teenager, she sleeps late, lounges on her overstuffed pillow, snacks all day, and generally considers the whole place hers.

I live in a carriage house behind a towering Victorian near the Denver Zoo and the Museum of Natural History. It's a perfect place for Sadie and me, a one-bedroom with a sunny kitchen and living room. The ceilings slant in all directions, somehow still managing to come to a point in the middle. I'd furnished it in overstuffed, used.

I let Sadie in and rummaged through the fridge looking for the leftover lasagna that I'd made the night before. I'm no chef, but I like sitting down to a decent meal after a day of eating on the run at one of Mack's favorite greasy spoons. Even at midnight I needed to sit in front of good food and shift gears. I filled Sadie's dish, poured a glass of cabernet, and thumbed through my mail as I ate.

I found myself thinking about Duvall. The guy seemed kind of distracted, not really in touch with the destruction in his office or the dead woman in the corner. People say there's nothing worse than losing a child. By the looks of Duvall, I'd guess it was true.

But there wasn't anything I could do about his loss. The only thing I could do was track down Greta's killer. It seemed pretty straightforward. I should have known better.

# Chapter 2

❧

Sadie recognized the signs. I'd spent ten minutes layering—snow pants and down jacket over wool sweater and leggings over long underwear, and earmuffs over my baseball cap. I took her leash off a nearby hook, her final clue. She went ballistic. For Sadie, heaven was Saturday morning in the park.

We'd almost made it out the door when the damn phone rang. I considered ignoring it. Probably a phone solicitor. I hate having my privacy invaded by an alien voice telling me I have just won an all-expenses-paid visit to someplace like Aspen or Steamboat Springs. All I'd have to do is take the two-hour tour and have enough money to buy a condo. Didn't they know I lived on a cop's salary? Worse yet, now computers do the talking, so you can't even cuss out a real person. Somehow swearing at a computer doesn't provide the same satisfaction, though I've done it plenty of times.

But it could be the office. Maybe someone had found a motive for Greta's murder.

"Hello." I tried not to sound as irritable as I felt.

"Hannah, it's Tom Kane."

"Tom, hi." Tom Kane calling on Saturday? Worse than a phone solicitor. I was scrambling to come up with an excuse to hang up before he did something stupid like ask me out again. "I was just on my way out."

"Sorry to bother you at home. I'm calling for George Duvall. He's pretty upset about Greta and the break-in yesterday. I suggested he speak with you. Can you come by his house late this afternoon, say around five o'clock? He apologizes for asking but says it's important."

By now sweat was pooling under my arms and dripping down my sides. Sadie was about to have a nervous breakdown.

"Okay, Tom. Where's the house?"

"Three-fourteen Clover. Just go down Colorado and—"

"I know the area," I interrupted, eager to end the conversation and get out into the cold. "I'll be there at five."

Sadie and I spent the morning in the park. The day had turned out as promised—crisp, sunny, and frigid. The snow sparkled like sugar crystals in the light. Sadie darted through the powdery stuff and caught the flimsy snowballs I tossed her.

When we returned, she went directly to her pillow in the sunny spot in the kitchen to lick the ice from between her paws. I hit the shower, then headed to the office, leaving a contented dog chasing imaginary rabbits in her sleep.

I spent the next couple of hours going over the reports of the break-in and Greta's murder. At this point there wasn't much. Fingerprints were still being run through the computer. Greta's autopsy was

scheduled for later in the day. Rodriguez and Brown
were out canvassing the shelters trying to track down
the bag lady and would be trying to locate anyone
who might have been in the building at the time of
the murder.

There had been no forced entry into Duvall's office. The door had been unlocked and the murderer
had simply slipped in. When Greta walked out from
the file room, the intruder had fired. No questions, no
hesitation. This was a cold-blooded, ruthless killer.
There had been no struggle, no attempt to subdue
her. I was sure that Greta had not been the target. The
killer had been after something in the office. When
Greta got in his way, he had eliminated her, removing
an obstacle that kept him from achieving his goal.
This was the worst kind of killer. Those that killed
out of passion or hate always made mistakes. This
killer murdered as a matter of course, as a practical
solution to an annoying problem. As simple as swat-
ting a mosquito that is buzzing around your ear.

By four-thirty I was on my way to the Duvalls'.
They lived in an upscale part of town, a section called
Cherry Creek. The street was lined with brick and
stone mansions, the cheap ones in the $500,000 cate-
gory. Rolling lawns ended at sidewalks canopied
under elm and magnolia trees. Now blanketed with
snow, in the summer this neighborhood would be
bursting with color, lawns finely manicured, gardens
filled with exotic mixes of shrubs and flowers.

I wondered why Duvall wanted to see me. He
couldn't possibly have discovered anything missing
from the disaster in the office. And why call me
rather than report it to the department? I'd thought
about calling Mack but decided to leave him in peace

on his day off. He and Sue were probably out in the middle of a frozen lake with fishing lines dropped in a hole.

The Duvalls' house was one of understated elegance, no colonnades or pillars, just big and well designed, with bay windows and dormers placed to let in light yet preserve privacy. A woman opened the door as I was about to knock. She was elegant, even in jeans and a turtleneck. Her silver hair was worn short and soft around her face, and a touch of color brightened her lips. Her eyes told a different story, though. Same look as Duvall's.

"Hello, you must be Ms. Sampson," she said. "I'm Caroline Duvall."

"Please, call me Hannah," I said, as I walked into a foyer the size of my living room.

"George is in the den. He has a fire going," she said, taking my coat.

I followed her back. The place oozed money, original oils under subtle lights, velvet chairs, and a crystal chandelier. But it felt as comfortable as my own. I knew it had to do with Caroline Duvall. I immediately liked her.

"Ms. Sampson," Duvall said, moving toward me with hand extended. "Thank you for coming. I'm sure that there are other things you'd rather be doing on a Saturday evening."

Right, I thought, like watching an old Bogart movie while devouring pizza. "It's Hannah. And it's not a problem. Tom made it sound kind of urgent."

"I hope I'm not overreacting," he said. "I was awake most of the night thinking about it. When Tom suggested asking for your help, it seemed like the right thing to do. He has a lot of respect for your work. I've been back and forth about it all day, telling myself I'm just reacting to grief. But Caroline agrees that we can't simply let it go.

"I'm sorry, please sit," he said, indicating a leather chair near the fire. This room, like the others, was elegant but lived in. Pictures of children and grandchildren graced the mantel and tables around the room. "Can I offer you a drink? A chardonnay or merlot, perhaps a beer, tea? Caroline and I are having martinis."

"A cup of tea would be great." I was a sucker for a good chardonnay, but I knew I had to return to icy roads.

"I don't know where to begin," he said.

"I take it this has to do with your son?" I said. "Maybe you can start there."

"Yes." He tried to mask the pain that crossed his face. "Michael was the youngest of the three boys. He would have been twenty-seven next month. He was filled with life. We'd worried about him more than the others. He had been so undirected in high school. In college he'd flitted from one thing to the next—music, psychology, anthropology, art, physics. He excelled in everything he tried. But nothing held his interest for long. And he was very busy having a good time, up all night partying."

"Things changed?" I asked.

"Yes," Duvall said. "During his junior year he took a marine biology class, of all things. It was one of those classes that every student wants to take, an off-campus three-week interim course in Jamaica. Fun in the sun for credit was the way Michael looked at it. We weren't about to pay for all the extra expense, so he used his summer earnings to go."

Duvall put another log on the fire, took a sip of his martini, and continued. "Michael came home hooked. It had not been fun in the sun but three intense weeks, up every morning for class at seven o'clock, all afternoon in the water with the professor and his assistant, identifying coral, sponges, fish, and invertebrates, in the lab or studying late into the evening. When he returned home, he became a certified scuba diver and then a master diver and rescue diver."

I knew the routine. I'd had the same training and more. I headed up the police department's scuba team. We were called in to do underwater retrieval and investigation. The calls were sporadic and easily managed along with my duties in Homicide. I'd signed up for the team because it meant a little extra money and because no one else would. After two years, I was promoted to team leader. I was the one who seemed to remain the most stoic under the horrible conditions that were inherent in the job. Really I was just expert at stuffing emotion into the recesses of my skull.

"Michael wanted to spend the rest of his life near the water and in it whenever possible," Duvall said. "He ended up getting a biology degree, with a focus on environmental science. He spent the summers in one internship or another. One year he studied crabs on an atoll out in the middle of the Pacific. Another he studied coral bleaching patterns in the Bahamas."

"What was he doing in the Caribbean?" I asked.

"He was in the British Virgin Islands working on his dissertation, looking at the effects of boating activity on the marine environment. Michael was passionate. He talked to anyone who would listen about the fragile environment in tropical waters and about how devastating an imbalance can be. Human activity has transformed parts of the world's reef into algae-covered rubble. To think that our grandchildren may never be able to experience such wonder."

. I didn't bother to mention to the Duvalls that I had never experienced any of that wonder myself. In fact, no one on the Denver team had ever done a recreational dive. Diving was business. One of my team members had been diving for twenty years and had never dived in the ocean. Diving was about retrieving evidence and solving crimes. We did not encounter beauty in the muck—just death and debris.

"How did Michael die?" I prodded. I really wasn't interested in a bunch of dead coral—just rocks, as far as I could tell. Seemed redundant anyway. I was pretty sure all rocks were dead, even those pet rocks that were such a marketing coup a few decades ago.

"He was diving," Duvall said. "Drowned. They found him in one of the wrecks, leg wedged under a heavy piece of equipment. He couldn't get out, ran out of air. A local fisherman noticed his boat tied to the mooring when he went out in the morning to check his nets. He didn't think anything of it. Michael was always out early and most of the fishermen knew him. But when he headed in that evening the boat was still there. He stopped to check—no one on board. He notified the police. The next morning they went out with divers and found him. They said that Michael should not have been out there by himself."

I could see how hard it was for the Duvalls to think about their son, gasping for air, trapped in a steel tomb, dying so alone and desperate.

"Michael took safety very seriously," Caroline

said, trying to regain her composure. "He used to get angry just talking about some of the divers he'd encountered, out trying to prove how macho they were. They'd talk about shark dives, carry all sorts of gear, pick up conch or starfish and leave them on the deck to die, touch when they just should be looking. They paid little attention to their dive buddy. They'd wander too far away and would never be able to assist another diver in trouble at a hundred feet."

"Michael had enormous respect for the ocean," Duvall said. "He usually dove with James, a local dive-shop operator. If James couldn't go, he would find someone else to fill in. When I went down to take care of his affairs, I spoke with James. He was extremely upset and could not understand why Michael had not been in touch with him. He usually called the night before or stopped by the dive shop."

"Surely there was some sort of investigation," I said.

"The local police asked a few questions," Duvall said, "interviewed some people at the docks, but they were convinced that Michael was just one of those foolish divers. We've been trying to accept that. Maybe Michael couldn't reach James and decided to go it alone this one time. But then this break-in at the office. I was so surprised that someone would go through the office that I didn't think much about it yesterday afternoon. But why would the intruder go though those boxes so thoroughly? They were clearly not part of the office files, but rather personal, postmarked from the islands."

"Maybe they thought they'd find something valuable in them," I said, offering what seemed pretty obvious.

"Well, I went back last night," he said. "It looks like some of Michael's research material is missing. When I'd packed his work, I'd been pretty upset. But I'd put all the research together, thinking I would pass it on to his dissertation adviser. There had been a stack of files. Each was labeled with the name of the site that Michael was surveying. I'm sure that there was one for the *Chikuzen*. It wasn't there last night. I probably would never have noticed that particular file missing except that Michael died at the *Chikuzen*."

"When did the boxes arrive at your office?" I asked.

"Just yesterday morning. I'd been at a meeting. When I returned, Greta said she had signed for them and had them stacked in the file room. They'd been there only a matter of hours."

I could see where all this was going. "You think the reason for the break-in was in those boxes?" I asked. "This all could be simple coincidence."

"Yes, and you could be thinking we are just two grieving parents trying to find some meaning in the meaningless death of our son."

"No, not at all," I lied. "But why are you telling me all of this? You should be reporting it to the police."

"Well, I did call Trujillo," Duvall said, referring to Donald Trujillo, my boss and chief of police. "I told him what I'd discovered and that Tom had suggested calling you. He said that right now the focus of the office break-in needed to stay local. He didn't think he could rationalize sending anyone to the Caribbean, and it would look bad to do so for the police commissioner. Of course he was right. But Caroline and I have to pursue this.

"So here's my proposal. You take a leave from the

police department. Go down to the islands and look into Michael's death. Caroline and I have personal resources. We can cover your expenses and salary. I've never put pressure on anyone in the department because of my position. But this is one time I'm willing to do it, and Trujillo will go along if the department is not directly involved."

"But why me? You could hire a private investigator."

"I've followed your work. I know you are the best diver in the city, and I've heard of your reputation, about how you will stick to a case long after everyone else has called it quits. What do they call you? Dead-End Sam?"

"I don't think it's meant as a compliment," I said.

"I know how it is in the department," Duvall said, "how fellow officers ride each other. I also know that there is a lot of respect behind it. And Tom Kane says you're the best. He's not about to go out on a limb, damage his good standing in my office. He's convinced you can help."

"I don't think I can just drop everything. I'm in the middle of cases."

"What I am asking is, if I can arrange it, would you agree to go? I won't pursue it with Trujillo if you aren't willing."

"Well, this is pretty sudden," I said, trying to think it through. Hmm, zero degrees and a foot of snow in Denver, a sunny eighty degrees in the Caribbean. Might be okay. Besides, I liked the Duvalls. Maybe I could help them finalize their loss by discovering what had happened to Michael, even if it turned out that he really had died in a careless diving accident. And more than likely that's just what had happened.

I mean really, who would want to kill a Ph.D. candidate who was studying slimy sea creatures and pieces of coral? But what the hell.

"Okay," I said. "Talk to Trujillo. If he agrees, I'll go."

# Chapter 3

The first half hour of my Sunday morning started just the way I like them to start—in bed, drinking coffee and reading the paper. Then my boss called.

"Sampson, it's Trujillo. I spoke with George last night. I'm okaying this harebrained scheme only because George is an old friend as well as the best police commissioner we've ever had. Normally I'd trust his judgment, but I think parenthood has colored it in this case. Go down to the islands. See what you can find out. I'm giving you two weeks. Then get back up here to work."

By ten o'clock I was back at Duvall's office. It looked bad. Greta's blood, now dried and blackened, had soaked into the papers that still covered the floor.

The investigation would continue but without me. People would be questioned, fingerprints run.

"I've made your reservations to Tortola. The flight leaves at seven-forty-two tomorrow morning," said Duvall, who had met me at the office.

Things were moving faster than I liked. Before the call from Trujillo, my only plans for the day were to take Sadie for her walk and get to the gym.

"Is there anything else you can tell me about Michael?" I asked. "Anyone have a grudge? Did he use drugs, owe the wrong people money?" Though Michael's death might have been an accident, I was now in murder mode.

"No. Michael was basically a good kid, certainly honest," Duvall responded. "He did experiment with drugs in college. I think it was fairly innocuous, as much as drugs can be. Weekend parties involved alcohol and probably marijuana. But once he started graduate school, he left all that behind. He said he'd done some pretty stupid things and felt lucky that nothing serious had happened. I didn't ask for details, but I think some of his friends had misdemeanor skirmishes with the law, driving under the influence, caught smoking marijuana, that kind of thing.

"Michael was a pretty responsible kid and people liked him," Duvall said. "I suppose he might have alienated some with his adamant defense of environmental issues. But I think most people respected him for it because he was practicing what he preached."

"Girlfriends?" I asked.

"Yes, a local woman, Lydia Stewart. We met her when we were down there in December. Had dinner. She is a native of the BVI, lived there all her life, though she went to college in the States. She works for one of the banks in Roadtown. She is a beautiful woman, black, of mixed Caribbean heritage. They had planned to marry."

The fact that Michael was involved in a relationship with a black woman didn't seem to faze Duvall in the least. I liked this man more every time we talked. No wonder he was so well respected by so many elements of the community.

"Michael was crazy about Lydia and I think she felt the same," Duvall continued. "She helped me go through his effects and I gave her some of his things, photos, a watch, a few mementos that were meaningful to her."

"I'll be talking with her," I said, jotting the information in my notebook. "Who else did he associate with?"

"Well, we didn't know many of his friends in the islands. Of course, his diving buddy, James. Michael interacted with a lot of the locals—fishermen, people in the boating industry. Sailing is big in the islands. Michael also talked about another scientist whom he collaborated with periodically. Works for the Department of Environment and Fisheries. We didn't meet him."

"Anyone else?" I asked.

"We went sailing one day with Michael and Peter O'Brien. He owns SeaSail, one of the big charter boat companies. He and Michael had gotten acquainted when Michael began inquiring about boat use. They spent at least an hour that day arguing about the damage the sailing industry was doing to the environment. Talked about bottom paint, holding tanks, moorings, anchor damage, the tourist economy. I was too busy enjoying the ride to pay much attention. We sailed around Tortola to a little bit of an island named Green Cay, ate on the boat, did some snorkeling, took the dingy to the island and lounged on the beach. It was a simply fantastic day—the last that we spent with Michael. We left the next morning for home."

"What about friends here in the States?" I asked.

"Well, that would mainly be the people at the university. His dissertation adviser, his roommate. I packed Michael's address book in one of those boxes. I'm sure you'll find the numbers."

He left as I started looking through the first box. By the time I reached the bottom of the last, it was getting dark, and I was starving. My right foot was numb from sitting on my heels for the past hour. I was surrounded by the remnants of a lifetime—photo albums, letters from home, correspondence from the university, shell and coral collections, a well-worn Nike cap, books, one called *Anchoring* that was filled with technical diagrams and directions about the skill of "dropping the hook." Christ, a couple hundred pages about putting a piece of iron in the sand. Evidently some kind of art in the sailor's mind. Peter O'Brien's name was scribbled on the first page.

At the bottom of the box, I'd found a copy of *Walden*, its edges bent and frayed. Michael had underlined passages on almost every page, including Thoreau's classic: "I went to the woods because I wished to live deliberately, to front only the essential facts of life, and see if I could not learn what it had to teach, and not, when I came to die, discover that I had not lived."

I'd practically memorized the book when I was twenty. Like Michael, I had been drawn to ideas about living life fully, finding joy in every moment. Somewhere along the line, though, I'd lost site of those goals. Like most, I was caught up in the rat race, my days consumed by the chase.

I'd guess that Michael's journey to the British Virgin Islands was motivated by the same idealism that motivated Thoreau, along with a tremendous respect and love for nature. The story these boxes told was of a sensitive man who knew the value of life and the world around him. It made me angry that Michael would never realize his dreams. What a waste.

I gathered the pile of stuff that I wanted to take with me—a thick collection of Michael's research notes, a draft of his dissertation, the address book, photos, one of Michael with his arm around a beautiful woman I assumed was Lydia. There were several miscellaneous shots—Michael working on a boat engine, folks on sailboats. One old photo didn't seem to fit. It was a black-and-white of three shirtless men around fifty, arms around each other. I'd found it stuck inside a book about scuba diving sites in the islands.

I wondered about that missing file. Had Duvall been mistaken about its being in with the other files? But then why would anyone have bothered to go through the boxes in the first place? I put everything that I wasn't taking with me back in the boxes, turned off the lights, and closed the door.

I'd been so intent on Michael's effects that I hadn't noticed how empty the building was. Now that I had what I'd come for I was anxious to get out of there. The building felt hollow, the hallway cold and deserted. My footsteps echoed off the hard tile floors as I rounded the corner to the elevators. I pressed the down button and waited. That's when I heard it: a door opening back down the hall. Someone coming in to get a head start on Monday's work? Maybe.

I crept quietly back around the corner and down the hallway. Duvall's office door, which I was sure I'd closed just minutes before, was ajar. I imagined every possible scenario, including Greta's killer waiting behind the door, ready to shoot. I stood at the door, heart pounding, gun drawn, listening. I could hear someone moving around in the office. Cleaning staff? Christ, the room was clearly labeled as a crime scene and off-limits. Whoever was inside knew he shouldn't be there. How could anyone have entered without my seeing him? Then I remembered the back stairs.

I opened the door just wide enough to slip inside. No one. The room was dark. I stood, blind, every sense alerted, waiting for my eyes to adjust to the blackness. I could hear a faint rumbling coming from the floor and then warm air started blowing across my face. The furnace in the basement had come on. A scent, something sweet and musky, drifted in the heated air. A familiar smell, but I couldn't place it. Suddenly the furnace quit and I was enveloped in silence.

I heard a noise in the file room, a kind of scraping sound. I moved silently across the soft carpet to the file room door, swallowing fear. I didn't like the situation at all. No Mack to back me up. Neither the time nor the means to radio for help. The back of my neck tingled; the nagging pain returned to my injured shoulder. A reminder—*Watch it, Sampson; this time it could be worse.* I rolled out my shoulder, an attempt to shake off the fear. I grasped the doorknob, cold in my clammy hand, and burst into the room, gun raised.

Inside, standing on a stool, was a man straining to pull a file off of the top shelf. Greta's killer stupid enough to return? I'd met plenty of stupid criminals in my years on the force.

He went flying when I'd rushed into the room. Now he lay sprawled on the floor as the contents of the file rained down around us.

"Holy shit!" he yelled.

Tom Kane. Now I recognized the smell—his aftershave. He looked up from under a blanket of papers, face ashen.

"Hannah, what the hell!" he said, shaken.

"What are you doing here?" I asked.

"I was looking for the demographics that I'd left with Greta. I've got to have that report done for the mayor by tomorrow. I wasn't disturbing anything else," he whined.

"Jeez, Tom, you know better than to disturb a crime scene," I said as we gathered the contents of the file. "Take this stuff and stay out of here until the investigation is complete," I said, handing him the file.

I could feel my heart rate slowing, the pain in my shoulder subsiding, my breath returning to normal. Now I was just pissed. Damn Kane. I should report him.

All the accolades that I'd imagined showered upon me for solving Greta's murder in record time vanished in the stale office air. Tom Kane was a jerk, but he was no killer.

By the time I got home, snow was falling again. Sadie greeted me at the door with her "where have you been all day?" attitude. While she ran in the yard sniffing every scent like it was something important, I headed for my landlords'. They live in the big Victorian in front of my place and were like a second family for Sadie. Scotty, ten, clairvoyant, and hopeful, answered before I could knock. There was nothing he liked better than having a dog to call his own for a week or two.

"Don't worry, Hannah," he said, "I'll give her a snack every day."

Sadie would be spoiled rotten and five pounds heavier when I returned. She'd be in dog paradise. I worried that someday Sadie would abandon me for Scotty and the good life. But she always greeted me when I returned with a kid's Christmas-morning excitement. She knew I needed her.

Sadie's well-being assured, I phoned Michael's former roommate at Berkeley and his adviser, Wayne Grishinski. Neither could tell me much. His roommate described Michael much the way his father had, as did Grishinski—friendly, outgoing, committed to his field.

Though the research was extremely valuable, Grishinski didn't really see it as threatening. "It would have taken a couple of years for Michael's results to be published and several further studies for verification," he said. "Even then, it takes pressure from someone more powerful than a Ph.D. candidate to institute change. Most people see research as purely academic, having no practical application, nothing to do with the real world. If Michael had been truly motivated, he would have had to take his findings to an individual or group with political clout. Though I suppose that he was just the sort to do it, and he did have some valuable connections through his family. All of us at the university are taking his death very hard," he said, voice faltering.

I spent the next hour reading Michael's dissertation. It was dedicated to his parents and Lydia Stewart. There was also a note of thanks to Peter O'Brien "for keeping me honest and reminding me about the big picture." I wondered what he meant.

By the time I turned the last page, I'd learned more than I really wanted to know about the million or so species that exist in the ocean: fish, shrimp, snails, worms, crabs, lobsters, urchins, sea stars, squid, sea plants, hundreds of coral species and sponges, and sea cucumbers, for chrissakes.

Seems like Darwin was impressed, though. He called the pyramids insignificant when compared to these underwater mountains of limestone. I guess it takes a naturalist. I dove to solve crimes, not to analyze the environment or admire my surroundings. Not that there was anything to admire. All I'd ever seen in the water were rusted vehicles, brown trout, and muddy, mucky lake bottoms. The only environmental issue I was concerned with was rotting bodies polluting Colorado lakes and rivers.

When Mack called, I'd been reading about coral colonies.

"Hey, Mack, did you know that coral is really a mix of animal, plant, and mineral? They are these colonies of thousands of tiny animals, coral polyps. They have tentacles that capture unsuspecting critters that float in water. The plant parts are the algae that hide inside the coral doing the photosynthesis thing and passing on sugar and oxygen to the coral. All this activity forms stony skeletons. That's the mineral part. Can you believe anyone would spend so much time studying this stuff?"

"Jeez, Sampson," Mack responded, "You really need to explain it all to me? What I want to know is how the hell you finagled a week in the Caribbean."

"Yeah, well, it wasn't my idea. Forty-eight hours ago I was relaxing on the massage table and planning a quiet weekend."

"Aw, Sampson, I really feel for you. While you're down there stretched out in the warm sand, you can think of me driving around in ice and snow."

"Okay. So what do you think? I guess Trujillo filled you in on the details."

"I don't know," Mack said. "Trujillo's pretty skeptical. But I have a lot of respect for Duvall. I just can't see him being that irrational. Though I guess where a kid is concerned, parents can get irrational."

Mack would know. He and Sue had raised four kids. One was twenty-eight and still living at home. He'd been diagnosed as autistic. They had taken him to every specialist in the West. It had been hard on a cop's salary.

"Anything on the break-in or Greta?"

"Nothing yet. Still have a bunch of people who work in the building to question. Brown and Rodriguez will be over there all day tomorrow. You know the procedure."

Yeah, I knew. There would be hundreds of pieces of information, most of it meaningless. But one small scrap might lead somewhere. It all had to be checked.

"Hey, call me if you need anything," Mack said. "Better yet, send for me. And Sampson, don't get burned."

# Chapter 4

❦

I was somewhere over the Atlantic. Or maybe the black stuff below was the Caribbean. At 35,000 feet an ocean's an ocean. All I could tell was that it was vast, empty, and deep. Boating, much less diving, in such a place seemed foolhardy—a kind of death wish.

Somewhere up ahead, about three hours away according to the voice from the cockpit, lay Puerto Rico. God, three more hours in this hot dog–shaped prison. Then I was scheduled on a puddle jumper to a place called Beef Island. I could just see it: some tiny island with pot roasts strewn under palm trees. So much for island paradises.

Desperate for distraction, I retrieved Michael's guidebook to the British Virgin Islands. The first thing I learned was that anyone who knew anything called them the BVI. According to the welcome letter from the chief minister, the BVI is the yacht-chartering capital of the world. The area is made up of some forty islands, cays, and rocks. They count rocks? Looking at the map, I'd guess that most of the forty were, in fact, rocks. About eight looked like they might classify as islands, and that was pushing it. Names ranged from the mundane to the plain weird— Norman Island, Cooper Island, Virgin Gorda, Big Dog, Cockroach. The largest, Tortola, is maybe eight miles long by four across, practically spitting distance to the other side. It's the seat of government, and most of the 16,000-some inhabitants of the BVI live there.

"Breakfast, ma'am?" I looked up to see the steward hovering with what he was calling "breakfast." He placed a tray containing a dried-out cinnamon roll and a bowl of fruit in front of me. The cantaloupe was crunchy and tasteless, the strawberries mushy. I decided to stick with the coffee.

"Not going to eat that roll?" the man sitting next to me asked. He was with his wife, who clearly planned to consume every morsel of her meal.

"No, please, help yourself."

"Thank you. Can never get enough to eat on an airplane. Meals just aren't what they used to be. Name's Gerald. This here's my wife, Patricia."

The woman next to him leaned over to shake my hand. Shit, I thought. I knew the signs. If I didn't act fast, I'd be doomed to small talk all the way to San Juan. I excused myself and made a quick escape to the bathroom.

As I walked to the back of the aircraft, I was assaulted by a five-year-old who thought I was the perfect candidate for a game of cops-and-robbers. I had just made it out of his grasp when I was tackled by an overstuffed shopping bag jutting out into the aisle. I narrowly avoided falling into the lap of the gentleman in the seat behind.

"Watch what you're doing," the owner of the shopping bag hissed as she pushed papers and files back inside and tried unsuccessfully to cram it under her seat. Like it was my fault.

She was a big woman, way too big to be wearing a god-awful bright green running suit. She looked like a giant lime. She was lucky that I wasn't one to rise to the occasion, exhibiting the airplane version of road rage.

I guess I would put air travel second on the list of things I hate, right after telephones, which have held first place for a while now. I'm a firm believer in the theory that all this high-tech stuff that was supposed to make life more pleasant and provide more leisure has simply made life more stressful. Now we can do everything we used to do in half the time, which gives us a lot more time to do more, faster. That all translates to a reduction in quality and to stress with a capital S, as far as I'm concerned.

My sister's the perfect example. She's got one of those high-powered ovens that will cook a meal in something like thirty minutes. We used to spend Thanksgiving chopping, mixing, playing board games, and savoring the smell of turkey growing stronger and more succulent as the day passed. Last Thanksgiving my sister and the kids spent the day at the mall and rushed home to mix up a box of stuffing and toss everything in the oven a half hour before our designated arrival with the appropriate side dishes. So much for family time and the glow of holiday to-getherness. I guess I shouldn't complain. At least she did most of the cooking.

Like everyone else, I have taken up the lifestyle, joining a bunch of strangers packed inside a tin tube, eating breakfast that came in shrink wrap and breathing recycled air. I splashed water on my face and ran a brush through my hair. I looked like I'd had about four hours of sleep, which is exactly what I'd had. My hair needed cutting and my skin had taken on the pasty glow of winter.

I returned to my seat, relieved to find Patricia asleep, with Gerald, head on her shoulder, mouth open, snoring.

In San Juan I boarded a tiny aircraft that actually had propellers for the forty-minute flight to Beef Island. The captain didn't even bother to close the cockpit door. Just before takeoff he turned around and asked, "Where ya wanna go?"

I wasn't sure whether he was kidding or not, and I had serious doubts about ever seeing my luggage again.

Forty minutes later we began to descend and mounds of deep green appeared. As we got closer, I could see sandy beaches and calm bays with a bunch of poles sticking out of the water. Finally I realized they were sailboats. I figured it was all a setup for those postcards—you know, those idyllic Robinson Crusoe–type places that exist only in the imagination.

We banked and started a steep descent. I didn't see an airport, no runway, no terrain dotted with pot roast, just water. At the last second, land appeared beneath the wheels and we touched down on a gravel strip that ended at the water's edge. A powerful reversal of the engines and we were there, in one piece.

Once inside the airport, two lines were forming, one for "residents and belongers" and one for visitors. Since I was pretty sure I didn't belong, I headed to the other line, where the immigration officer took me through the standard routine and stamped my passport. I grabbed my luggage, which by some amazing stroke of luck had arrived before me.

The terminal was one flat building with three deserted ticket counters, a little snack bar, and a gift shop displaying a rack of dusty postcards and plastic place mats. With a few long strides, I was outside.

The trees were green and bursting with red and yellow flowers—in January. Chickens scattered from beneath my feet and croaked at my audacity. I guess I was invading their space. Across the way a baby chick was trying to keep up with its mother and at the same time avoid being run over by cars whose drivers were unconcerned about the wildlife in the road. The only other building in sight was a shack across the dirt roadway that said "Airport Restaurant." Four or five goats were milling about the structure, keeping the grass short. There are airports and then there are airports.

It was hard to believe I had been fighting the crowds at DIA a few hours ago. The only stressor here was that little chick in the road, and I was pretty sure I was the only one worried about it when a little boy, wiry and barefoot, scooped the chick up and put it in the grassy area with the others.

"Taxi, ma'am?" asked a man in a yellow, green, and red Rasta beret, from which a tangle of matted hair protruded.

He took my bag and I climbed into his beat-up brown station wagon. It reeked of marijuana. I considered finding another cab. Funny, back in college I'd have paid extra for a marijuana-saturated taxi. But it ruins a law officer's image. People tend to question a cop who smells like a character from *Reefer Madness*.

I was about to seek out other transportation when

the driver held out his hand and with the most disarming smile introduced himself, "Name's Robert. Welcome to our beautiful islands! Where ya wantin' ta go?"

Oh, what the hell. "Treasure Chest," I said.

"No problem, mon," he said as he ground into first gear and screeched out of the airport, somehow managing to miss every chicken and goat in his path.

"Next time you comes down, you be coming into our new, modern airport." He pointed to a huge cement structure nearby.

"I kind of like the one you've got," I said.

"Lotsa folks say dat. Called progress, though. You be comin' here ta sail?"

He was surprised to find that I wasn't. According to Robert, I was the only person he'd picked up today who was not getting on a boat. "This be a sailin' paradise," he said. "You be needin' ta try it out while you be here."

"Do you sail?" I asked.

"Sure, I be sailin' since I be walkin'. Gots myself a little boat. Can't afford any of dem big boats. I sails in all da small boat regattas. I wins mosta dem too!"

Robert's long hair hung in tangled ropes over the back of the seat and almost touched my knees.

"Nice hair," I said, hoping to illicit some sort of explanation for why a young male would sport hair no woman could run her fingers through. Hey, cops want to know stuff like that. Could be important.

"Dreadlocks," he said. "I be Rastifarian. You be hearing of dat?"

"Just the name," I said.

"Well, Rastas be worshiping Haile Selassie as da African redeemer. Ya know dat Marley song, 'Africa

Unite'? He be talkin' 'bout dat. Lotsa Rastas smoke the ganja weed, don't eat no animals, got dreads. Dread means God-fearers," he said.

And I'd thought it was just a fashion statement. Instead it was politics, religion, marijuana, and hair all mixed into a life philosophy.

Our conversation turned into a monologue, Robert doing all the talking as he sped up hillsides to incredible vistas of the ocean meeting quiet turquoise harbors and then coasted down into little enclaves of homes, roadside stands, and shops. I was too busy trying to stay upright in the seat to enjoy the views, much less carry on a conversation with Robert. Every time he came up to a slow-moving vehicle or a cluster of livestock, he would honk and swerve around. Whoever was coming the other way had better watch out. Thing was, Robert was just keeping up with everyone else on the road, where the speed limit seemed to be defined as "go as fast as you can without running into anything."

"Too bad you not be sailing," Robert said. "This be perfect sailing weather. Wind been steady all week."

"What about rain?" I wasn't really interested in the wind, for chrissakes.

"No rain for a month," he said. "It be dry. Cisterns almost empty. But no worry. God be providin' when da time comes. No problem."

Robert seemed to be a true advocate of the "nothing to worry about" principle. I guess that accounted for his driving.

"Dis here be da place," he said. The Treasure Chest was unassuming—none of the fountains or canopied doorways that I associated with Caribbean resorts.

"You be needin' a taxi, I be out front here mos' da

time," Robert said. "I'm da best tour guide on da island."

Robert honked and waved as he pulled away. I walked into the lobby, where I was greeted by the clerk, Bernadette, according to the brass name tag that perched above her ample breast. Like the exterior, the reception area was designed for business. No plush lounging areas with deep cushioned couches that were made so you didn't want to get up and couldn't anyway.

There was no one around. I had the feeling that people didn't spend a lot of time lingering in the hotel. Behind Bernadette's head was a board that said "Owners in Port" and then listed a bunch of names: Commodore Riley on *Molly B*, Captain Johnson on *Rainbow Chaser*. She informed me that these were the boat owners who were sailing their boats this month.

"They like to know who's here so they can keep a watch out for each other, sail together, do some racing, share meals," she explained.

"Not many people staying in the hotel?" I asked.

"Oh, sure," she said. "They're around. Most of the folks who stay here are boaters. They come in for a night or two before and after their charters. They stay real busy, though. Don't see too many people lazing around at the pool."

She handed me my key and an old guy with a couple of teeth missing insisted on carrying my bag and showing me the room.

"Lester," he said, offering a leathered hand. "Welcome to our beautiful islands."

We walked through the lobby, which opened to the water on the other side. It was stunning. No wonder no one spent any time sitting around in the lobby. Row upon row of masts swayed in unison, the sun setting behind them. There must have been a hundred boats of all shapes and sizes in this harbor. Soft laughter drifted from a few people lounging on their decks.

Lester hefted my bags down to the end of a cement sidewalk, stopping at the last room on the end, right on the water. He gave me the complete tour of the place, turning on lights, pointing out the coffeemaker, and the extra towels and blankets, a wide, toothless grin filling his face. He seemed almost embarrassed when I tipped him.

"You be needing anything, you just call on old Lester," he said, handing me the key and hobbling back down the sidewalk.

The room was nice—a couple of rooms, actually, one with a tiny kitchen and sitting area, the other with a queen-sized bed and bath. It was definitely island chintz, with terra-cotta floors, rattan chairs, and pictures of fish adorning the walls. Fish? The curtains and bedspread were teal, yellow, and blue, with an occasional parrot perched among green fronds.

A breeze blew in through the sliding glass doors. Not too secure. It would take a toothpick to gain entrance. Doors like these would never have been an option in downtown Denver.

I walked to the ocean's edge, just feet from my door. The water was like glass, reflecting lights from the shore. I tossed a couple stones into the deep. Then I took my shoes off and waded along the shallow, sandy edge, lulled by the peace. I could see how people became addicted to places like this. It was easy to get caught up in the beauty and serenity.

But there was more ebbing beneath the surface. Things hidden, dangerous, unknowable. Out of the corner of my eye I saw something big and dark break the surface, then disappear.

# Chapter 5

❧

Next morning I wandered down to the marina, cup in hand, working on my daily caffeine fix.

Boats with names like *Celebration* and *Sea Wish* lined the docks. The place was a frenzy of activity. Water tanks and gas tanks were being topped off. Supplies were being stowed. Ropes were flying and dockhands were yelling directions in a language that only they understood. Up at the top of one mast, a rigger was trying to untangle a nest of rope. The boat was swaying from side to side, as he dangled from some kind of pulley-type gizmo. I thought he was probably swearing but it was hard to tell.

Ahead, a man wearing a T-shirt that said "Sail fast, live slow" was loading groceries onto his boat. *Blow Me*, Pittsburgh, Pa. was etched on the back of the boat.

I couldn't resist. "That takes balls, I said pointing to the name.

The man laughed. "Morning," he said. "Name's Richard Head. I figured I might as well maintain the theme."

"Dick Head?" I asked.

"Yeah, that's me." He smiled. "Great name for a boat, don't you think?"

"Yeah, it is," I said.

"Hell," he said, "life's too short to take too seriously. The marina wasn't excited about the name, but couldn't pass up a paying customer. When I'm not using her, they put her way over on D dock, where the charterers don't see her. Fine with me. Keeps her out of harm's way, no unskilled helmsman likely to come crashing into her. What boat are you on?"

When I told him I wasn't among the multitudes there to sail, he shook his head. "You can't visit the BVI without sailing. Be a disgrace. You want to take an afternoon sail, you give us a holler. Wife and I are down here on the boat for the winter."

I told him I just might consider it and headed to the lobby. Robert, the Rasta cabbie, was parked out front just where he said he'd be. By ten I was sitting in the office of Tortola police chief, John Dunn, a tall black man with a bit of a belly hanging over his belt. He wore a white shirt and dark tie. His suit jacket hung on a hook behind the door. In spite of the sweat stains expanding under his arms, he somehow managed to look cool and collected. He had that "I'm an official doing official business, so don't expect me to be friendly" kind of attitude that I had also noticed when I went through customs—courteous yet distant.

The office was decorated in drab, chipped linoleum, dirty bare walls, a metal desk, a couple of hard metal chairs. The one he offered me was in a corner next to a huge window, directly in front of a noisy air conditioner that blew cold air onto the back of my neck. It felt good for about two seconds. I figured it was calculated, my chair strategically placed for maximum discomfort. Dunn's chair faced the window with a view of the ocean and framed with a kaleidoscope of blossoms.

Unlike Robert, who had said "no problem, mon" about twenty-two times between the airport and the hotel, I could tell that the man in front of me was going to find a problem. Funny, though—something about him reminded me of Mack.

"As I told you on the phone, Chief Dunn," I said, taking the same businesslike approach, "I am here at the Duvalls' request. They're having a difficult time accepting their son's death, and the recent break-in at Mr. Duvall's office renewed their concern that perhaps Michael Duvall's drowning was not an accident."

I thought that sounded pretty official, but he wasn't buying it and he was really good at the "keep your distance" patter.

"I'm afraid you have wasted a trip down here, Ms. Sampson, though of course you will find our islands beautiful. My staff and I conducted an investigation. In spite of what his parents may think, it is clear that the Duvall boy drowned.

"I've heard it dozens of times before," he continued, folding his hands in front of him on the desk. "Friends and relatives who simply can't believe that their loved one could die on these sun-drenched beaches or in these crystal waters. This is an idyllic place, no doubt, but there are dangers.

"Just last week we recovered a body out at the Indians, a snorkeler who had been thrown into the rocks by the surge while trying to swim between the pinnacles. He was knocked unconscious and drowned. No one could reach him in the churning surge and rocky outcropping. His wife and kids, who snorkeled not fifteen feet away, were smart enough not to try to follow him through. Michael Duvall was just another of the reckless and unlucky."

"His parents can't accept that," I said. "They say he had a lot of respect for the ocean, spent hundreds of hours in and above the water."

"Of course, that's the parents' perception, a son who can do no wrong. I did not know Michael Duvall, but after his death I talked with his friends and associates. He was known to smoke pot, drink a bit too much some weekends, decide to skinny-dip off his neighbor's dock. Like most young men, I believe he could be somewhat impulsive and in fact reckless. Fortunately most come through it unscathed and wiser. He was one of the unlucky ones."

"I'd like to look at the file," I said.

"Look, Ms. Sampson, I'm not too keen on some scuba-diving cop from Denver, who's hardly put her big toe in salt water, coming down here and second-guessing our findings about accidental deaths in paradise."

Clearly Dunn had done his homework about my background.

"I understand. I'd feel the same if you were invading my territory, and you're probably right about Michael Duvall. But I'd like to put it to rest once and for all. I think his parents deserve that. I'll make it quick and I'll stay out of your way. Hey, if you're right, I'll buy you a steak," I said, trying to lighten things up.

"In da islands, mon, you buy Mai Mai and plenty of Heineken," he replied, a quick smile crossing his face. "I'll look forward to the meal. My secretary will get you the files. They cannot be removed from the office."

By the time I got up, my head felt like it was perched on top of a Popsicle stick. I could hardly turn my neck, but damned if I'd let Dunn know. I had the feeling he'd been enjoying my discomfort.

He escorted me to the back office, asked his secretary to get me the Duvall file, wished me luck, and left.

I couldn't place her, but I'd seen Dunn's secretary somewhere before.

"Lorna Simms," she said, extending fat, stubby fingers. "So sorry I was rude—you know, on the plane."

Right, the nasty woman in the lime-colored suit with the shopping bag on the airplane. How could I forget? In spite of the smile, her eyes were wary. I'd guess that life had been hard for Lorna Simms.

"I was visiting my sister. She was real sick. Kind of an emergency trip," she said. "Came back yesterday. I'm afraid I was tired and cranky. A long trip."

"I hope she's okay," I said.

"She's going to be fine," she said without further explanation. "Understand you are looking into that Duvall boy's death. Terrible thing. I feel real sorry for those parents. Guess I can't blame them for doubting things. Hard to accept a boy just dying like that so young. Parents never plan to outlive their kids."

I hadn't mentioned Duvall's parents or an investigation to Lorna, but I had the feeling she didn't miss much of what went on in the office.

"That boy shouldn'ta been out diving by hisself," she said, shaking her head. "Kids that age they think they're gonna live forever."

"Did you know Michael?" I asked.

"Oh, not to speak of, just to say hello in passing. Seemed like a nice enough boy," she said.

She brought the file and ushered me to another office as drab as Dunn's but without the window. This was government frugality at its most efficient.

"How about coffee and a doughnut? Got a whole box. If you and the chief don't eat 'em, I'll have to," she said. Clearly she had been forced to eat her share over the years.

"Just coffee would be great," I said.

She returned moments later with a mug and hovered. I buried my face in paper and she finally got the message.

"Let me know if you need anything," she said as she closed the door.

Christ, the woman made me uncomfortable. I pegged her for the nosy, gossipy type. I figured the whole town would know who I was by nightfall.

There were no real surprises in the police report. The fisherman, on his way out to check his traps, had noticed Michael's boat off an island called Great Camanoe. Didn't think much about it. Most of the fishermen knew Michael and saw him frequently anchored around the islands. But he thought it strange when the boat was still there late in the afternoon. He'd gone alongside and hollered but did not board. Seemingly boarding another's boat is a lot like walking into someone's home uninvited.

He reported it to the local police. Dunn went out and boarded the boat. Everything was in order. A couple of dive tanks, both full. The gas tank was half-full, engine in good working order. The boat was tied to a mooring buoy that had been placed at the site by one of the dive companies.

With darkness coming on, Dunn had left the boat where it was. He spent the next morning checking with folks around the docks and at Michael's apartment to see if for some reason Michael had come to shore with another boater, leaving his boat in open water.

By late that morning, Lydia had called to report him missing. He was supposed to have met her for dinner but never showed up. At first she thought he had probably gotten absorbed in his work and forgotten, but when she had been unable to reach him the next morning, she got worried. He would have called her with all sorts of apologies.

That afternoon Dunn returned to the boat with a couple of divers, Harry Acuff and Edmund Carr, to begin searching. It didn't take Acuff and Carr long to find Michael in the wreck, hopelessly caught under the heavy cooling unit, his tank empty.

The divers said that it looked as though Michael had been exploring the wreck and had dislodged the compressor, which had wedged his entire lower leg against the hull of the ship. His regulator was floating in the water above his head. More than likely, at the end of his air supply and in complete panic, Michael had removed the useless device from his mouth and his last attempt at a breath had been to fill his lungs with water.

He'd probably known that he would die in the steel structure seventy feet under the ocean. I could imagine his terror. I'd been trapped underwater once. It had started as a routine training dive under two feet of ice. We'd cut a hole through the frozen surface with chain saws and axes and I'd dropped in, the goal to find my way to another hole some fifty feet away using a compass. I'd been doing fine until my regulator froze. I panicked and headed straight to the surface, hitting hard, blue ice. Just on the other side was sunlight, blue sky, and life-giving oxygen, completely out of my grasp. I scraped at the undersurface and pushed against the thick mass. It was like trying to push past a concrete wall.

In my panic I'd forgotten I was tethered to the safety line. All I needed to do was follow it back to the hole in the ice where my fellow divers waited. Within seconds I was out, lying on the ice, sputtering, gulping frigid air into starved lungs, and cursing the useless regulator. I won't ever forget seeing that open water rippling above my head or those hands reaching out to me. Michael had not been so fortunate.

The divers brought his body to the surface shortly after they found it. I wondered whether they had followed procedure during the recovery. Probably not. They would not have even thought about the area being a crime scene. Even if they had, few rescue divers anywhere have been trained in underwater investigation. In the past, the focus has been on getting the victim out of the water and collecting evidence from the body on the surface. Only recently have law-enforcement agencies in the States recognized the importance of rigorous underwater crime-scene investigation.

The operating procedures for the Denver dive team called for underwater photos, scene sketches, measurements, compass readings, and a thorough examination of the area before the body was taken to the surface. It also involved careful handling of the body. While still underwater, the hands, feet, and head would be enclosed in plastic bags and the entire body placed in a body bag with mesh panels for water drainage.

My team had been trained in postmortem physiology and the techniques of meticulous observation and documentation of the underwater crime scene. They knew how to examine the victim as well as the area on the bottom for any signs of vomit, and understood the need to check the mouth for any inhaled debris, such as vegetation or silt—all indications that the victim was probably alive and breathing, at least for a while, under the water. They would record body position, injuries, and the degree of rigor mortis. They realized that once the scene was disturbed and the body brought to the surface, significant forensic evidence would be lost, washing away as the water was disturbed or affected by exposure to the air.

I would dive the site of Michael's death, but I didn't expect to find much, given what I assumed to be a haphazard recovery process and the fact that it had been almost a month since the body had been recovered. Any evidence that had existed would probably have been contaminated by the divers, washed away in the current, or eaten.

The autopsy report indicated that there was bruising on Michael's right arm and torso. His leg had a deep gash, but little else could be determined because the area around the wound had been nibbled away by fish, crabs, and other tiny marine creatures attracted to the open flesh. They had also begun to feed on his lips and ears. Though it didn't say, I assumed that his eyes had been protected by his face mask. Next would have been most of the exposed flesh on the face and neck, which had not yet occurred.

In the warmer water of the Caribbean, decomposition occurs more rapidly. The body showed signs of what pathologists call "washerwoman's skin," extreme wrinkling on the palms and soles. The skin was white and soft, taking on a greenish cast in the lower quadrant of the body. In some areas it had begun to loosen and darken, the blood pooling. Rigor mortis had set in.

The coroner estimated that Michael had been dead and in the water about twenty-four hours. Blood tests showed no alcohol or drugs in Michael's system at the time of his death.

The coroner had ruled the cause of death as drowning. He'd found no indication of poison, disease, wound, blow, or other trauma, except for the bruises and the gash on Michael's leg. There was no record that the coroner had examined the lungs beyond the simple observation that salt water had been present. Apparently he had not autopsied the lungs, in which case he might have found signs of drowning, such as tears in the alveoli or small hemorrhages on the surface of the lungs from overdistention.

It seemed clear to me that immediate assumptions had been made about how Michael had died. The coroner's procedures had been perfunctory, simply confirming those assumptions—Michael had pulled down the compressor, gotten trapped in the wreck, and drowned. Without a thorough autopsy it was impossible to know whether that had in fact been the case. The coroner's findings could just as well mean that Michael was dead before he entered the water and that the water in his lungs had seeped in after death.

It was possible that someone had killed him and left his body in the wreck to make it look accidental. If the compressor had been dropped on his leg after death, there would have been a gash but no bleeding or bruising. The damage by sea animals made that impossible to determine. The bruising on the rest of his body may have been caused as the unit had fallen on him or in his struggle to free himself. Then again, maybe they were inflicted by his killer or killers.

I wondered if anyone had checked Michael's diving equipment or his boat. There was no record of it. I made a note to examine both.

Dunn had questioned Lydia, a couple of the dive shop operators, anyone who might have relevant information. I wrote down the names of the two divers, Acuff and Carr. They may have noticed something that they thought unimportant or that never made it into the file. You just never knew. Sometimes the most mundane comment or unlikely piece of information turned out to be the key to an entire case. Sometimes people didn't tell the same story twice.

# Chapter 6

❧

I waved to Lorna on my way out the front door of the police department. She was busy talking on the phone while simultaneously inhaling the last of the doughnuts. I'd arranged to meet Lydia, Michael's fiancée, later in the afternoon. With some time to kill, I decided on a brisk walk along the waterfront and into town. I'd quit running several years ago. The constant pounding had taken its toll on knee and ankle joints, and I just wasn't as compulsive as I once was. Somewhere along the line I'd backed off. Didn't have so much to prove to myself. Didn't need to run fifty miles a week. Turns out I enjoyed walking a whole lot more. I'd actually started to look at the world around me. These days my workouts included three or four days a week at the gym and long walks with Sadie.

Now, though, I could feel the tightness. My joints felt stiff, and my shoulder ached. I needed to get out and walk fast, swing my arms, get some circulation going. I headed down to the water, hoping to find a walkway that would take me along the edge of the ocean. Not to be. Much of the waterfront was fenced off and unreachable. Sporadic stretches of sidewalk were interrupted by restaurants jutting out into the water or by mom-and-pop stores. I found myself taking a zigzag path, diverting down narrow streets, past offices, through the outdoor market. A blue Honda Civic, with a broken headlight, seemed to be following the same aimless route. Every time I zigged, it did too. Some wayward tourist trying to find his way through the same maze.

Finally I grew tired of walking the labyrinth and started back to the hotel. So much for brisk walks, taking in the fresh sea air. Mostly I'd been breathing exhaust. Making my way toward the hotel, I found myself crossing the main street at least a half dozen times in order to avoid deep ditches that cut through my intended path. Every crossing was like a game of chicken. Could I make it to the center then over to the other side faster than the speeding vehicles bearing down upon me, horns blaring?

I stood poised to make the final dash across the street to the quiet of my hotel. About the time I stepped off the curb, I saw it—a blue blur out of the corner of my eye. It was coming right at me, bearing down at about fifty miles per hour. Christ, I didn't know whether to dash back to the curb or try to make a run for the center median. I felt like the proverbial deer caught in the headlights. I froze, trying to decide which way the car was going to go.

As it turned out, it was going whichever way I was going. As I ran back to the curb, the damned thing swerved right at me, jumping the curb inches behind me. I took a flying leap over a row of trash cans lining the sidewalk, caught my toe in one, and ended up on my ass on the cement, covered in pieces of rotting lettuce and carrot. Behind me the car plowed into tin, throwing the rest of the trash all over the street, and sped off. The blue Honda. I watched it disappear around the corner as I stumbled to my feet, picking brown slimy stuff out of my hair.

Rasta Robert had been sitting in his cab in front of the hotel and raced across the street to help. "Crazy drivers," he'd said, pulling me to my feet. "Jus' never watchin', thinkin' anything on da road jus' better be getting' outta da way."

The driver of the Honda had certainly wanted me out of the way—for good.

By the time I arrived at Lydia's, it was late in the afternoon. Robert had insisted on taking me to her small bungalow in the hills above Roadtown. He'd known exactly where she lived. In fact, he knew Lydia.

"Oh, she be one beautiful woman," he'd exclaimed. "Family be livin' on Tortola for many generations. Her father owns half the island, I think! He be very traditional. Not likin' his chilin takin' to outside ways. Especially Lydia gettin' engaged to that American. He be real angry. Wantin' her marrying one of da rich local fellas. Dat Lydia, though, not many around a match for her. She be headstrong, independent. And smart! That girl can do math, I'll tell you."

"How do you know her so well?" I'd asked.

"Oh, folks on da island, we know. Most of us grew up together. Goin to the same market, same churches, same schools, grandparents, great-grandparents, parents, den dere kids and dere kids' kids."

Given Robert's description of Lydia, I was surprised to find myself standing at the door of a traditional Caribbean structure, a peach stucco with white trim typical of the pastels that dotted the hills of Tortola.

The woman who answered was gorgeous. She was small-boned but tall, with finely crafted features and mahogany skin. Her hair was pulled back into a sleek bun. She was dressed in a gray business suit, no shoes.

"Hi. Hannah Sampson here to see Lydia Stewart. I called this morning?"

"Yes, hello, I'm Lydia," she said, extending her hand. "Please, come in."

It had been less than a month since Michael's death. I could see the pain still etched in her face. I wondered how long it would take for the signs to fade.

Her home was a wonderful mix of old and new. The pastels of the exterior were repeated in the artwork inside—Caribbean scenes painted by local artists—the furniture an eclectic mix of comfortable overstuffed chairs, wicker, wood, and steel.

"I'm sorry to bother you," I began. "I know it must be difficult to talk about Michael."

"Actually, it's not," she said. "It's harder not to talk about him, which is the way a lot of my friends and family have reacted. Trying to pretend it never happened, that he never was. That hurts more. Let's talk out on the veranda. There is a cool breeze and a fantastic view of the channel."

*Fantastic* hardly described it. Falling away from the balcony and off down the hill was a splash of colors, the vividness matched only by the fragrance. Barely visible through the trees were red splotches of the tile roofs below and farther out the boats in Road Harbor. In the distance I could see several islands, small green mounds surrounded by deep blue. Sailboats tipped in the wind in the open channel, while others were anchored in glassy harbors.

"That stretch of water is called the Sir Francis Drake Channel," Lydia said. "Drake navigated these waters in the late fifteen hundreds, along with Christopher Columbus. The island directly across is Peter, and the one to the right is Norman. You can make out the Indians just there off Norman, a very popular snorkeling spot, so many fish there, and sometimes a nurse shark happens by. Off to the distant right is St. John, one of the U.S. Virgin Islands.

"They found Michael's boat out that way," she said, pointing to the far left.

"What do you think happened?" I asked.

"That's hard," she said. "Michael's parents probably told you that he didn't dive alone. Usually that was true. He was very safety conscious when it came to diving. But he was a fanatic about his research. He also lived fully and was fearless. It was one of the things I loved about him. He had a 'go for it' mentality that kept things interesting and challenging. I knew life would never be dull with Michael. He talked about going to the Galápagos, trekking around Ecuador, spending a summer volunteering for Habitat for Humanity. I was game for it all."

I could see the regret. She pulled her legs up under her in the patio chair, hugging them to her, trying to find comfort.

"How did you meet Michael?" I asked.

"Actually, I met him because of his research. He needed help crunching numbers. That's my field—statistics. I received my B.S. in math from the University of California and stayed there for graduate work in statistics. I liked being in the States but always intended to return home. Offshore finance is big business here, bigger than tourism. I came back to the islands a couple of years ago and took a job with one of the international companies here in Tortola.

"I'd heard that Michael was looking for a statistician through a mutual friend," she continued. "It sounded like fun, and I missed doing the statistics, so I agreed to help him. I was to be listed as a contributing author on the final publication. No money but lots of glory," she said, smiling.

"You must know a lot about Michael's research."

"Yes. You know I've lived with the ocean outside my door my whole life. I guess I kind of took it for granted. But Michael saw the miracle of it all. I learned so much from him. Like him, I am worried about exploitation and overuse. It's such a delicate and fragile environment. Did you know that two-thirds of the Caribbean reef is in jeopardy due to overfishing and the high levels of nutrients that smother the coral? The nutrients come from sewage."

"What exactly was Michael studying?" I asked.

"He was focused on the effects from boating. As you've probably seen, the BVI is world-renowned for sailing—beautiful anchorages and wonderful snorkeling and diving. As a result, there is a lot of boat traffic in the islands. Unfortunately there are few regulations."

"So what's the problem?" I was having a hard time seeing how any of this would lead to murder. Maybe it wouldn't.

"Well, one is the pollution. Can you imagine the impact of having fifty boats crammed into an anchorage the space of a football field all flushing their sewage into the calm water? By definition, good anchorages are sheltered from the wind, wave action, and currents. That means quiet water that doesn't circulate quickly and sewage that is slow to wash out to deep water. One solution would be to outfit the boats with holding tanks and at least require boaters to empty their tanks out in deep water. That's what occurs in California. In fact, the tanks there contain dye, so if a boater dumps in restricted areas, the coast guard will fine him."

"You said one of the problems Michael studied was pollution. What were the others?"

"He was looking at the effects of boating in general. It had to do with sheer volume. People drop their anchors in coral beds, damaging and eventually killing the coral. Imagine the devastation from the cruise ships and big freighters. In a matter of seconds, their anchors and chains can crush a coral reef that took thousands of years to grow. Add to that the antifouling paint that is used on all of these boats. It is highly toxic. Has to be to keep organisms from growing on the bottom."

Gazing out at a vast ocean that spread to the horizon, I was having trouble believing that a little paint on a boat would have much effect.

"Snorkelers and divers add to the damage," she went on. "Many are novices and have trouble keeping their feet off the bottom or controlling their fins. They end up kicking against the coral and breaking it. Then there are those who feel compelled to touch and to bring underwater creatures home as souvenirs. They see a beautiful conch, take it out of the water, and leave it up on the boat, never considering that an animal might live inside. The conch dries out and dies, produces a horrible smell, and over the side it goes. Many will insist that it's just one little conch or one small piece of damaged coral, but the popular dive and snorkeling sites can see a couple of hundred people a week, maybe more, depending on the season. Michael followed the reports. Just last year the Global Reef Monitoring Network reported that thirty percent of the coral reef worldwide had already been destroyed. They predict that if trends continue, sixty percent will be decimated by 2030."

"I'm convinced." I had to admit I was about as interested in hearing about shit in the water as I was about dead conch. I'd seen conch on someone's plate in the hotel restaurant. It looked like a curled-up piece of old tire.

"Sorry," she said, "I'm afraid Michael's passion was contagious. His research revealed the true extent of the problem in terms of boating and tourism, problems that locals talked about only anecdotally. Like the owner of Underwater Adventures talking about the dead turtle he found off Cistern Point with plastic wrapped around its bill."

"How did Michael gather his data?" I asked.

"He spent most of his day taking water samples, measuring visibility and water temperature, examining and taking photos of coral colonies. He'd record bleaching. That's when the coral gets stressed and expels the algae that give the coral its color. He would compare the data to the data about boat traffic and the use of the land nearby, looking for correlations. Then he would move on to the next area and do the same."

"Do you know why he was diving out at the *Chikuzen*?"

"Michael took water samples and dived at all the dive sites. He had been consumed by the *Chikuzen* site lately because he had discovered some dead fish there. It had been a onetime occurrence and he was trying to figure out what had killed them."

"Why would he have gone out alone?"

"If Michael had wanted to dive the wreck and no one was available to go with him, he wouldn't have waited around. I think it's easier for me to accept Michael's death because it was always a possibility, given the fact that he lived so fully."

"He took risks then?" I asked. Maybe his death was just what the coroner reported—accidental drowning—and my trip down here was a wild-goose chase.

"Yes, in certain situations, he did."

"What do you mean, certain situations?"

"He was completely confident about his diving skills, a fanatic when it came to the environment, and determined when it came to an unanswered question. He'd dive without hesitation if he thought he'd find an answer in the water."

"Can you think of anyone who would want to kill him?"

"I can't imagine who," she said. I thought I saw a flash of doubt cross her face, but she said nothing else.

"Could his research have been a threat?" I asked.

"It could have an impact on the charter industry down here," she said. "Michael would have eventually made a case to the local government and to the tourism board. He thought he could convince them that the damage to the reef and the water pollution would eventually impact tourism. They could force charter companies to address the problem by installing holding tanks on boats and providing pump-out stations. This would be quite costly.

"More costly yet, they could start putting quotas on the number of boats chartered each year, which would have huge financial implications on the larger charter fleets. They can't afford to have boats sitting idle in port."

"When you talk about the charter companies, how many do you mean?" I asked.

"Well, there are three or four large ones, over one hundred boats in each of their fleets, and there are scores of smaller operations scattered around the island. Then there are the companies who run day charters. Approximately four hundred thousand people visit the islands every year to sail, snorkel, and dive."

"Chief Dunn talked about Michael's marijuana and alcohol use." I didn't mention the skinny-dipping. I had been known to engage in that activity myself whenever the opportunity arose, which unfortunately wasn't often. "Could there be some drug connection? Someone he owed money or an unsavory local dealer?"

"No," she said. "Michael's drinking and drug use was minimal, a weekend party, a quiet night sipping wine and smoking on the beach. We both enjoyed it once in a while, always moderate though. Maybe we spent a hundred dollars a year on pot, bought it from a friend who grows it in her garden."

"You're right. It doesn't sound like any motive for violence," I said. But I wouldn't rule it out. People were seldom honest about their use of illicit drugs, especially when talking to a cop. Lydia would be no exception.

"Where were you the morning Michael died?"

"Me?" she asked, incredulous and hurt. "You can't possibly think that I was involved in Michael's death."

I didn't really think so. Her devastation seemed real. And even though she was an experienced diver, she didn't look strong enough to overpower Michael under the water, unless of course she had help.

"Have to ask," I said.

"I was at work all day. I start at eight and leave at five. You can check with anyone at the office. I went straight home afterward to wait for Michael."

"When was the last time you saw him?"

"I talked to him the night he returned. He'd gone down to speak with the port authority about the *Chikuzen*. He was kind of abrupt on the phone. Didn't want to talk at all. Said he couldn't come by. He seemed distracted, not really listening to me. Said he was going to dive in the morning and we made a date for dinner. He never showed up. When he didn't answer his phone the next morning, I called Chief Dunn. He went out to the *Chikuzen* with a couple of divers and they found Michael."

"Who else should I be talking to?" I asked.

"You'll want to talk with Peter O'Brien," she said. "He owns SeaSail Charters. He and Michael were very friendly in spite of their differences. They spent hours sailing and arguing. Also Ralph Maynard. He works for the Department of Environment and Fisheries. Michael and he had worked closely on several projects, sometimes dove together. The list from Dunn is pretty complete otherwise."

Lydia insisted on taking me back to my hotel, and damned if her driving didn't mirror Robert's. I began to wonder if the driver of the Honda had simply been another typical island maniac behind the wheel. To take my mind off the possibility of death at every turn, I silently composed what seemed the local rules of the road: drive as fast as you possibly can, especially around curves. Don't slow for pedestrians, goats, or chickens that stand by the side of the road. Be sure to honk and wave at your friends; stop in the middle of the road if they need a ride. Pass other slow-moving vehicles even if you can't see what's coming from the other direction, and do not for any reason consider wearing a seat belt.

Lydia found humor in my obvious discomfort. "It takes getting used to," she said, "but this is the island way. I guess you'd call it carefree, a 'no-worry' attitude. The people of the Caribbean are a wonderful and unique breed, so much a product of their environment. It's hard to put it in words. They drive fast but are never in a hurry. They are dependable people that you can count on. If they have an obligation at eight o'clock, they do not arrive at eight-oh-one or at seven-fifty-nine. It's eight o'clock. Yet they are a relaxed and happy folk. Americans call it 'laid back.'"

"One more thing," I said as we pulled up to my hotel. "Do you know what happened to Michael's diving gear or where I might find his boat?"

"I don't know what happened to his gear," she said. "I never even asked. The *Lucky Lady* is in a slip down at the marina at Wickham Two. I haven't been on her since Michael died. His parents wanted me to keep her, but I can't. We spent a lot of time together

on that boat. Without him . . . well, you know. I need
to sell her."

"I'd like to take a look at her," I said.

"Sure. She's in slip twelve. Anyone at the marina
can show you."

"Thanks." I opened the door.

"Thank you—for getting involved." She gently
touched my arm. "And thanks for letting me go on
about Michael."

"You're welcome," I said. As I watched her pull
away, I couldn't help feeling that in all the talk, there
was something Lydia hadn't said.

I walked through the lobby and out to the end of
the dock. It was too beautiful to go back to my room
and I needed to think. Brooding came easier without
the restriction of walls.

It was possible that Michael's research had re-
sulted in his murder. From what Lydia said, he could
have pushed someone's buttons with his vehemence
about the destruction of the reef. Or threatened a
thriving charter business by forcing restrictions on
boating activity. But she'd said that Michael was not
as careful as the Duvalls wanted to believe. Maybe
his recklessness when it came to the environment and
diving had gotten him into trouble. He could have
pulled that compressor down looking for some environmental hazard. This entire trip could be a waste of
my time and the Duvalls' money. But Lydia was hiding something. I was sure of it. I'd seen that expression before during an interrogation.

I sat at the end of the dock for a while, feet hanging off the end, arms propped behind me. I had forgotten how vast and star-studded the night skies
could be. As a kid growing up in Illinois, I'd spent

hours lying in the grass waiting to wish on the first star. But the brightly lit Denver skies didn't afford such a view, and these days I never took the time to look anyway.

# Chapter 7

❧

Only nine-thirty and damn, it was hot. About five minutes after I walked out of my room, my tank top was already sticking to my back. I wore tan hiking shorts, an old pair of Birkenstocks, and the tank, a sherbet deepening to orange where the sweat soaked through. I was headed around to the other side of the harbor to talk with one of Michael's dive buddies, who owned Underwater Adventure.

The shop was hard to miss. The building, deep pink with a green awning, looked like a watermelon perched on the water's edge. Rows of dive tanks lined the side of the building. Dozens of wet suits, buoyancy vests, and regulators hung from a metal bar, drying.

Stepping inside was like stepping into an aquarium. There were fish everywhere—fish T-shirts, bikinis, mobiles, magnets, paperweights, jewelry, pink, yellow, and turquoise fish.

"Good morning," a huge black woman greeted from behind the counter. "May I help you?"

"Hello, I'm looking for James Constantine," I said.

"He be here somewhere. James? James!" she hollered toward the back room.

"No need to shout, woman; I'm right here," came a voice from around the corner. A tall black man, tattoos gracing each bicep, gave the woman a surreptitious pat on the ass as he moved past her.

"I'm James, help you?"

"I'm Hannah Sampson," I said. "Denver police officer. Michael Duvall's parents asked me to come down to check out a few things. I know you and Michael were friends. Can we talk a minute?"

"Sure, let's go out back. I'm repairing equipment. We can talk while I work," he said, leading the way. A small outdoor shop was littered with dive gear. The long hoses of dive regulators in various stages of devastation were tangled on the workbench like a nest of snakes.

"It's a constant battle keepin' da equipment workin'," he said, noticing my amazement. "We gets people renting the gear don' know how to take the proper care. Biggest problem's the hoses. Start leaking around the tank attachments and mouthpieces. People finish their dives, they leave tanks attached to regulators and buoyancy vests. Drop the heavy tanks on the regulators. Then they complain 'cause they have a faulty breathing system."

"What can you tell me about Michael?" I asked. "How did you two meet?"

"I met Michael at the Jolly Roger, just down around the pier. We were both drinking a beer. Started talkin'. Found out he was a scientist, lookin' at the water and the reef. Turns out we had a lot in common. Dive operators in the BVI know about protecting da reef. Been helpin' put in mooring balls at the dive sites to keep boats from anchoring in the coral."

"What's that got to do with Michael?" I asked.

"Mike and me, we went out a couple times a week. I'd help him collect his samples; he'd go along to help me check moorings. Help me repair 'em. Stuff like that. We be friends and dive buddies. He was a good man to have alongside at one hundred feet— comfortable in water, levelheaded. I sure do miss havin' him around."

"What do you think happened?"

"Same's the police," he said. "Mike got hisself caught in that damn wreck. Outta air and seventy feet down is a bad combination."

"Was there anything that seemed unusual about it?" I asked.

"Naw, not really," he said. "Some of the guys wonder how he managed to get hisself caught. Edmund Carr for one. He was one of the divers that went down and found him. But depends on da situation. I wasn't there. But Mike wouldn'ta panicked."

"Why do you think he went out there alone?"

"Well, that's somethin' I've wondered about. He hardly ever would go out by hisself unless nobody else could go. Usually call me or one of the other guys to go, always someone wantin' to go out. Sometimes Lydia."

"Did he call you that day?" I asked.

"That's the thing," he said. "He never called me."

"What's the site like?"

"Well, wreck's in about seventy to eighty feet of water," he said. "Hard to find unless ya know where it is. Not too many divers out there, but lotsa fish, lotsa sponge, coral. Not so disturbed as wrecks like the *Rhone*. Guess that's why Mike was interested. He'd been out there coupla times in the weeks before he died. Kind of unusual really. Him spendin' so much time at dat wreck."

"Any chance you could take me out?" I asked.

"Well, sure, any excuse to drop these chores," he whispered, nodding to the door. "But it's no novice dive. You been diving much?"

I gave him the rundown: police diver in Denver, hundreds of dives in water so cold hypothermia would set in within minutes without protection.

The kind of diving that I did was in an underwater world unlike Constantine's. It was a suffocating, claustrophobic place, made worse by the cumbersome equipment. Not one inch of skin was exposed to the hazards of cold and contamination. First came a heavy thermal underlayer, then a dry suit, a thick, loose-fitting rubber ensemble that looked a lot like kids' pajamas with the feet in them. The neck was de-signed to fit to a point just short of strangulation, and the rubber hood was guaranteed to remove huge chunks of hair upon removal. Then came the dive vest with the tank and regulator, which supplied air from the tank to the face mask. The mask snugged tight around the entire face and had an earphone and speaker in it for communication with the shore. Last were fins and weights, some twenty to thirty pounds, enough to sink the diver to the bottom.

Once in the water we swam blind in liquid thick with green and brown slime. Sediment and pollution limited vision to about two feet from the tip of the nose, sometimes less.

Physical stresses from cold, cramping muscles, pressure on ears, and constraining equipment exacerbated the psychological impact. Anxiety could work its way into total panic. Monsters appeared out of the muck; water crushed into the chest; breathing became strained, then impossible. Reason vanished; fear could turn to unadulterated terror. Then only one thought prevailed—"Get the hell out of the water!" I'd learned to swallow it, talk myself back. I don't know why I kept doing it. Maybe just to prove that I could. That I was capable of that kind of emotional and physical control.

The dive and recovery team was mobilized whenever there was a report of a victim in the water or foul play that involved underwater recovery of evidence. There was nothing glamorous about the job. Seldom were we in rescue mode. By the time divers were called in, the victim had gone under for good.

Only once had I actually brought someone up who had been revived. We'd been training out at Rocky Mountain Lake. We were practicing search patterns, which involved a starting point from which we took ever-increasing arcs to cover the search area. I'd been in the water with one of the novice divers when the call for help came. A kid, playing near the edge, had disappeared. We were at the site in minutes. I went down and started sweeping the area. As usual, visibility was nonexistent. I swam along the bottom, arm outstretched, brushing against rocks and debris—a washing machine.

I'd almost missed the kid, just the tips of my glove brushing against fabric as I swam. I turned, reached out, and found something soft—arms, a face, hair flowing in the current. Her eyes were open, but unseeing. I grabbed her around the waist, kicked hard for the surface, and started CPR the instant I saw daylight. By the time we got her to shore, she was shaking and whimpering. Alive. Mostly, though, I'd pulled bodies out of the lakes and reservoirs of Denver.

"I've never had the luxury of diving in warm water or in conditions where I could see more than five feet in front of my nose," I said, handing James my worn dive certification card.

"No problem. You be in for a treat. Da waters here be like one of dem Disneyland places."

Disneyland. Christ, these people were fanatics about their ocean. Nothing could be that spectacular. I'd seen underwater pictures. I was sure they were shot just like the postcards of sun-drenched beaches. That's what photographers get paid for. They place the huge hotels just out of the frame and the busy highway behind them. Same thing with the underwater shots. They get a shapely diver, wearing a bright yellow wet suit, hair flowing behind her, and wait for a pretty fish to swim by. I kept my cynicism to myself.

"Think one of the divers who helped recover the body would come along?" I asked.

"I'll make a couple calls, see who I can round up. Plan on about one o'clock. What gear do you need?"

"Regulator, weights, and tank," I said, regretting the fact that my regulator was still in the shop in Denver being reconditioned. They'd promised to have it ready within the week, then called to tell me they were waiting for a part. Right. I put that excuse in the same category as "the dog ate my homework." I didn't relish using one of the devices that lay tangled on James's worktable.

He noticed my discomfort. "No worry; I never be

usin' equipment that's not in da best workin' condition," he said. "I don't want nobody getting hurt on account of my gear."

I didn't like diving without my own regulator. I knew its idiosyncracies. And I kept it in perfect working order, every gasket, fitting, and hose in top condition. Constantine's equipment was probably okay, but I felt a familiar twinge of uneasiness. I should have paid attention.

Instead I agreed to meet Constantine back at the shop in a couple of hours and walked back to the hotel. I settled at a quiet table beside the pool for lunch. I'd brought the diving guide that I'd retrieved from Michael's effects. I wanted to know as much as I could about the site of his death before I ventured beneath the surface. The pages detailing the wreck of the *Chikuzen* were worn, passages underlined, notes in the margins.

According to the guide, the wreck sits in open water nine miles off of Mountain Point, Virgin Gorda. The ship was a 246-foot steel-hulled Korean refrigeration vessel used to service Japanese fishing fleets and later as a floating warehouse on Saint Martin. When Hurricane Henry threatened the island, government officials told the owners to get the decrepit ship out of the area so that it would not damage the docks or sink in the harbor. The owners set the ship on fire and sent it adrift, hoping it would sink offshore. Instead it drifted seventy miles to the BVI. When it became apparent that the ship was headed for Tortola, she was towed out and sunk. That was over a year ago. Since then she has become home to a vast array of sea creatures. For those who are able to locate her, she is considered a premier dive.

Michael had written a question mark by the description of the boat as a warehouse, a date in the margin—August 2—and a name—Derrick Vanderpool, Port Authority, Saint Martin.

"Hannah Sampson?" I had not noticed the man until he was standing at my table.

"Yes?" I responded, startled.

"Peter O'Brien. Lydia mentioned you, said you are here about Mike. I own the marina, the SeaSail fleet," he said, gesturing around him. "Live just up the hill. The desk clerk said you were out here. Thought I'd introduce myself."

To say that O'Brien was handsome would be like saying that skiing Devil's Crotch at Breckenridge was challenging; it was more like a death wish. My stomach did a quick flip. God, that hadn't happened since I was sixteen. O'Brien was about six-one, deeply tanned, with chiseled features, a strong chin, and eyes the color of the pool. He reminded me of the guy who plays James Bond. He wore beige shorts, an olive-green polo shirt, and scuffed boat shoes, no socks. Sunglasses hung from a rope around his neck.

"I'd invite you to join me but I'm just on my way out," I said. "I'd like to talk with you about Michael. Lydia said you were friends."

"We were," he said. "Why don't we talk over dinner? I'm known to be an excellent chef."

"All right," I said. Probably a stupid move. O'Brien was way too good-looking, and he was a part of my investigation. But what the hell. I did need to question him; might as well be over food.

"About seven o'clock?" he asked. "I'll meet you here at the pool and we can walk up to the house."

"I'll be here."

He stopped to talk with the maître d' on his way out. I never got the bill for lunch. That ended up being the best part of the day. It went straight downhill from there.

# Chapter 8

❧

I didn't think it could get any hotter. It had. By one o'clock even the lizards had taken shelter in the shade. One scurried further under a hibiscus bush as I walked down the sidewalk and back to the dive shop.

James and another man were loading the tanks onto the boat. Sweat ran down their faces and dripped onto the deck. They hardly seemed to notice.

"Hannah," James said, "this is Harry Acuff."

"Hello," I said, shaking the man's grimy hand. He was small, wiry, and reminded me of the island dogs that roamed the beaches and streets. He had a tattoo of a naked woman on one forearm, on the other a map of Puerto Rico, etched in blue and red.

"Thanks for coming," I said.

"No problem," he said. "Always happy to help a pretty lady."

Christ, I thought, what a condescending jerk, but I managed to keep it to myself.

"Harry helped recover Michael's body. He be workin' around the marina and over at da boatyard," said James.

"Yeah, hands in engine grease all day," Harry said.

I stepped aboard and James headed the dive boat into the main channel. Outside the breakers, the breeze picked up and the temperature dropped at least ten degrees. No wonder people came here to sail. Hiking the islands could only lead to heatstroke and certain death.

"Down there, dat distant island, that be Virgin Gorda," James said. "That group off to the left is the Dogs. We'll head between them and Scrub Island, and then it's about five miles to the wreck. Take about half an hour."

A dozen sailboats glided past, most of them with the SeaSail logo. Clearly Peter O'Brien's charter company was doing well. I wondered how detrimental Michael's research might be to his business. Proof of the damage from boating could cost him plenty in reduced business and in refitting the entire fleet with holding tanks.

The boats were beautiful, tipping in the breeze. Every so often one would suddenly alter its course, ropes creaking and sails flapping until the wind caught them from the other side and pulled them taut again.

"Coming about," James explained. "It's how a sailboat makes its way against the wind. Nothin' like an engine, if ya ast me. Gets ya there about ten times faster."

I had the feeling that for sailors, getting there was not the point.

We passed a batch of tiny uninhabited islands that James identified as Great Dog, George Dog, and West Dog. They looked a lot nicer than they sounded. Quiet coves nestled along their shores. Pelican fished in water that turned from ink to indigo to turquoise to crystal aquamarine. I spotted a couple of mooring balls scattered in some of the coves.

"Those be the moorings we put in to keep boaters from anchoring in the coral," James said. "Some great diving around those islands. That's the Chimney over there. Has underwater canyons and a huge arch covered with coral polyps. Over there's Bronco Billy. Bunch of canyons and ridges, can see lobster, eel, lots of anemone, sponges, coral, all kinds of fish."

Another few minutes and James was throttling back on the engine. "This is it," he said. I wondered how the hell he knew. We were out in the middle of the ink. It looked deep and I couldn't see anything until we were just about on top of the slime-encrusted mooring ball that bobbed up and down on the waves.

"How do you find this place?" I asked.

"Come out here enough, ya know where it is. These days, though, anyone with a GPS can find it. Just get the coordinates from the Internet. Used to be easier to spot. Ship had white paint on the hull. Now it's getting covered with sea life."

As James moved the boat slowly up to the mooring ball, Harry stood on the bow with the boat hook and grabbed the line attached to the mooring. He tied it around a cleat and James cut the motor.

"Let's go," he said, dragging tanks and dive gear out of the locker and pulling on his wet suit.

I did the same but not with the casual enthusiasm of James and Harry. I have never been able to dive without spending a couple of seconds silently questioning my motivation. I mean, it was stupid, really. I was about to jump into a vast, watery underworld where the act of breathing went from being the most

automatic thing humans do, to one in which every inhale and exhale was a noisy and unnatural event.
Forces would push on my body and I would be enveloped in equipment that limited movement and visibility. And every dive I'd ever done had uncovered
tragedy: drivers caught inside vehicles, kids caught in
the weeds at the bottom of a lake, shooting victims
weighed down with rocks or stuck under bridges.

I checked the regulator, unscrewing the cover of
the second stage where the mouthpiece is attached. I
could see that it had been recently serviced—no cor-
rosion inside, the rubber exhaust valve smooth and
soft. It looked like James had completely refurbished
the device. I snapped my air tank in place on the back
of my dive vest and attached the regulator to the tank.
Then I turned the knob to begin the flow of air from
tank to regulator. I checked my air-pressure gauge,
making sure the tank was full. It showed 3,200
pounds, enough for forty-five to fifty minutes at a
depth of seventy feet. We would try to limit our bottom time to forty minutes. Otherwise we would have
to do an eight-minute decompression stop at fifteen
feet to eliminate the excess nitrogen in our blood-
stream that can cause the bends.

I breathed through the mouthpiece to ensure it
would deliver precious air to my lungs. These activities always managed to assure me—the rote stuff took
my mind off the monsters of the deep.

James briefed us on the dive. He'd lead, with Harry
bringing up the rear. James and Harry would carry
the underwater lights. I had my camera strapped
around me and carried an evidence bag.

The plan was to go down the anchor line together.
Once on the bottom, we would swim along the deck,

around the bow, down the hull, and back to the stern. Michael's body was found in a compartment just past one of the main refrigeration holds. When we got there, Harry would take the lead to the exact place.

We made our way to the back of the boat, put our regulators in our mouths, and rolled backward into the sea. We each gave the okay signal, fingertips on head, and began releasing air from our vests in order to start the descent.

Not ten feet below the surface, we were sinking through a huge school of barracuda. Shit! Nothing like this ever swam around a Colorado lake. I resisted the urge to scrabble back to the surface and into the boat. James and Harry were continuing to descend, clearly unconcerned, into the darkness below.

Knowing I would be unfamiliar with the environment, James had given me a quick summary of the sea life we might encounter. "Probably see a few barracuda, maybe a shark. They're harmless," he'd said casually.

A few! There were at least a hundred of the damned things. Now I understood his earlier Disneyland reference. This had to be the Haunted House part. These fish looked mean. I was smack in the middle of a million razor-sharp teeth. We were out of the pack before panic took over completely. But the barracuda continued to trail us as we swam to the wreck.

On the bottom we scared up a sting ray, covered in sand. He suddenly darted from his hiding place and disappeared into the blue. James pointed to the ship, barely visible up ahead. The mast and crow's nest tipped, dark against the water; rigging lines draped down into the sand. Eerie. A death ship.

As we swam closer, I could see that the wreck was

teeming with life—fish of every size and color drifted in the rigging and darted through portholes. A blanket of color covered the hull: red, purple, and yellow coral. An octopus slithered over some orange sponges and disappeared in a hole. Okay, it was pretty down here. Actually it was captivating. I had never seen anything so stunning under the water.

I'd almost forgotten why we were down there until Harry motioned for us to stop. He pointed to a square of black about six by eight in the midsection of the ship: the entrance to the refrigeration hold.

We started in. Harry took the lead. Inside was pitch-black. He switched on his light, illuminating the interior, a cavernous space filled with hundreds of fish. We swam to the other side, where Harry's light found another opening about four feet square. Again Harry led. He entered the narrow entrance and I followed, James behind me. Our path was littered with debris. Wires hung from the ceiling, and pieces of metal jutted from surfaces. We moved slowly, avoiding contact with anything that might snare our equipment or slice through a hose. Every once in a while one of our tanks would brush against the steel structure, echoing through the dead ship. We were making our way deeper and deeper into the wreck. It was claustrophobic. Should equipment fail here, getting out of the ship and back to the surface would be just about impossible.

Harry directed the light into the black. I could see several openings that led off this passage into others. It would be very easy to get disoriented, lost in the maze. The hall seemed to go on forever, the end somewhere in the darkness out of reach of his beam.

We were about ten feet down the passage when

Harry stopped ahead. An old generator, encrusted in barnacles, blocked the way. Less than two feet existed between it and the ceiling. I could see what we'd have to do to get past. Scuff marks marred the ceiling where other divers—Michael, Acuff, and Carr—had squeezed through.

Harry unsnapped his vest with the tank still attached, slid it off, and held it out in front of him, keeping his regulator in his mouth. Then he swam up and over. I was next. I unbuckled my vest and pulled it and the tank over my head. I'd done this before, but this was nuts. My only connection to my tank was the mouthpiece attached to the hose, stretched out ahead of me. If I lost my mouthpiece or the hose were cut or broke loose from the tank, I would be out of air, down seventy feet, inside a steel death trap. I'd never make it out without help. The same was true for James and Harry. We were placing our trust, and possibly our lives, in one another's hands. And what the hell did I really know about these guys anyway?

My heart raced, anxiety level peaking. I could feel the pressure building in my chest. I'd be hyperventilating in a minute. I knew the signs. I forced myself back from the brink, took control, and squeezed over the damned generator, working my fins hard, and came out the other side. James followed. We clipped back into our vests and kept moving. Suddenly Harry stopped, pointing his light to the left, the rays disappearing into a void. He'd come to the entrance of the next compartment. It was smaller than the first compartment, maybe eight by eight, but after the confinement in the passage, it felt like a ballroom.

Once inside, Harry pointed to a tangle of lines hanging from the ceiling and then to the compressor that lay below in the corner. It had been the force that had held Michael Duvall in this tomb.

Before touching anything, I wanted pictures. I unstrapped my camera and took several wide-angle shots of the entire scene, then moved in and took close-ups from every possible angle. Again and again a photograph had revealed something that had not been apparent when I'd examined an underwater crime scene, and photographs were solid evidence in a courtroom. Though in this case, because the scene had been contaminated by divers, I doubted any photo would be admissible in court. Besides, it had been weeks since the body had been recovered. Any number of recreational divers might have been down in the wreck since then. Had this been a professional underwater investigation, the scene would have been kept off-limits until all evidence had been collected, a process that would have been completed quickly and thoroughly.

Next I searched the compartment for anything that seemed out of place in the wreck. Pieces of heavy equipment were scattered about, an old freezer, another big compressor. Junk littered over the bottom, all of it parts from the ship, long covered in a thick layer of sediment and sand. An entryway led into the dark—maybe to crew's quarters or galley.

I swam over to the compressor and pushed, then put my weight on it, fins anchored on the bottom. It wouldn't budge. I could see why Michael had been unable to free himself. The thing must have weighed five or six hundred pounds.

How could Michael have ended up underneath it? Unless it had been unstable to begin with, it would have taken leverage to bring it down. Why would he have done that? Was he looking for something up there? I swam to the ledge where the unit had sat. Fish scurried from their hiding place when I pulled the loose wires back. Nothing up there but water.

I could see what looked like fresh marks on the unit, just developing a new layer of sea life. Some of the marks would have been made by the divers when they had freed Michael's body. But there was a separate set on the other side. Michael had probably made them. But with what? I hadn't seen any notes in the file about a wedge or crowbar being found.

I motioned to James, who had brought a crowbar for just such a chore. He moved the unit onto its side. Underneath lay a metal pipe. I was about to retrieve it when damned if Harry didn't pick the thing up. He'd just added several sets of prints to any that might have been on the pipe, possibly obliterating any that had been there. Though the chances of lifting prints from an item recovered in salt water were remote, especially after a month, it was not out of the question. I took it from him, grasping it by the end, and put it in the PVC container I carried in my evidence bag for that purpose. I made sure the container was filled with water and capped it on both ends. Otherwise the pipe would begin to oxidize the minute it was exposed to the air.

I spent a few minutes measuring the depth and water temperature and took a water sample. We'd been down about thirty minutes, and I'd seen enough. I checked my pressure gauge. I was surprised to see that I still had plenty of air—1,300 psi, far from the 500 red zone. I was sure that my heart rate and breathing during this dive would have doubled my air intake.

I signaled James. Time to head to the surface. He

took the lead, swimming out of the compartment and back down the passageway. He looked back to make sure we were following, then disappeared over the generator. Harry was right behind me with the light when it suddenly went out. I was enveloped in black. It was like being pushed into a coffin.

# Chapter 9

❧

At first I thought that Harry had mistakenly switched the light off. I expected it to come back on at any moment. It didn't. Damn Harry. Where was he? We had been making our way out of the compartment and back down the narrow passage. I managed to somersault around in the confined space and swim back into the black interior, looking for Harry, straining to see any sign of light from his flashlight. Nothing. Could the battery have died? Was he lost or hurt somewhere? Tangled in lines?

I'd done plenty of diving blind. Instinct and training took over. I kept one hand out in front while I felt along the side of the passageway with the other until the surface became a void under my fingers. I was back to the compartment in the interior. I banged on my tank with the end of my dive knife. The sound reverberated through the water. No return signal. I banged again. Waited. Nothing.

I quickly devised a haphazard search pattern and swept the inside of the compartment. No Harry lying inside unconscious. I was sure that the space was empty. Where the hell had he gone? It was time to get out. Though I couldn't see my gauge, I knew by now that my air would be moving toward the red zone. I'd have just enough to find my way out of the ship and to the surface.

I felt around the side of the interior compartment until I located the passage and made my way back down the black tunnel. At the generator, I again slipped out of my vest and tank and squeezed over. It would be another ten feet to the big refrigeration hold, and then out to open water. I kept moving slowly down the passage, feeling my way in the dark, brushing against the tangle of lines and jagged metal that we'd encountered on our way in. Finally the walls of the passage gave way to the next compartment.

That's when my regulator sputtered, gave me a few final bursts of air, and quit. Shit. I had to get the hell out of there. But I couldn't see the opening out of the compartment. I should have been able to see a dim gray square of light in the black. I scanned the area, turning 360 degrees—nothing. Precious seconds were passing, the store of oxygen in my system diminishing. I wasn't even sure which way was up. All of the indicators were gone, no gravity, no visual clues. Now even the bubbles, exiting my regulator and rising to the surface, were gone.

I twisted and turned in the water, searching for that damned gray square. My head struck what I thought was the ceiling of the compartment. Again I did a 360. There it was, up above my fins, for chrissake. I had somehow ended up upside down, at the very bottom of what I realized was a deep, cavernous space. What I'd thought was the ceiling was actually the floor. I swam hard, knowing that once I made it out of the ship, I still had to make it to the surface.

Just as I cleared the wreck, someone grabbed me, ripped the useless regulator from my mouth, and shoved in another. It was James. He held the mouthpiece to my face and I breathed. He watched as I regained composure, then pointed to the surface. We managed to do almost the full eight-minute decompression stop on James's limited tank of air, then surfaced to glorious sun and blue sky.

"What the hell!" James yelled as we climbed into the boat. Harry was already there, lounging on the bow, drinking a beer.

"What the hell," he yelled again as he jerked the beer out of Harry's grasp. "What are you doin'? Where were you?"

"What ja mean, mate?" Harry asked. "I been here."

"I mean below. She almost drown down in the compartment. Where the hell were you? You were supposed to be last out with the other light." James was about to take a swing at him when I grabbed his fist.

"Damn, James," Harry said. "You were way ahead. She was behind you. I came out the other side. Tight squeeze but shorter. You blokes were fine. Wat do ya mean, drowned?"

"That's the last time I dive with you, Harry," James said. "You're stupid, careless. One day it'll catch up with you. You'll end up same's Michael 'cept you'll deserve it!"

I struggled out of my vest, too tired to join the fray. James set the gear on the deck.

"What happened?" he asked me.

"What happened was Harry left me in that passage

in the dark. When the light went out, I went back for him. Thought he might be caught or hurt. Finally I realized I needed to start out. I had just made my way to the refrigeration hold when my air quit. The pressure gauge had indicated thirteen hundred when we'd started out. It should have been plenty. Glad you were there, James."

"When I realized no one was behind me, I went back," James said. "Saw you coming out of the hold, knew you were in trouble. Shouldn'ta been nothin' wrong with your equipment."

He picked up the gauge. "It's empty," he said, flicking his finger sharply against the glass cover. "I don't understand how that could be."

I looked carefully at the pressure gauge and mouthpiece. Everything looked fine. I ran my fingers along the each of the low-pressure hoses that went to the mouthpiece, the spare mouthpiece, and the vest. They were all new, flexible, and in perfect shape. At first glance the high-pressure hose looked good too. It's the hose that goes directly to the pressure gauge. Designed to withstand up to 5,000 psi, it provides an accurate pressure reading from the tank to the gauge. It was split right at the fitting.

"Look at this." I handed the regulator to James.

"Jeez, that explains why you ran out of air. That thing would have been losing air like crazy. But these hoses are designed to withstand the pressure."

"It must have happened when I came back down the passageway. It was too dark to see anything. I must have sliced it on a piece of metal."

"It shouldn't have come apart like that, even if you brushed up against something razor-sharp. The high-pressure hose is thick and hard. It wouldn't split." He looked again at the hose. "Man, this ain't a high-pressure hose."

"What?"

"I don't make that kinda mistake. How could a low-pressure hose end up on here? No wonder it split. Jeez, I am sorry. I can't understand this."

James seemed completely flabbergasted, but he was the one in charge of the equipment. Had he sabotaged my dive?

"Where did you put this after you refurbished it?" I wondered who else might have had access.

"I finished with it after you left the shop this morning. Put it on the dive boat along with my gear and went to lunch. You think someone tampered with it?"

"Possible, unless you used the wrong hose."

"Can't be. I'm real careful with all the gear."

"Guess you're getting senile in your old age." Harry had been sitting on the edge of the boat without a word.

"How the hell did you get out of the ship?" I asked, turning to him.

"Jus' went down the other way, mate. The passage leads to the mess hall and up to the bridge. No problem."

"Guess you've spent some time exploring the wreck," I said. He had to be very familiar with the maze of passageways to make his way out so easily.

"Sure, I've dived it a couple of times. Never know what little souvenir ya might find."

"Isn't that illegal?" I asked. I knew that many of the sites in the BVI were designated national parks and that collecting artifacts was against park regulations.

"What's a little coin or spoon here and there?" he said, smirking. "Besides, who's to know?"

What a cocky asshole. I refrained from comment, but James was really angry. He'd be waiting for Acuff to make a mistake selling something that he shouldn't have in his possession.

I spent the return trip querying Acuff about finding Michael. He wasn't particularly helpful.

"Went out with Dunn and Carr that afternoon," he said. "Carr and I kept working our way into the interior of the ship till we found him."

"Who actually located him?" I asked.

"Was Carr that went in first. I was right behind. Duvall was in that compartment like I showed you, just kinda swaying in the current, leg caught under that refrigeration box."

"Do you think it was an accident?"

"Oh, yeah, absolutely," he said. "Stupid move. Pulled that compressor right over on hisself. Not much chance a gettin' out from under. All he could do is wait for his air to give out."

"The police report said that his regulator was out of his mouth, floating in the water."

"Yeah. Thing was floating above his head. I figure he ran out of air and thought he was a fish, ya know, could breathe water." Harry was actually gloating, as if there were no way it would ever happen to him.

"Did you notice anything on the body or in the water around the body?"

"Just a bunch a fish and shrimp feeding on him," he said, smiling.

"What about blood or vomit, foam around the mouth?"

"Didn't see nothin' like that."

"Did you look?"

"Hey, my job was to get down there, look for the

guy, and bring him up if I found him. That's what I did."

"Why do you think he went out by himself?" I prodded. This guy was a fountain of information.

"Beats me," he said. "I hardly knew the guy."

"Where were you the morning Michael died?"

"You expect me to remember where I was a month ago? Guess I was workin' like usual."

"Where would that have been?"

"Hell if I know. I work for lotsa people down here. Freelancing is what I call it. Fixin boats for whoever wants to pay me good, mostly over at the boatyard, sometimes for SeaSail. Don't think that be none of your damned business, though."

"If it's murder, it's my business."

"Yeah, well, like I said, Duvall got careless and drowned."

By the time we tied the boat to the dock, Harry had consumed the entire six-pack that he'd stashed in the cooler.

"Hey, Ms. Sampson, think about it this way," he said as he swigged the last of his beer and walked unsteadily down the dock, "least you didn't end up like Duvall. Besides, it builds character and makes a great story for all your friends in the U.S. of A."

"Thanks, Harry, but I think I've had enough character building in my life already."

When I got back to my hotel room, I called Mack, mostly because I needed to hear a friendly voice. I had come close to dying in that wreck, and I wasn't at all sure it had been accidental. At this point, I didn't know whom to trust. Constantine had seemed innocent enough—upset that his equipment might have been faulty. And he had come back for me. But he would have known that once I'd made it to the opening, I would have made it to the surface. It could all be an act on his part. Maybe he and Acuff had conspired to get me out of the way. Was I really that much of a threat? I had absolutely no proof that Michael's death had been anything but an accident.

Mack picked up on the second ring. "Sampson, good to hear your voice. You've only been down there a couple of days. You miss me already?"

"Actually, I do." I told Mack about my near-death experience diving and what I'd discovered so far.

"Jeez, Sampson, sounds like I need to come down and watch your back."

"Any leads on Greta's murder?" I asked.

"Nothing much," he said. "No surprises in the autopsy. Her only injury was the bullet wound to the chest. Weapon was thirty-eight caliber. We haven't found the gun. We questioned the husband. He's pretty devastated, and friends report the marriage solid. Evidently they had just renewed their vows. Course, you never know what goes on behind closed doors, but I'm just not seeing him as the killer."

"What about fibers, fingerprints?"

"Nothing yet. We're working on it."

"Well, let Trujillo know I called, okay?"

"Sure. Look, you be careful down there. And I'm serious about the backup. Call me if you need me."

# Chapter 10

❧

I was in the bar, a double gin and tonic in hand, watching the sun dip into the water, when Peter O'Brien arrived.

"You look lovely," he said.

I'd showered and made an attempt to pull my hair up, though stray wisps hung helter-skelter. I told myself it was the natural look and left it at that. When I'd packed, I'd jammed a crushable dress in my suitcase, an afterthought. It was a sexy affair—black, calf-length but skimpy on top and formfitting. I wore it now in an attempt to regain some equilibrium, prove I was fully alive, after my near death. The turmoil in my stomach was finally subsiding—more to do with the double gin than the dress.

O'Brien didn't look bad himself: black Dockers and a beige gauzy shirt that implied the muscled body beneath. He still wore the boat shoes, no socks. I had to remind myself that this was business and that everyone was suspect in Michael's murder, if it was murder. I was pretty sure it was. I'd been on the island less than forty-eight hours and I'd almost been hit by a car and drowned out at the *Chikuzen*. Accidents? Possible, but more than likely someone was trying to subvert my investigation. And Lydia. There was something she had not wanted to say when we spoke yesterday. Tonight I would find out about O'Brien.

I was describing the day's dive when the waiter arrived and set a martini in front of him. I hadn't seen him order. "They know me here," he said in response to my bemused look.

"I've known James a long time," O'Brien said. "When it comes to diving, he is strictly professional. His is the first shop I recommend when charterers want to hire a dive company. I'm surprised things got out of hand."

"What about Harry Acuff?" I asked. "Do you know him?"

"Only in passing. He hangs around the dive shops, the marina. He's always looked a bit seedy, a bit too hungry, if that makes any sense. He works over at the boatyard and does some freelance work as a diver. He's very experienced. Dunn uses him; so does the Parks Service. He occasionally works on my boats doing the underwater repairs. Do you think he abandoned you in the wreck on purpose?"

"At this point, anything is possible," I said.

"Well, I'm certainly glad you found your way out of there," he said, smiling—or was it a smirk?

I wondered how glad he really was. O'Brien had plenty of motive for killing Michael. He was friendly with Constantine, knew Acuff. He could afford to pay them well to ensure I never made it out of that wreck.

"How about some famous O'Brien cuisine?" he said.

He offered me his arm and we strolled up the hill to his house. It fell more into the villa category: a huge

white stucco with peach-colored trim on a rolling hillside. Inside, it was airy and spacious, decorated taste-
fully in an island theme. The floors were tiled with
Spanish pavers. The furniture was wicker and rattan.
Framed charts and pictures of sailboats decorated the
walls. I picked up a photo from a nearby table that
caught my eye. An athletic couple stood on an old
wooden sailboat with a young boy between them.

"My parents," O'Brien said. "That was our first
boat, named for my mother, the *Catherine*. She was
headed for the salvage yard when they bought her for
almost nothing. A lot of sweat and love went into her
restoration. She's a classic, brass fittings, teak decking.
And she can really move through the water. Just not
made like that anymore. These days, most boats are
made of fiberglass."

"Do you still have her?" I asked.

"Yes. I'll never sell her. She's docked down at the
marina."

We walked out to the pool where an elegant table,
a vase of island flowers in the center, was set for two.
The lights from the marina glittered below. The sultan
overseeing his kingdom, I thought.

"I've made a typical island meal, grilled red snapper with Caribbean rice and beans. Thought you
should experience island cuisine," he said as he
opened a bottle of chardonnay and poured. "Relax
and try to forget the day. Give me a few minutes in the
kitchen."

The wine was finishing the job that the gin had
started. I could feel the tension begin to ease; the pain
that had been throbbing down the side of my neck
and into my injured shoulder subsided. I'd better
watch it, I silently warned myself.

O'Brien returned, plates in hand. I was impressed that he had cooked himself and wondered if there was a chef hiding in the kitchen.

"I don't cook often," he said, reading my thoughts. "Mostly I depend on Marta, but it's her day off."

"It looks wonderful. I'm impressed."

"Just my intent," he said, lifting his glass to mine.

Why, I wondered, would it be important to impress me? I hardly knew him.

"How did you end up in the islands owning a marina and a charter business?" I asked.

"Actually, I grew up here in Tortola. My parents started the company. My father had been a successful businessman in L.A. He was fed up with the hassle and the cutthroat environment. He and my mother had always sailed in California. They decided to sell everything and come down here. I was only five. They bought the *Catherine*, fixed her up, and hired her out. They crewed it, did the cooking, and gave lessons to those who were interested. The boat and their services were in such demand that they bought another. It just grew from there, now over a hundred boats. They came in at an opportune time; sailing was just catching on down here. And my father was an entrepreneur to the core. He knew what it took to be successful."

O'Brien refilled our glasses and continued.

"I grew up on sailboats, from little sunfish to sixty-foot sloops. When I turned sixteen, my parents insisted I go back to the States for high school. I didn't want to leave them or the islands, but they weren't giving me a choice. They wanted me to get a good education.

"It wasn't just financial success that concerned

them. They placed a lot of value on being well-read, thoughtful, questioning. So I went to boarding school in the East and returned home for holidays and summers. Prep school provided the foundation. I went to Stanford, then to Berkeley for graduate school. One September day, I had just begun the semester when I got a call. My parents were missing, presumed dead."

O'Brien shifted in his chair, took a sip of wine, trying to mask the sadness.

"What happened?" I asked.

"Hurricane. Common down here in the fall. When these storms threaten, the base personnel kick into high gear. They round up charterers that are out on the water, take the boats to hurricane holes. We use a small lagoon just east of the marina. The boats are protected there by land and the mangroves. Other boats are rafted together. The idea is to keep them in the water, where they are the safest, and not allow them to be blown into shore. Every available dockhand was busy. The folks in the marina too, trying to find accommodations for all the sailors that had to come in off the boats. People end up sleeping in makeshift beds in offices. It's total chaos."

"Your parents were out in it?"

"Yes. One of the charterers, a couple with their two children, was unable to get in. They were out past Virgin Gorda with the storm bearing down. My parents insisted on going. They were the best sailors in the fleet, and they knew there was little chance this couple would be able to survive out there. They took one dockhand and the fastest speedboat we had. By the time they got out there, the wind was really picking up. They got the family loaded into the speedboat and the dockhand raced them into shelter at Gorda Sound,

getting in just minutes before the storm bore down. In
the meantime, my parents stayed on the boat, planning to weather it out aboard. They had been in
storms before and were skilled in handling the forty-
footer. They knew better than to try to bring her in.
They would have headed the boat straight out to open
water and just tried to keep her directed into the wind
under the power of the engine. The eye passed right
over them. More than likely it blasted over the side
along with hundreds of gallons of water and turned
the boat over. I spent a week out there looking for any
signs of them. Recovered debris, seat cushions, boat
fenders, not much else."

"I'm sorry. That must have been hard."

"Yes. But it was the way they would have wanted
to die. They were not the type to sit aging in rockers
on the porch. I stayed after that. Got the base back in
shape, repairing roofs, surveying boat damage. Most
came through intact. In the entire region, two other
boats went down, one off of Saint Croix, one off of
Saint Martin. Three people were picked up by the
coast guard; four perished, my parents among them."

"Your parents must have been very special people," I said.

"They were. They realized early on what was important. SeaSail and the islands were their lives. I am
determined to carry it on. It's the legacy they left me."

I wondered how determined O'Brien might be.
Enough to kill to protect it if Michael's research
threatened his business?

"Wife? Kids?" I asked. I knew there weren't. This
was the home of a single man.

"No. There was a woman at Berkeley. She tried it in
the islands for a while but it didn't work. She was in

law school, gearing up for the big time. The pace down here didn't match her ambitions. And I wouldn't leave. Guess neither of us was committed enough to the relationship to make sacrifices. No one serious since. What about you?"

I gave him the ten-minute version of my past, omitting Jake, and worked him back to the real reason I was there.

"How well did you know Michael?" I asked.

"Michael and I were friends," he said. "I think the best kind. We could argue heatedly for hours and come away from it respecting and liking each other. At least that's the way I saw it. I think Michael did too. His death was hard. I know that people think I should be relieved to have him gone. Sure, his research could have had a negative effect on my business, but I consider myself an islander and I'm concerned about the environment."

"I read Michael's dissertation. What did he mean about you keeping him honest, something about the larger picture?"

"The problems here are more complex than just sailboats," he said. "That was one of our constant arguments. Michael would get so focused on the sailing industry that he'd lose sight of the bigger issues. The cruise ships are a good example. Several years ago one cruise ship passenger videotaped a long chain of plastic garbage bags being thrown over the side in the dead of night. Shampoo bottles and other plastics embossed with cruise line names are frequently found on coastlines around the world. Not to mention the damage from their anchors and oil and gas seepage."

I could see his anger rising. O'Brien seemed as passionate about the damage to the reef as Lydia had been.

"Even more problematic," he continued, "is the sewage and sedimentation that comes from shore. The reef needs water that is warm but not too warm. It needs sunlight and clear water, free from sediment and nutrients, which promote the growth of algae blooms. Development in costal areas means increases in sediment from excavation and increases in nutrients from fertilizers, septic systems, and irresponsible disposal, not to mention the spills from huge oil tankers. Global warming is only multiplying the problem. Many blame the big incidence of coral bleaching in 1998 to warmer water temperatures."

Clearly O'Brien had spent a lot of time studying the issues. I guess he would. His business depended on the quality of the environment. But there had to be trade-offs financially.

"Wouldn't the regulations that Michael wanted have cost you a fortune, maybe even put you out of business?"

"It would be expensive, yes. But the business would survive. I'm willing to make changes in the charter business because I know that change has to occur on every level," he said. "I'm in the process of refitting all my boats with holding tanks. It may actually help my business. I'm developing a marketing strategy: Rent from the company that cares about the reef. I'm lobbying other companies to do the same."

O'Brien took my plate, refusing any help from me. "Enjoy the view. I'll be right back."

I was thinking more about what O'Brien had said than noticing the view. I wondered how much of his environmental rap was smoke screen. After all, he could reason to any suspicious police officer, why would he kill Michael when they were on the same side?

O'Brien returned balancing coffee cups and brandy snifters. A bottle of Hennessy was tucked under his arm.

"What can you tell me about Lydia?" I asked as I sipped coffee. I was passing on the brandy.

"Oh, Lydia cared very much for Michael. They were good together. Directed in the same way, smart. Her family wasn't happy about the match. Her father is a powerful businessman in the islands. Tried to run Michael out, insinuated to Chief Dunn that Michael was dealing drugs. But Dunn is a good man, not the kind to bow to authority. He looked into it and told Arthur to let it alone. Arthur was really angry. Tried to have Dunn booted out of office without any success. When Lydia found out what her father was up to, she quit talking to him, refused to see him."

"I got the feeling there was something Lydia wasn't telling me," I said. "I wonder if it has anything to do with her father."

"It's possible. When all is said and done, family is the core of life in the islands, and without Michael it's all she has now."

"Do you think her father could have been involved in Michael's death?" I asked.

"I don't know. It's nothing I would have ever considered, but then Michael's death was determined an accident." He was quiet for several moments. "I suppose it's possible," he said finally. "Arthur is volatile and he's used to things going his way. But killing? I don't know."

"There are ways to arrange such things that make

one feel pretty removed, maybe even not responsible," I said.

"Maybe," he replied reluctantly.

"Where were you the morning Michael died?" It was time to press O'Brien harder.

"Of course, I know you consider me a suspect. I would have reason to want Mike dead."

"That's right. So where were you?"

"I'm afraid I don't recall. My days are pretty much the same. I usually go into my office first thing in the morning, then down to the marina in the afternoon. I suppose that's what I did that day."

"I need to know. How about you give it some careful thought, check your calendar for that day?"

"I'll do that and I will let you know. I have nothing to hide. As I said, Michael and I were friends."

It was past eleven o'clock by the time we headed back to my room. O'Brien walked me to the door. I could tell he considered kissing me but then thought better of it. I had to admit I was a little disappointed. Damned if I wasn't attracted to him.

"Watch out, Sampson," I whispered as I closed the door behind me.

# Chapter 11

❧

I lay in bed staring at the light patterns moving across the walls as the sun reflected on the blades of the circling fan. A sweetly scented breeze drifted across my body. I was determined to enjoy the sensation for a while. It was only six A.M. I'd stay in bed another hour. My appointment with Edmund Carr, the other diver who had helped retrieve Michael's body, was not until one o'clock.

So far I really had nothing concrete to indicate that Michael's death was anything but an accident. Maybe it was just the aftereffects of being trapped in the wreck that had my senses alerted, but I knew that I had to follow those instincts. Every once in a while my gut leads me to something important.

Almost anyone could have dived into the wreck when Michael was in there: O'Brien, Acuff, Lydia Stewart, James Constantine, all were qualified divers. I had called Lydia's office. She'd been at work all day the day Michael had died.

I'd encountered only a couple of people who had motive. According to O'Brien, Lydia's father had very real and personal reasons for wanting Michael eliminated.

Friend or not, O'Brien himself had reasons to want Michael out of the way. No matter what he said, he would certainly feel the financial repercussions of Michael's finding. He'd made a good case about being as concerned as Michael about the damage that boating was doing to the environment. But then, O'Brien was smart. He knew what needed to be said.

Then there was Harry Acuff. He was distasteful in the extreme but he had no obvious connection to the case except that he'd found Michael's body. He was just some seedy lowlife who was sucking whatever he could from the local economy with as little effort as possible. But neither he nor O'Brien seemed to be willing to tell me where they'd been the morning Michael had gone out to the *Chikuzen*.

So much for sleeping in. It was six-fifteen and I was wide awake. After a quick shower and cup of coffee down at the docks, I found Robert out in front of the hotel and got him to drop me off at Stewart Trust. I wanted to pay a visit to Arthur Stewart. Lydia had said he was president and CEO of his own company, which formed and administrated offshore companies, international trusts, and mutual funds. Stewart was in the right place at the right time twenty some years ago when the BVIslanders gained citizenship separate from the British. Since 1984, more than sixty thousand international business companies have incorporated in the BVI. These businesses were attracted by the ease of obtaining tax-exempt status and by the islands' reputation as a law-and-order society. Stewart's was one of the first of scores of trust companies that sprung up in response to the world of international finance. According to Lydia, her father had also made a fortune in real-estate development.

Stewart's office was on Wickham Cay I, along with several other trust companies. It took up a good half of the first floor. To call it pretentious would have been an understatement. It looked like the office of a London barrister. Heavy brocaded curtains hung behind velvet couches in the reception area. The burgundy carpeting was at least four inches thick. Though perfectly suited for the cold climates of old-money London, it was stuffy and out of place in the Caribbean. Obviously it was made to impress, and probably effective with Stewart's clientele.

Stewart's secretary informed me that Stewart was not available. I wondered if he was behind the enormous oak doors that she seemed to be guarding.

"Mr. Stewart is in a meeting," she said. "Did you have an appointment?"

"No, I thought I might just catch him free. I spoke with his daughter yesterday. She said she was sure he'd be able to see me."

I was lying through my teeth, of course. But I could tell Stewart's secretary was one of those protective types and maybe a bit afraid of her boss. She was in her sixties, hair tinged with gray. She wore a brown silky suit, just a shade lighter than her skin. It was held together over a full bosom by pearl-and-gold buttons. She was probably intimidated as hell by Arthur Stewart. I hoped the reference to Lydia would soften her up a bit. No point telling her that I was a police officer investigating Michael's death.

"Mr. Stewart won't be in the office until this afternoon," she said. So Stewart wasn't lurking behind closed doors.

"I'm sorry," I said, resorting to my most sincere, "I'm a nice person who's just trying to help" tone. "I haven't introduced myself. I'm Hannah Sampson. I'm trying to pull together some loose ends about Michael Duvall for his parents. Help Lydia with some closure." It worked.

"Poor dear. I have a daughter about Lydia's age. Already married, with three children. I hope that girl can find herself another man real soon. I am Ruby Chalwell," she said, offering her hand.

She was gloating. Her daughter already had a family while Lydia was still single and alone. I picked up the thread and started to pull. "Yes, I hope we can help her get over Michael and move on," I said, implying that the *we* included Ruby.

"How can I assist you?" she asked, actually eager.

"Well, maybe you can tell me a little about Mr. Stewart before I talk with him. What's he like?"

"Oh, well . . ." She hesitated, peering at those closed doors, then went on, "Mr. Stewart is a businessman."

"What do you mean?"

"He keeps his distance. Never lets anyone get the upper hand. Guess that's why he's so successful. Lots of others, the bankers and such, are afraid of him. But that doesn't keep them from doing business with Mr. Stewart."

"You think he's unethical?" I probed.

"I didn't say that," she said, wary now about the way the conversation was headed. "He's in business," she rationalized.

I backed off a bit. "Did you know Michael?"

"Oh, yes. He seemed like a nice boy, but he wasn't an islander."

"Do you think that was a problem?"

"Well, I'll tell you one thing: My husband would not have stood for it. Of course, our daughter would never have even given one thought to marrying an outsider."

"Did Michael ever come into the office?"

"Once, only once," she said softly.

"Why only once?" I prodded. That's all it took. She was dying to tell the whole story.

"Must have been about a month ago. Michael came by. I could hear him even behind those heavy doors. Mr. Stewart was yelling at Michael to stay away from Lydia. Said if he saw her again, he'd never see anything else. I couldn't hear what Michael said. He kept his voice real low. But whatever he said, it must have been the wrong thing. I heard a crash; then Michael came out of the office, his eye cut, blood dripping down his face. I rushed in to make sure Mr. Stewart was all right. He was standing there furious. I've seen him angry before but never like that. He just glared at me and told me to forget what I'd heard."

That's when Ruby realized she'd said too much. "Well, I'm sure Mr. Stewart was just worried about Lydia. I'd best be getting back to my work," she said, standing. "I'll tell Mr. Stewart you were here."

"I'm staying at the Treasure Chest. Please ask him to call me there."

Ruby still didn't really know what my business was with Stewart. I'd led her to believe I was a friend of Michael's and Lydia's. Okay, I admit it: I'd been a bit disingenuous. It's what I get paid for. Besides, I'm a firm believer in the end justifying the means.

"You can tell him I'm a police officer, looking into Michael's death for his parents."

Outside I found myself in the midst of children on their way to school, girls wearing blue jumpers and white blouses, cornrows and barrettes adorning their heads, boys in neatly pressed white shirts and blue trousers, backpacks, books, and basketballs in tow. They jabbered among themselves in patois, some combination of English and island chatter that I could not understand. Every once in a while a familiar word emerged, but nothing made any decipherable whole.

When I stopped one of the older kids to ask if he could direct me to the library, he spoke in perfect English. "Yes, ma'am," he responded, "just there at the circle, turn right on Fleming. The library will be at the end of the street. It is the white building with blue. The library is on the second floor."

"Thank you," I said.

"My pleasure, ma'am," he said, then ran to catch up with his friends, yelling, "Jambala, ketch upwidal wat."

I would have never found the place without the kid's help. It was located right in the middle of chaos, housed above a grocery store and next door to a bar from which a steady bass emanated. As I climbed to the second floor, a guy standing on the balcony next door nodded, tipped back a Heineken, and then belched.

I figured it was pretty unlikely that I'd find a shred of useful information in this ramshackle island library. The book collection was limited to current paperbacks and several shelves of reference books. But they were well along on the information highway. Several computers with Internet hookups as well a couple of microfiche machines lined the exterior wall of the second room. All of the newspapers from the various islands, as well as the *New York Times*, *Wall Street Journal*, London *Times* and others, were neatly organized in file drawers.

I started on the Internet but found little about the *Chikuzen* that wasn't already written up in Michael's dive book. Perhaps the local paper. I located the *Saint Martin Times* in the last cabinet, and since Michael had jotted August 2 in the dive book, I pulled the reel marked June–August of 2001. The *Chikuzen* had been towed out of port in August right before the hurricane. I scrolled through the reel until the headlines on August 16 caught my eye. The front page was filled with warnings of the hurricane that was bearing down on Saint Martin, accompanied by photographs of people attaching huge pieces of plywood to windows, nailing down storm shutters, tying small craft to piers or towing boats to protected coves, and anchoring small outbuildings with stakes and ropes. The *Chikuzen* was mentioned only in passing: "Determined too dangerous to leave in port, the government is forcing the owners to get her out of the harbor."

The paper was predicting the hurricane to be one of the worst in recent years, with winds between 125 and 130 mph and gusts between 145 and 150 mph, classifying it as a category four hurricane. The storm had developed seven hundred miles east of the Leewards and had steadily been moving west while increasing in severity. It was expected to hit Saint Martin sometime in the early-morning hours. People were being evacuated from coastal homes and businesses.

The hurricane had hit with a vengeance the following morning, splitting telephone poles, destroying coconut palm trees, wrenching shutters from windows, stripping roofs. A fourteen-foot surge from the sea had swamped beaches, tearing boats from their moorings and breaking them on the rocks. Six inches of rain had fallen, causing flash flooding. Some 25 percent of the homes had been damaged, leaving fifteen thousand homeless.

The storm had proceeded on its path with equal ferocity to the Virgin Islands. Saint Croix and Saint Thomas sustained extensive damage, every house, hotel, school, and factory flooding. Power lines had been severed. With reports of looting, troops were being brought in along with financial assistance. The storm made its way to Puerto Rico, then up South Carolina, finally dissipating in the cool temperatures of Canada.

News of the cleanup filled the papers for the next week, then gave way to more mundane events: a report of graft in the governor's office, an upcoming regatta from Saint Martin to Saint Barts. One short blurb on the back page said that jewels stolen from the Emerald and Diamond Emporium were still unrecovered and were considered lost in the tumultuous waters produced by Hurricane Henry. Interesting stories, but hardly relevant.

The August 2 date that Michael had written in the dive book bothered me. Why that date? The *Chikuzen* had been hauled out of port on the sixteenth. I needed to get in touch with Vanderpool at the Saint Martin port authority, the guy whose name Michael had jotted in the book, to find out more about the *Chikuzen*.

By the time I left the library it was almost noon. I'd have just enough time to grab something to eat before I headed over to see Carr. I wandered down to the harbor and stopped at a seaside vendor's.

"Afternoon, ma'am, try my famous calamari?"

"Sure," I said.

He handed me one of those red-and-white-checked cardboard containers overflowing with deep-fried tentacles. These were the same little guys I'd seen at the wreck. Five or six of them had been swimming around there, changing hues to blend with their surroundings and ejecting spurts of defensive ink. What the hell, maybe with enough catsup they'd taste like onion rings or french fries.

"Did you know Michael Duvall, the American who drowned down here in December?" I asked. It was possible that someone down at the docks had seen him going out.

"Naw," he said. "Saw him around but never talked to him."

"Ever see him down here with anyone?"

"I never gets down to the docks till after eleven. Most the fishermen, divers, they likes to get out early mornin'. Check with ol' Capy down at the end of the pier. He practically lives down here. Useta be the best fisherman around till he started hittin' the bottle, hittin' it hard. Got hisself haunted, is wat I think. The sea demons done captured him. Got so no one would go out wid him. Then he got hisself caught out there in a nasty storm. Lost his boat and that was that. Mos' folks calls him touched," he said, pointing a finger to his head. "They gives him a wide berth, but he's harmless enough, and ol' Capy knows the docks."

As I approached, I could here Capy singing, "Ples don' ya rock ma bot, 'cause I don' wan' ma bot ta be rockin'."

"Hi, there," I said. "You a Bob Marley fan?" I'd collected all of Marley's albums.

"Sure, mon," he said. "Dat man can play dem tunes."

"Yeah, too bad he died so young. No telling what he would have gone on to do," I responded.

"He dead? Now, dats a cryin' shame. When he die? Maybe I'll go to the funeral."

"Oh, well, I think it's been a while ago now." Like about twenty years, but I decided not to break that news to Capy.

"Damn sorry to miss dat service. How'd he go? End up in the deep blue?" he asked.

"No, I think he got sick," I said. "Cancer, you know."

"Oh, yeah, that's nasty stuff, dat dere cancer, grows in you like a monster. Think I gots that cancer in me. Some kinda monster I picked up in the sea. One night I was out alone not too far from dat wreck off Mountain Point when a bad fog settled on me. Couldn't tell which way was home, couldn't tell up from down, water so calm you could see the color of your eyes in it. Boat hardly moving. Splish-splashing in the calm. Then I heards it. Sometin' in da water. Sometin' flashing by looking like a giant snake, me looking close over the side and dat damn thing comes out the sea almost takes my head off. See dem scars?" he said, holding his arm up. "Dat where dat thing stuck me. Been out on dat water since I learnt to walk, almost sixty years, never seen nothing like dat."

"Wow, that's an amazing story," I said. I wondered if he'd really seen something out at the wreck. An underwater light, maybe. Maybe just the ravings of a drunk.

"Ever see that monster again?" I asked.

"Naw, los' my bot after that; don't go out on dat

water anymore," he said, and took a long drink from the bottle in his hand. It smelled like rum.

"Name's Marvin Hofsted. Mos' folks calls me Capy," he said, holding out a scarred and callused hand.

"I'm Hannah, Hannah Sampson," I said, taking his hand.

"Nice ta meet ya." He offered me a sip from the bottle.

"No, thank you, Capy, but help yourself to some calamari. Are you down here on the docks a lot?"

"Sure thing. I live over there," he said with a mouth full of crispy tentacles. He pointed at a shack just a few yards away.

"Did you know Michael Duvall?" I asked.

"Well, I sees lotsa folks come and go 'round here."

"He was American, a young man, blond, about six feet tall. You might have seen him going out with diving gear. Maybe you would have seen him with Lydia Stewart."

"Oh, sure, dat white boy. Lucky man. Fact, I called him Lucky. His bot be da *Lucky Lady*, but I called him Lucky 'cuz dat Lydia a real beauty. Dem both good kids. He done helped me patch dat dere roof last year. Brought some black paper, some shingles. Worked all day on it. One of dem kids would bring me fresh fruit practically every day. Den one day he go out, never come back. I figure dat monster gots him. I tolds him better not go down under dat water. Dat dere snake gonna fin' ya sooner or later. Kept telling him he ain't dat lucky. Damn shame. You know when dat funeral is?"

"I think it was a while back, Capy."

"Damn, I mist dat service too!"

I wondered if I could believe anything this man told me, but I persisted. "Did you see him go out?"

"Sure, I always helped him untie his lines. Least I could do."

"Anyone with him?"

"Naw. He was goin' out by hisself real early. In a hurry. Kind of got the idea he was meetin' someone out there. Said no time to stop at da market, but Lydia be 'round later. Seems like he was headed to dat wreck. Guess so, 'cause dat's where they found him, caught in dat monster."

"Did he say anything else to you?" I asked.

"Not much. He was kinda quiet. Seemed kind of worried."

"See anyone else around?" I asked.

"Dat time the mornin' not a lot of folks about. Always a couple of the fishermen going out early to check their traps."

"Do you remember seeing anyone else at all?"

"Well, yeah, there was Jimmy. He almost always goin' out in the morning. Best time to dive, calmer, not so much wind."

"Jimmy?"

"Jimmy Constantine, owns da dive shop. He and Pete O'Brien went out together. Think it be da same day. I remembers 'cause they be havin' trouble getting the boat started. Harry Acuff came by givin' dem all kindsa grief about it. Dey finally got it going and headed out."

So Constantine and O'Brien were out diving on the same morning that Michael had been out there. Why hadn't O'Brien remembered that? And if he did, why hadn't he wanted to tell me?

"How long after Mike left did they go out?"

"Jeez, maybe half hour, maybe less."

"Anyone with them?"

"Don't know. Didn't see nobody else. Coulda been."

"Did you see Acuff or anyone else go out?"

"Didn't notice nobody else. Ya know, I kept tellin Lucky don' go in dat water. I tole him and tole him. He not listenin' to me, not listenin' to the warnin's in da sea neither. Jest not listen, not listen . . ."

It was almost one o'clock. Capy had managed to finish off the rum as well as my lunch and was nodding off at the end of the pier when I left. What had he told me? Michael had left early in the morning, alone. Seemed worried. Maybe meeting someone. O'Brien and Constantine had left shortly after. Could Capy be mistaken about it being the same day? How much could I believe from a man who was sloshed on rum by one o'clock, saw sea monsters, and was disappointed to discover that he had missed Bob Marley's funeral?

# Chapter 12

❦

I found Edmund Carr in his office at Central Bank. He was a small man, about thirty-five, balding, neatly dressed in a conservative business suit. He immediately rose from his desk and flashed a warm smile, extending a delicate hand in a surprisingly firm grip. I introduced myself and told him why I was there.

"Have a seat," he said.

I settled into an overstuffed tweed affair and pulled out my notebook.

"Don't know how I can be of help, but be happy to answer any questions," he said. "Mike was a friend."

"How did you end up as part of the recovery effort when Michael was reported missing?" I asked.

"I volunteer for BVI Search and Rescue," he said. "Since there's no coast guard in the islands, Search and Rescue was formed to provide twenty-four-hour coverage in the BVI. We're all trained in CPR, and the boats are equipped with emergency equipment. Went out with Chief Dunn and Harry Acuff."

"Why Acuff?" I asked. "Is he also with Search and Rescue?"

"Used to be. He was asked to resign just a couple of weeks ago."

"Why is that?"

"Oh, let's just say he likes his liquor. Usually he's either hungover or drunk. Not an ideal state for diving. He is unreliable, missed volunteer meetings, and is not disciplined in the water."

After diving with Acuff yesterday, nothing Carr said came as much of a surprise.

"How did he end up going with you to the *Chikuzen*?" I asked.

"It was one of the few times that he was actually in the office monitoring the phone. He took Dunn's call. I was the other diver on call, so Acuff called me. We always take at least two divers along with a boat handler and, if necessary, a medical tech. In this case, though, it was just the three of us—me, Dunn, and Acuff. Actually I was surprised that Acuff went. He was always finding excuses. Never wants to do anything he doesn't have to."

"What do you remember about the rescue?"

"Well, we got out there about ten o'clock that morning," Carr said. "Lucky Lady, Duvall's boat, was still tied to the mooring ball. Kind of eerie—that boat just bobbing there in the swells. Nothing seemed out of order. I could see the keys still dangling from the ignition, a couple of dive tanks propped in the rack, a bottle of sunscreen on the console. Just felt weird."

"Then what?"

"Dunn stayed on the rescue boat and Harry and I went down," Carr continued. "We searched the exterior of the ship first, looking around the hull. Next we started on the interior, checking the wheelhouse, then into the refrigeration holds. We found him in the middle section, in a smaller compartment way back inside the hold."

I knew exactly where he meant. I was feeling lucky that Carr wasn't down there retrieving my body instead of sitting across from me describing the scene of Michael's death.

"He was just floating there," Carr said, "his leg caught under that refrigeration compressor. He looked bad. You know, bloated and gray. Leg torn up, cut to the bone. Fish were nibbling on the body. Funny, though, in all the horror there was something peaceful in his eyes."

"Did you know Michael well?" I asked.

"Sure, we'd dived together several times. He was also a Search and Rescue volunteer. In fact, we'd dived just the week before on a rescue. Guy had a heart attack while he was diving. His dive partners already had him out of the water. We did CPR and got him to the hospital. Guy did okay."

"I've been told that Michael was safety conscious and an expert diver."

"Can't think of anyone I'd rather have along in an emergency. Mike was levelheaded, calm under pressure. Loved the water, was completely at home a hundred feet down. Maybe that's why he could accept it as his final resting place."

"Anything seem unusual down there?"

"You know, I've gone over it again and again. I just don't really see how that compressor could have come down that way. Mike would have to have been really tugging at it. Why would he do that? And when it came loose, why hadn't he been able to get out of the way? Dunn is right, though. We will never know why. Just takes a freak set of circumstances. Maybe Michael had seen something behind the unit and was determined to get at it. He was always looking real close at stuff, checking under boulders, peering under crevices."

"How did you get him out?" I asked, wondering whether they had used the pipe I'd recovered from the wreck.

"Acuff and I had to wedge the compressor off of the body with a bar."

"Did you use a metal pipe?" I asked.

"No, we went up to the rescue boat and got a crowbar that's kept on board. Why do you ask?"

"I examined the site yesterday," I said. "I found a piece of piping underneath the compressor. It was about an inch and a half in diameter, maybe four feet long. Do you know where it could have come from?"

"You know, I remember seeing that lying there when we freed the body. Tumbled that compressor on top of it without thinking much about it. Think that's what Michael used to pry that thing loose?"

"Possible. Ever seen pipe like that around?" I asked.

"It could have been a piece of the shaft from a boat propeller. Suppose you can find them in any of the boatyards. Wonder why Mike would be using something like that. He had all kinds of tools on board for collecting samples—hammers, small pickaxes, crowbars, you name it. Maybe it was dropped by another diver before Michael dived there."

"What did you notice about the body?"

"Well, jeez, he looked bad."

"Tell me exactly what you remember. Everything, whether it seems important to you or not."

"Like I said, he was floating there, with his leg

caught, a big gash in it. He had been chewed up pretty good by sea life." He hesitated.

"Go on," I said. "I've seen it all before. I try to think of it as part of nature's recycling system."

In fact, from the description in the police file, Michael's body had been found in relatively good shape. I'd seen a lot worse. The term is *anthropophagy*, and all experienced recovery divers have seen it. Crustaceans—crabs, shrimp, lobsters, crayfish—are the most voracious. Not to mention sea lice. For the uninitiated diver, finding a half-eaten body—eyes protruding from sockets devoid of all flesh, and teeth exposed in a freakish grin—can be horrific. I suppose I should be concerned that it had all become routine for me.

"His hands were being nibbled on by juvenile fish," Carr said. "His face . . . jeez, there were a bunch of shrimp feeding on it. Man, it was horrible. His lips and ears were really torn up. I just wanted to get him out of there. When we moved him, a lot of blood seeped out from all the wounds, coloring the water around his body."

"What about around his mouth or in his face mask? Did you notice anything at all?"

"Well, there was just all that blood around his mouth. His face mask was covering his nose and eyes."

"Could you see anything in his mask?"

"His eyes. They were open, staring right at me."

"What about around his nose?" I didn't want to lead Carr, but I needed to get him to see again what he had seen down in that ship. At this point, he was the only reliable witness I had who had been at the scene. I'd already written off Acuff.

"Yeah," he said, "there was this foamy stuff around his nose. I remember that. It got washed away when we took him to the surface. His mask came loose."

"Did you notice any color in the foam?"

"It was pinkish. That mean anything?"

"Possibly." Actually, the appearance of foam was a good indication that Michael had drowned. It occurs as the result of mucus secreted from the tracheal and bronchial glands when water is inhaled. The pink tinge would be produced when the alveoli in the lungs ruptured.

"What about rigor mortis?"

"He was stiff, if that's what you mean. Stiff as a board. It was a real struggle getting him into the boat. It took all three of us and we still banged him up a bit."

"Did you take any photographs or measurements?"

"No, nothing like that. Sorry."

"What about the compressor? Did it look like it had fallen straight down from the ledge?"

"Pretty much. We tipped it away to free him."

"Did anyone examine the area closely?" I asked. "Pick up anything at all?"

"Don't think so. We just took Mike to the surface and got him into the boat. Dunn and I rode back together with the body, and Acuff followed with Mike's boat."

"Did you notice anything unusual about the boat?"

"Nothing I haven't told you, but I never got on board. Guess Lydia will try to sell her. It's down at the marina. I'm about done here for the day. Be happy to take you over there."

The *Lucky Lady* looked just as Carr had described it. The sunscreen still lay on the console. The boat was wood with a wooden top that framed the windshield and covered the cockpit and steering wheel. It was about twenty feet long and wide enough to provide lots of working space. Painted green and white.

"Boat once belonged to one of the dive shops," Carr said. "Michael bought it cheap when the shop decided to upgrade its fleet. He painted it and modified it to meet his needs."

I stepped aboard the front part of the boat, not an easy task in Birkenstocks. I almost lost one in the water. I crab-walked from the front and stepped around the windshield and into the cockpit. A cooler was there, Pepsis and bottled water floating in stagnant water. The boat was rigged to be functional. Dive tank racks holding three tanks were lashed on one side. The other side was made up of bins of various sizes, covered with worn and faded seat cushions.

In a heap on the floor were a wet suit, a regulator, tank, and a dive vest. "Was this Michael's gear?" I asked Carr.

"Sure looks like his. We took it off him in the police boat. Guess it got dumped here."

"Did anyone check his equipment?"

"Just his air supply. His tank was flat empty. Gauge registered zero."

"Did you try his regulator?"

"No reason to. His air had to have been flowing through it okay for his tank to be empty that way. It seemed pretty obvious that his equipment had been working fine. He was trapped under that compressor, after all. Breathed until he ran out of air."

I was sure that Carr was right, but I would have checked it. I held my breath, counted to ten, and tried not to blame Dunn. He had been convinced, even before the body had been brought up, that Michael had died because he had been a careless diver. He'd seen no reason to check the equipment or preserve evidence.

I knelt down on the deck and untangled Michael's gear. His regulator was still attached to the tank. At this point the issue of fingerprints was irrelevant. By now the equipment had been in the hands of Carr, Acuff, Dunn, and probably several marina employees. And the boat had been sitting out in the sun and rain for a month.

I twisted the knob on top of the tank to open the valve, allowing air into the regulator, and checked the gauge. The needle didn't move. The tank was flat empty, just as Carr said. When I hooked the regulator to one of the spare tanks and opened the valve, the pressure-gauge needle flipped to 3,000 psi. When I breathed into the regulator, air flowed freely. So Michael's equipment was functioning when he drowned.

"Look at this," I said to Carr. A piece of netting, dried and salty, was caught on the knob on the top of Michael's tank. It was just a small strip, about four inches long and maybe two inches wide.

"Looks like an old piece of fishing net," Carr said, peering closely at the netting. "Stuff is all over the place. You see it spread out in the sand and draped over wooden frames drying out. Every fisherman on the island uses it."

"How would a piece of it end up tangled around the tank?" I was wondering aloud.

"Good question."

I retrieved tweezers and an evidence bag from my backpack, gently untangled the netting, and placed it inside the bag.

"I'd better get going," Carr said, and stepped ashore. "Let me know if I can help you with anything else. You can always reach me at the bank."

"Thanks for your help," I said. I meant it. Carr had been able to provide some significant information about the recovery of Michael's body.

I picked up Michael's wet suit, which lay in a heap under his weight belt. It was old and worn and had a tear in the shoulder seam. The tear could have been there for months or it could have happened in the struggle to free himself from the compressor. Then again, maybe Michael had torn it trying to get untangled from a net. It would be a good way to disable a diver, keep him contained until he ran out of air.

I searched the rest of the boat, pulling the cushions off and looking into the lockers that lined each side. One held an anchor, boat bumpers, ropes, life jackets, a bucket, and a brush, along with the array of tools that Carr had described, including a small crowbar. Inside another were extra fins, a mask, weights, an underwater flashlight, other dive paraphernalia. In the last were three boxes. I opened the lids of each using a pencil I'd had in my pocket. It wouldn't hurt to ask Dunn to dust the protected areas on the boat for prints. One of the boxes was filled with test tubes and vials, hemostats, and water droppers. Another box contained a heating unit that was designed to hold the test tubes, and the third box held a centrifuge. Both devices were designed to run on the boat battery. Michael obviously was doing some of his sample preparation while he was still out on the water.

Just to the right of the steering wheel was a glove box, the latch broken. It looked like it had been forced with a screwdriver, the marks fairly fresh—shiny, no rust. I sifted through the contents with the pencil. I found boat papers, a nautical chart of the BVI, and a notebook. I fished the notebook out by the spirals and flipped it open. It was filled with dates, locations, water temperatures, depths, visibility. The last entry was at a place called Angelfish Reef. There was no entry for the date Michael died. Either he had not gotten started on collecting and recording data or he had not been to the *Chikuzen* to collect data.

I wondered if whoever had broken into the glove box had found what they were looking for. It was possible that Lydia or even Dunn had forced the lock. Maybe it was Michael himself, having lost the key, or Acuff looking for anything of value on the boat.

I was putting the seat cushions back in place when one tore at the zipper, the nylon fabric rotting and dried from sun and salt water. As I tried to pull the material back around the cushion, a folded piece of heavy paper slipped to the floor. It was brittle and water damaged, and tore as I unfolded it. I ended up with three separate pieces that I laid out in the bottom of the boat. It was a diagram of a ship, a maze with every detail outlined and labeled, the location of charts, crew quarters with bunks, and storage lockers, the galley with bins, drawers, and storage cabinets. The diagram had scores of tiny symbols written all over it that indicated the exact location of the ship's contents—eating utensils, pots and pans, food bins, linens, diesel oil, even mops. There were so many labels that they confused rather than clarified—it was like camouflage. I could see the three big refrigeration holds along the right side. It had to be a schematic of the *Chikuzen*.

# Chapter 13

❦

Ralph Maynard of the Department of Environment and Fisheries was a caricature of what I would have expected if I'd been thinking about it at all. Which I wasn't.

Instead, I was contemplating the Honda. I'd spotted it about a block down from Maynard's office, idling at the curb. I'd walked quickly in that direction, hoping that I could get to it before the driver saw me and took off. No such luck. I was about a hundred yards back when I saw the guy look into his rearview mirror, slam the thing into gear, and skid around the corner.

I'd actually chased it for about four blocks, running down the middle of the street in my Birkenstocks. I had to quit wearing the damned things. When I finally stopped, sweat was seeping from every pore. I looked like I'd just stepped out of the shower with my clothes on. I stood in the middle of the street, pulling steamy air into my lungs, and watched the blue turn into a speck in the distance and then disappear. I never got a good look at the driver, and the plate was rusted and covered in mud—only a 3 and an H visible.

By the time I got back to Maynard's office, my heart rate had just about returned to normal but I looked like hell. Maynard was sitting behind his desk. Like I said, he was working to fit the image. I'd dated a Parks Service guy for a while. He was what my friends called "a hunk." His uniform consisted of worn jeans, a flannel shirt in winter, T-shirt in summer, and hiking boots. He worked out every day, muscles hard as the rocks he climbed. He belonged in his rugged environment. It turned out we made better friends than lovers. We'd continued to climb together after the romance part ended.

The man in the chair in front of me seemed to be the Caribbean version—sporting cargo shorts and a shirt covered with yellow orchids and red parrots against a green background. It reminded me of the curtains back in my hotel room. Maynard was working hard at the look, though. His clothes were spotless, pressed and just too right, like he should have been modeling for some kind of outdoor clothing catalog. All he needed was one of those safari hats with one side snapped up against the brim.

He made a big show of looking at his dive watch, which covered a large part of his wrist. I figured its main function was to impress the impressionable— that is, anything in a bikini under the age of twenty. Okay, I admit to being a bit resentful. I've never been comfortable wearing the damned things.

"Hannah Sampson, I presume. You're late," he said, rocking back in his chair.

"Sorry," I said as I glanced at the clock above his

head. It said 3:03. Our appointment was at three o'clock.

"I've got to do some sampling over at Jost Van Dyke before it gets dark. I'm on a very tight schedule." He actually pronounced it *sedual*. Christ.

"Well, you did say three o'clock. I'll be quick, but I expect a few minutes of your time." I'd learned a long time ago not to let some jerk walk all over me. The more you give, the more they take.

"As I said on the phone, I am investigating Michael Duvall's death at his parents' request," I said.

"The police say he drowned. What are you investigating? Mike was a nice guy but he was plain careless. Any reasonable diver would never have gone into that wreck alone." He started to get up.

"A few more questions, Mr. Maynard. I've been told that you and Michael worked together. What did that involve?"

"We shared data. Sometimes went out together to collect samples. The Environment and Fisheries Department in conjunction with Water and Sewage has been monitoring bacterial water quality since 1988. The government owns the seabeds and therefore the coral reef within the territorial sea, which is the area all around these islands. The major pollutant is sewage, from land and boats," he said.

I got the feeling he had memorized some government manual.

"Mike was looking at the boats," he continued. "Obviously, with the increased number of boaters every year, there's more waste disposal in the water. Add to that the anchor damage and the damage from divers and snorkelers. It all adds up to damage to critical habitats—coral reef and sea grass beds. Mike was assessing the extent of the problem and was trying to determine the carrying capacity in terms of boating. Right now the charter companies will put as many boats out as they can rent, and they keep advertising to promote more boating. Then they buy more boats to meet the increased demand. At some point there won't be any interest because the water will be a mess."

"Where were you the day Michael drowned?"

"Hey, I was not even on Tortola. Was up at Jost Van Dyke, taking water samples all day. In fact, I went up there the night before."

"Anyone see you?"

"Hell, yes. I was with two other guys from the department the whole time. Ask them. Their office is right across the hall."

"I'll do that." I pulled the diagram out of my pack and showed it to Maynard. "What do you make of this?" I asked.

"Looks like the schematic for a ship," he said, spreading the parchment out on his desk and examining it carefully. "Where did you get that?" He didn't seem that surprised when I told him.

"It looks like the *Chikuzen*," I said.

"Suppose it could be," he said. "Hard to say. Could be any of the wrecks down here. There are hundreds of them. Maybe it's not even a wreck."

I pointed out the refrigeration holds. "Couldn't be many around like the *Chikuzen*. Why would Michael have a diagram of her?"

"God knows. Mike was into all kinds of off-the-wall stuff. Interested in historical documents. Once showed me his collection of old navigational charts and drawings of whaling vessels, some from the eighteen hundreds."

I remembered seeing the drawings and charts in the boxes at Duvall's office.

"Why do you think Michael would have bothered to hide the diagram?" I asked.

"Damned if I know. Might have just stuffed it in the cushion to keep it dry," he said, folding the diagram and placing it on his desk.

"You know, you ought to be checking out the people in the boating industry around here. They're the ones that would be threatened by Mike."

"You said you believe he drowned."

"I do, but if you've got to look, look at the likes of Peter O'Brien."

"Why O'Brien?"

"He didn't like what Mike was up to," he said. "They argued all the time."

"That's not the impression I got from O'Brien. He said they were friends. That he was all for the changes Michael advocated."

"Well, that's what ol' Peter would say. You know the PC thing. All he cares about is SeaSail, preserving his family heritage. A rich kid trying to get richer. Most of the yachtsmen are the same way. Come down here, live in the lap of luxury. Christ, most of 'em don't even do their own sailing. They hire a crew, a captain, cook. All they do is sit on their you-know-what all day, basking in the BVI sun and living off their interest. Same with O'Brien and the other owners. Getting rich from tourism while the rest of us beat our heads against the wall trying to make a living."

"Seems like tourism would be good for local folks," I responded.

"Well, I'm not getting any richer."

"Most of us don't get rich; we just live comfortably and don't end up under bridges," I said, trying to follow Maynard's logic. The only common thread seemed to be an intense hatred for the wealthy. "Seems like a good thing for the islands in some ways."

"Yeah, well, it's a lot better for some," he said.

"How did you end up in the BVI?"

"I grew up in the Leewards. Parents came down here from the States when I was young. Went to college in Saint Thomas, majored in chemistry, got a job here on Tortola."

"How long have you been with Environment and Fisheries?"

"What's any of that got to do with Mike?"

"It's habit," I said. "I ask questions."

"I just got hired on here last July."

"Why here?" I asked.

"Good a place as any. Look, I've got to go." He stood and moved around to the front of his desk.

"I'll need that diagram," I said.

"Of course." He handed it back to me.

I checked with the guys across the hall on my way out. Maynard was where he said he'd been over at Jost Van Dyke. That was one loose end tied up. Maynard hadn't been anywhere near the *Chikuzen* that morning, and besides, nothing he'd said translated into a motive to kill. I wondered why he was so resentful. He probably did his soliloquy about the rich to anyone who would listen. I'd bet it was something that had been fermenting for a long time. I knew a lot of people who thought life owed them.

I walked by Underwater Adventure on my way back to my hotel room. James was outside filling tanks. He remembered going diving with O'Brien that day, just as Capy had said.

"We'd been hearing reports about a humpback whale hanging around out past Norman Island. Don't get to see them much in these waters. Pete, me, Richard Head, and one of my master divers went out. It was a real treat getting in the water with that whale. Big fella, musta weighed fifteen tons."

"Did you see Michael that morning?"

"No, but we'd headed south out of the channel that morning. Mike woulda been going in the opposite direction."

I walked down to *Blow Me* to talk to Richard Head. He'd been thrilled to be on that dive. "Never thought I'd get that close to a whale in the wild. Unbelievable. O'Brien was almost close enough to touch it."

So O'Brien had an alibi. How the hell had he failed to remember that diving expedition? Still, he could have sent someone else after Michael. The dive would have been a good cover. Besides, he and Arthur Stewart were the only people I'd found with motives.

I wondered about the diagram of the *Chikuzen*. Had Michael hidden it on the *Lucky Lady* or had he simply slid it into the cushion to keep it from getting soaked by sea spray or from blowing away? Perhaps it was just one of Michael's diversions, used to satisfy his curiosity about the old ship.

Back at the hotel, I called Derrick Vanderpool of the Saint Martin port authority. He didn't want to give me any information at all over the phone except to say that Michael had been down there. I figured a personal appearance, badge in hand, would do the trick. Maybe he'd know why Michael had the tattered diagram of a useless old ship.

# Chapter 14

I was about to bite into a forkful of tuna steak when I spotted the angry black man steaming into the restaurant. He was about six-two and carrying about 250 pounds under an impeccable linen suit and tie. I took a quick glance around, hoping that he was going to storm on someone besides me.

"Hannah Sampson?" he asked.

Should I deny it?

"Yes," I admitted, trying on the friendliest smile I could muster. I didn't think it would work. It didn't.

"You need to damn well stay out of my business," he thundered. "I am not some local yokel you can walk all over. You'd better watch yourself. I am a respected man on this island, and I know people. I'll have you booted out of here so fast you won't know you were here."

Had to be Arthur Stewart. He seemed to believe he could remove anyone he liked from his island. "You must be Lydia's father."

"That's right, and I want you to leave her and me alone. It's time she forgot Michael Duvall."

"Please sit down, Mr. Stewart," I said, in the most

reasonable monotone I could muster, given the fact that I was ready to slap this overweight dictator in the mouth.

He just stood there fuming.

"Look, we can talk now, or I'll be camping out at your office tomorrow. Your clients might be a bit reticent to do business with you when they realize a police officer is sitting out in your waiting room."

He yanked a chair out, scraping it across the floor, and sat down. By now we had the attention of everyone in the restaurant. He waved to the waitress, who was cowering in the corner nearby. She came quickly and took his order—a double bourbon on the rocks. Fine. Maybe he'd calm down a bit.

"I am not here to cause more trouble for Lydia," I said. "But I am going to get at the truth about Michael Duvall's death."

"The truth is that he drowned. It's apparent to Dunn and everyone else, including Lydia. Why are you down here opening the whole nasty business up again?"

"His parents have doubts about their son's death. Surely, as a parent, you can understand that they want to know what really happened."

"Yes, I can understand that, but I don't want my daughter hurt any more than she already has been." He was starting to calm down, a combination of my appeal to his parental instincts and the bourbon. He had downed the first and was signaling the waitress for a refill.

"Your daughter is a strong woman," I said, "and I think she wants to know the truth." Of course, if Stewart had been involved, he would want just the opposite. It was pretty obvious he loved his daughter.

If she found out that he had killed Michael, she would be devastated, not to mention the fact that he'd be invited for an extended stay in prison.

"I heard you tried to have Michael arrested for dealing drugs," I said.

"That's right, and I'd do it again. I know he and Lydia were smoking ganja."

"How would you know that?"

"I smelled it when I went to Lydia's house. He was there, sitting out on the patio, playing innocent. Lydia never did anything like that until he came along."

Stewart was either naive or lying to himself.

"Duvall was bad for Lydia in every way. She got involved with him and she didn't have time for her family anymore. Came around the house less and less. Gave up the values we taught her all her life. Missed Sunday services. The family always goes together. Until Duvall, Lydia always attended, and she respected her parents. Do you know she called me a racist? Me, a black man!"

"Your secretary told me that you and Duvall had a fight. That he'd left your office bleeding."

"My secretary talks too much," he said. "Duvall and I had an argument and I settled it. I told him to stay away from Lydia. He leaned over my desk, swearing at me. Nobody curses at me."

"Do you dive, Mr. Stewart? Or did you have someone else follow Michael out to that wreck and kill him?" I was pushing him, hoping he'd make a mistake.

"No, I don't dive, and if you think I had anything to do with his death, think again. Though I'll tell you what. The day he died was one of the happiest in my recent memory. He would have ruined Lydia."

"Father, stop it!" Lydia had just walked in, followed by O'Brien, frustration and embarrassment deepening the color of her mahogany skin. "I'm so sorry, Hannah."

"Sorry!" Stewart blustered. "Who the hell does she think she is, coming here and accusing me? I won't have it."

Lydia was silently crying behind him. I could see him soften when he turned to her. "Okay, baby. You know I don't mean it."

"I know you mean it, Father, and I know you'll never believe that Michael was the best thing in my life. Don't think for a minute that because he's gone I'll settle down here and have five grandchildren for you. You just never got it. I was with Michael because we were compatible. We wanted the same things. He wasn't leading me anywhere I wasn't already going. Fact is, sometimes I was leading him."

"Stay out of this," Stewart said, standing and turning his fury back on me. I could see he needed a scapegoat. He couldn't direct his rage at his daughter. "Get off this island. Go home and tell his parents Duvall got in over his head." A sarcastic grin crossed his face, and he stormed back out the way he had come in.

"Hannah, I am sorry," Lydia said.

"Hey, don't worry about it." I motioned to the empty chairs at the table.

"Hello, Peter. What are you two doing here?" Lydia and Peter? I was jealous for about a second before my cop antennae came up. Was there something going on between these two? Maybe Michael's death was all about love and lust.

"Hello, Hannah. I was out at the docks, ran into

Lydia outside, and thought she might need a bit of help with her father."

"Mother called me," Lydia said. She was worried. She said my father was furious and on his way over here. Evidently Ruby had called to tell him about your visit to his office. I know you think Father might be involved. For a while I thought so too. Though I tried to convince myself otherwise.

"After I talked with you the other day, I decided that I had to confront him. We talked a long time, and I believe him when he says he was not involved in Michael's death. Even though he hated Michael, he assured me that there were lines that he would never cross, murder being one of them. And I realized that was true. I've watched my dad operate my whole life. He can be ruthless in business but he maintains a level of ethics that he has defined for himself."

"I have to agree with Lydia," Peter said. "I don't think Arthur would compromise his value system."

"Even when his daughter was involved?" I asked. "I've known parents to cross all kinds of boundaries when they thought they were saving their children."

I told Lydia that I had been down to the *Lucky Lady* and asked her about the lock on the glove box. She was surprised to hear it had been broken. Neither she nor O'Brien could shed any light on the diagram of the ship. Though Lydia didn't think it unusual for Michael to have such a diagram in his possession, she didn't know why he would have had it out on his boat.

Lydia and Peter talked as I ate. Cold tuna was really not too bad. They were taking turns telling me about the places in the islands I had to see, their patter turning into a friendly battle about which were the best.

"The Baths contain the most outstanding boulder formations in the islands," Peter said.

"Too crowded," Lydia countered. "Sandy Cay is much nicer."

"Every time I go to Sandy Cay someone's anchor lets loose and a boat runs afoul," Peter countered. "A couple of weeks ago I watched a big catamaran crash into another boat anchored nearby. Guy on the cat didn't know what to do. Stood on the bow yelling and waving his arms. Too many charter companies are letting unskilled helmsmen rent their boats. Half of them don't even know how to set an anchor."

They were both in hysterics, but I could tell there was an underlying sadness about the changes that were occurring in their islands. Soon Lydia left and I was alone with Peter O'Brien.

"I heard about your dive with the humpback," I said. "Hard to believe you didn't remember being out there that day."

"Of course I remember the dive. I guess it could have been the same day Mike went out. How did you discover that?"

"Capy, old guy who hangs out down near the marina, saw you and Constantine go out. I talked to James Constantine and Richard Head. They both confirmed it."

"You work fast, Hannah."

"Yeah, well, that's my job."

"Seems you're good at it. Though I would never have pegged you as a cop. How did you ever end up in a job like this?" he asked.

"Anger," I said. I had a degree from the University

of Illinois in English, and had been working on a graduate degree in women's literature at the University of Chicago. God knows what I would have done with an advanced degree, probably taught.

But I'd gotten sidetracked at Chicago, living in an educational fortress, protected by locked gates from the violence and poverty surrounding it. Any student who wandered alone outside the campus was thought to have a death wish. The longer I was there the harder it was to accept. The people who lived in the neighborhood would never have the opportunity to get the education that was offered behind the nearby gates. I started enrolling in sociology, psychology, anthropology courses, searching for understanding about societies and subcultures.

Then one spring day, I missed my connecting bus back to campus from a trip to the art museum downtown. It was a warm day, trees greening, daffodils sprouting from window boxes along the concrete street. What danger could there be on a fine Saturday in May? I was just a few blocks from campus and decided to walk. This kind of weather brought people out. Neighbors sat on stoops talking and smoking. A boom box blared from a window. Three little girls drew chalk designs on the sidewalk ahead, their mothers watching from the steps.

I stopped to admire their work. I hadn't paid much attention to the teenagers standing in the shadows over on the basketball court. Suddenly two other boys appeared from the alley next to me. Before I understood what was happening, gunfire echoed off the buildings and one of the little girls lay at my feet, a yellow piece of chalk still grasped in her tiny fingers.

The shooting was between rival gang members.

The only ones hurt were the ones that got in the way. They never caught any of the boys.

"It was all so senseless," I said. "A six-year-old child, killed by some seventeen-year-old boy who probably lived down the block. I ended up getting a graduate degree in criminology. So I guess the short answer is that I was converted into a police type."

"You still angry?" he asked.

"Yeah, I am."

O'Brien insisted on walking me to my room. Again we were standing at my door, but this time he pulled me toward him and I let him. He had a tenderness that few men could duplicate: giving, confident, and in tune. We were inside and on the bed before I realized we had stepped over the threshold. He was slowly unbuttoning my shirt, and I was letting him. In fact, I was about to start on his.

But damn. In the light of day, this would seem like a big and embarrassing mistake. It always did.

"I can't do this," I said.

He understood immediately. Smiling, he slowly started buttoning my shirt. It took all my will to let him do it.

"You know," he said as he stood at the door. "I'd like to take you sailing. You have to experience these islands from a sailboat. Let's go out this weekend."

"I'd like that, but I'm flying over to Saint Martin in the morning," I said, trying hard not to regret the fact that we would not be sharing my room tonight.

"I've got a boat that needs to be delivered over to our Saint Martin base. A couple of my crew were going to take her. Why don't we do it? It's an overnight sail. We can leave in the morning, do a little diving, and head out at sunset. I'll give you some sailing lessons on the way. If you bring that diagram, I'll have a look at it. And I promise, nothing but sailing unless it's okay with you."

"Sounds okay," I said. I knew it was a bad idea. Maybe he hadn't been at the *Chikuzen* that morning, but the more time that I spent with O'Brien, the more reasons I had to suspect him. With Michael out of the way, his business would be secure and he'd have an open field with Lydia. Now he wanted to look at the diagram. What was I thinking? Problem is, I wasn't. I hoped I didn't regret it.

# Chapter 15

❦

I was stretched out on a blanket. The last warm rays of sun had just found their way beneath a distant cloud. The sky was streaked with fuchsia, gold, purple, orange. The breeze was warm against my tanned and naked body. A nearby picnic basket held the remains of Gruyère, summer sausage, French bread, berries, mangoes, grapes. A half-full bottle of merlot lay in the sand along with two wineglasses. I turned on my side and gazed into eyes the color of a Colorado sky.

I knew it was a dream. I kept working on it, and the guy finally removed his swimsuit and snuggled in next to me. Our bodies tangled, silky against each other. He slowly glided his hand up my body, over my hip, and up to my breast. Then he moved on top of me, heavy, delicious, smothering. . . .

Smothering. I couldn't breathe. I felt like I was buried in sand. He was pushing something thick and soft into my face. Suddenly the dream had turned to nightmare.

I awakened to the heavy thickness pressing against my nostrils. Someone was on me, pushing a pillow into my face. Someone big. It was not the handsome guy from the beach. It was not Peter O'Brien either.

I realized that in a matter of seconds I would lose consciousness. Darkness already penetrated the edges of my brain. Do something, Sampson. Do it now!

I was scratching ineffectively at the intruder with the one hand I had managed to free from beneath the covers. I couldn't reach anything vital, nothing that deterred him from his goal, which seemed to be to end my life.

I reached for the nightstand, grasping for anything that I might find to hurt the guy. My fingers found a pen. Somehow I managed to grab it and bring it down hard into the mass of flesh on top of me. It was enough. He loosened his grip, and I brought my knee up hard into his groin. Contact. We were both momentarily out of commission. While he was doubled over in pain, I was sucking in oxygen.

About the time the dark edges faded from my vision, he had come to his senses and was on his way out the door. The nerve of this guy to invade the best dream I'd had in months. I was pissed. I was also in my underwear. I threw on the sweats and T-shirt I'd left on the chair and was just seconds behind him. No shoes, but my Smith & Wesson in hand.

He was heading for the docks. I caught sight of him briefly before he disappeared into the marina. Wrong choice. He was going right down a dead end. I'd be able to corner him at the end of the dock.

The marina was deserted, the boats dark. It had to be two or three in the morning. The only sound came from the water lapping against the shore. I moved carefully down the narrow boards, stepping silently in bare feet. It was dark, the moon obscured by heavy cloud cover.

A barely audible splash sounded just under my feet. I stopped, heard it again right below me under the dock. I waited, gun drawn, scanning the water for a shadow. Five, ten seconds passed—another splash and movement. He had somehow made his way under the dock. I tensed, alert to every sound, waiting for him to make a mistake. Finally a movement, and then a pelican glided out from under the wooden slats and took off into the night sky. Christ, I'd almost shot it.

I continued down the dock. The boats were ghostly shapes against the gray sky. He had to be down here somewhere. Careful, Sampson, I reminded myself. I saw something move up ahead, one boat that was swaying out of sync with the others. It was huge, had 502 etched on the side and under it the name *Jubilation*, out of New York.

I stepped silently on board. The companionway was open, a black hole into the space below. I was going to have to make my way down. I crept across the cockpit, which for some reason had two steering wheels, one on each side. I didn't take the time to try to figure out why.

I peered into the opening but could see absolutely nothing. I waited, trying to get some feel for the space below, hoping for some indication of where he might be. I knew he was on this boat. Then I heard it—a click. It sounded like it came from right at the bottom of the stairs.

I started down, thankful now that I had left my shoes behind. As I touched the bottom step, moonlight filtered into the cabin, illuminating the galley and eating area. The boat smelled musty, like wet beach towels left in a heap for a week. Evidence of recent inhabitants littered the countertops—cereal boxes, a peanut butter jar, opened cookies, some over-ripe bananas. The only place one could hide in the main cabin was under the table. Squatting, I discovered only a Snickers wrapper.

That left the four doors, one off each corner of the main cabin. I checked the nearest, which was behind and to the left of the stairs. A quick glance revealed a compact space with a double bunk and a small bench. No one inside. Another door opened off the sleeping quarters. I opened it quickly, gun ready. It was the damned head, about the size of a refrigerator, with a sink and toilet. Empty. I checked the cabin and head on the other side of the stairs. They were a mirror image of the first. Again nothing.

Okay, I thought, he had to be in one of the other two in the front section of the boat. I could sense his presence. At the third door I turned the handle and was about to burst in quickly with my gun raised when the door was pulled from my grasp and the man nailed me fullback fashion. I ended up on the floor between the table and the seats, tangled in sticky plastic cushions. I'd managed one shot, which I knew had missed. Someone was not going to be happy about the hole I had put in the bottom of the boat.

I could hear him up top as I scrambled up the steps. When I reached the cockpit, he was jumping onto the boat alongside. I followed, making it onto one boat as he jumped to the next.

Lights were coming on belowdecks, and confused and angry voices mumbled, "What the hell was that?" I supposed people didn't like having others scrambling around on the bows of their boats in the middle of the night in a peaceful harbor.

Pretty soon we had run out of boats. We were at the end of the line, so to speak, on the deck of the last boat in the row. He had no place to go but into the water. He turned. He had a wrench in hand but immediately realized it was no match for the gun I had pointed at his chest.

"Hold it right there," I said, hoping he would not jump and that I would not be forced to fire at him in the water. I didn't like shooting at people whose motives I didn't know. After all, this could be some punk after my loose change, but then I remembered the pillow.

"Okay," he said, fear and resignation crossing his face, "Don' be shootin me, ma'am."

About then I saw his expression change and his eyes focused on something at my feet. Shit.

The next instant, my feet were yanked out from under me. I caught a blurred glimpse of the other man, standing in the dingy alongside the boat, right before my head made contact. You know how it is when your feet fly out from beneath you on the ice? Only then it's usually your tailbone that is fractured and bruised for months. My head made hard contact with the steel cleat and then the metal edge of the boat. I was aware for only an instant of the salty liquid that flushed into my lungs.

# Chapter 16

❧

I awoke to that same awful salt. I was sputtering and coughing it all over the front of my shirt. A drenched Richard Head, hair stuck to his brow and water running down his face, leaned over me. Obviously he had been practicing his CPR.

"Jeez, I didn't think you were going to come back for a minute there," he said, breathless.

A circle of boat shoes and flip-flops surrounded me. I recognized Dick's wife. The others were strangers, no doubt the owners of those disgruntled voices, awakened by gunshots and the pounding of feet across their decks.

When I tried to sit up, a wave of nausea and pain swept over me.

"Better just lie still," Dick's wife said. "You've got a really nasty cut above your eye, probably at minimum a concussion, maybe a skull fracture, not to mention all the bruising. We've called an ambulance."

"Oh, I don't think I need an ambulance," I said as I pulled a bloody hand away from my forehead and turned to deposit digested tuna steak on the dock.

"Sure," she said. "You're lucky to be alive. You

were in the process of sinking to the bottom for good when Dick dove in and pulled you out. You're in no shape to return to your room. You need to be X-rayed and monitored for twenty-four hours."

"Emma has raised four sons," Dick said. "Been through it all, broken arms, fractured ribs, concussions. She's not about to let you go anywhere but the hospital, so you better just lie back and relax."

I was beginning to think they were right. I was barely holding on to reality as the world kind of swirled around me.

Next thing I knew, I was lying between crisp white sheets in a room I did not recognize. A large woman with a British accent was taking my blood pressure.

"About time you joined us for this fine day, love," she said.

"What time is it?" I asked.

"Gettin' close to four o'clock in the afternoon. You've been out for a good twelve hours. The doctor will be in soon."

I felt like shit. My mouth was not only salty but dry, and my head felt like it was filled with wet cotton and gripped in a vise. A strip of bandages was wrapped above my ears. I hoped they'd used something colorful.

Before I could respond to the tap at my the door, an Ichabod Crane look-alike came in. "Hello, I'm Dr. Hall. How are you feeling?"

"Oh, great," I said. "I'm ready to be freed."

"You've had a serious concussion. You're fortunate there was no fracture and there is very little swelling. It took eleven stitches to close up the wound. It would be best if you spent the night, just to make sure that swelling doesn't develop. Besides, you're going to feel pretty punk for the next few days."

He did a bit of poking and prodding, shone a light in my eyes, said he'd check in with me in the morning, and left.

As he walked out, he ran into John Dunn.

"Ms. Sampson," Dunn said. "Glad to see you're alive. Not even a week in our fine country and already in the hospital. I'd say trouble follows you."

He planted himself in the chair next to the bed, opened the box of chocolates he'd brought, and helped himself to one before setting it beside my bed. This guy was reminding me more of Mack every time I saw him.

"How are you feeling?" he asked.

"I'm fine. Thanks for the chocolate."

"You don't look that great," he said, choosing a peanut cluster from the box. "Want to tell me what happened? I've talked to the folks down at the marina, guy who pulled you out, a couple of others. They couldn't tell me much. Most of them heard a gunshot and the footsteps across their bows. By the time anyone was above deck, the speedboat was pulling away. No one got much of a look. Most agree it was one of those sleek racing affairs, fast and low in the water. That describes about five hundred boats in the region."

I told him about the guy in my room. I figured the naked Adonis of my dream wasn't relevant and started at the point when I woke up to a pillow crushed into my face. "Last thing I remember is someone grabbing my ankles."

"Can you describe the intruder?" he asked.

"It was pretty dark, but I think I'd know him if I

saw him again. He was big, black, around twenty-five or thirty. He obviously had a partner. God, I walked right into it. How did he get into my room?"

"The lock on the sliding door has been jimmied. It didn't take much, probably just a quick turn with a screwdriver. Did you get a look at the other man?"

"It happened too fast. One minute I've got the guy cornered and the next I'm in the water. Never heard or saw anyone."

"He must have been waiting out there the whole time. Was probably standing down below you in his boat, grabbed you, and pulled you down and into the water. Then they both took off."

"I guess someone doesn't like my being here, asking questions about Michael's death," I said. "Unless of course you think this was some random act of violence. Robbery." I hadn't mentioned my encounter with the blue Honda to Dunn.

"Have to admit it doesn't happen much down here. Sure, we have plenty of burglaries, but usually of empty residences, and there are no murder attempts. Just what have you come up with, anyway? It would have to be important. Otherwise all they're doing by attacking you is raising more questions about Michael Duvall's death."

"Maybe I wasn't supposed to be around today to talk about it," I said. "You know, just disappear, dispose of the body out to sea. Then spread the word that I had returned to the States."

"Who have you talked to?" Dunn asked.

"Peter O'Brien, Lydia Stewart. Her dad came into the restaurant last night raging at me. The guy was ballistic."

"Yeah, Arthur," he said. "He's a tyrant, all right,

and he's used to getting his way. He'll never control Lydia, though. It eats at him. Anyone else?"

"Couple of guys down at the dock, Ralph Maynard over at Environment and Fisheries, James Constantine, Harry Acuff, and Edmund Carr."

"No one you've mentioned stands out as trouble, except Stewart," he said. "Though by now, half the island knows who you are and what you're up to. By tomorrow the other half will know too. I'll do some checking. Maybe someone else saw something last night."

I hadn't bothered to tell Dunn about the pipe I'd retrieved from under the compressor, or about the piece of netting and the schematic of the ship I found on Michael's boat yesterday. I'd intended to have the pipe checked for prints without involving Dunn. When I mentioned it now, he was angry that I hadn't turned evidence over to him the moment I'd found it. But damn, I'd been sure he'd just dump the stuff in a closet. So maybe I'd been wrong.

"You must have uncovered something or threatened someone," he said. "As soon as you're up and around, we need to have a long conversation. I want to be kept informed."

"Okay, Chief," I agreed. I told him about the Honda and asked him to run the partial plate number and to dust the *Lucky Lady* for prints.

"Must be a couple of thousand blue Hondas on the island, but I'll have it checked. See what comes up. And I'll have someone over to dust the boat today."

"One other thing. Can you get Michael's phone records?"

"I'll work on it," he said. "And I want that pipe. I'll have it checked for prints and try to find out where it might have come from." He grabbed a couple more chocolates on his way out the door.

I found my clothes without a trace of salt or blood neatly folded in the closet. It was a real chore getting into them. Every once in a while things started floating around me, kind of like the feeling you have when the Tilt-A-Whirl has stopped and you're still moving. I spent a good ten minutes pulling on my pants and shirt.

I was sitting on my bed working on restoring equilibrium and bemoaning the fact that I had no shoes when Peter O'Brien walked in.

"Hannah, are you supposed to be up?" he asked. He held a bunch of pink and purple flowers in one hand. In the other, he held a pair of flip-flops, same brilliant hues.

"I was here earlier. You were asleep. Nurse told me you were shoeless when you came in, so I picked these up. Didn't think you'd need them right away, though," he said, noticing my amused look. "Hey, it's all I could find on such short notice. I thought they were kind of colorful. My practiced eye estimated a size seven."

"Good guess." Somehow I wasn't surprised that O'Brien knew his way around women's clothing. "Thank you, and also for the flowers."

"You don't really look like you should be getting dressed."

"I'm okay. Just a little tipsy now and then. I need to get out of here. I hate hospitals, and you should see the doctor. He looks half-dead himself. He gave me the okay to leave," I lied.

O'Brien insisted on driving me back to my hotel and on staying until he knew I was not going to pass out on the way to the bathroom. He actually tucked me under the covers for a nap.

"You make a good mother," I said.

"I've asked the staff to keep an eye on things and to call Dunn if anyone seems suspicious. The hotel has repaired the lock on the sliding door, and it's been re-inforced with a metal bar across the bottom. I'll check on you later," he said, pulling the door closed and ensuring that it locked behind him.

I was asleep when Dunn came by to pick up the pipe. "You're lucky I'm not going to charge you with withholding evidence," he said. I thought he was joking, but with Dunn it was hard to tell.

I retrieved the pipe, still preserved in seawater inside the PVC tube, from the shelf of the closet. Then it dawned on me. I'd been too out of it to notice when I'd gotten back to the room.

"Damn," I muttered. I checked the bathroom, tore the bedcovers apart, looked under the bed, then searched the entire place again as Dunn watched in confusion.

My backpack, with the ship's diagram inside, was gone.

# Chapter 17

❧

The side of my face, from hairline to just below my cheekbone, looked like the ugly paisley skirt that I'd considered cool at sixteen. After Dunn left, I slept for another twelve hours.

I felt better than I looked, just a vague throbbing behind my left eye and down the side of my face. I wondered if the skin would ever return to normal flesh tones. An ugly gash started at the inside of my left eyebrow and ended somewhere in my hair. A neat row of stitches held the skin tight.

I was trying to cover up some of the purple with makeup when Dunn showed up at my door.

"How are you feeling this morning?" he asked, settling into a chair.

"Amazing what a couple of aspirin will do. Were you able to lift any prints from that piping?"

"I'm afraid not. I've got one of my deputies taking the pipe to a couple of the boat shops to see if any of them use that particular kind. Chances are they all use it. May have something to report later today."

"What about the boat?"

"We lifted several good prints. Most of them probably belonged to Michael. Only one set that came up in the data base."

"You're kidding. Whose?"

"Harry Acuff. He has a record. Used to live in Puerto Rico. Was arrested for drunk driving and a fight in a bar. Served three years for robbery. After he got out, he moved down here. Seemingly he's stayed out of trouble since. His prints were all over the boat, on the glove box and inside the lockers. Since Acuff brought the *Lucky Lady* back in after we recovered Michael's body, I'd guess he decided to take the opportunity to scour her for anything of value. Figured no one would ever notice."

"Yeah." That Acuff had a record wasn't surprising. But his prints in the boat didn't make him a killer. We needed more.

"One of the maids said she saw a guy hanging around the hotel all afternoon on Thursday," Dunn said. "She didn't think much about it. She believes his name is Billy, and that he drives one of the ferries on the run out of Soper's Hole to Saint Thomas. She figured the ferry was held up for repairs and that he was killing time flirting with the help. I am heading over to Soper's Hole to talk to the guys at the ferry dock there. They'd know whether one was out of commission Thursday and who was on the schedule that day. Feel up to taking a ride over there with me? See if you recognize anyone?"

"Absolutely," I said. I called O'Brien first, and we agreed to sail to Saint Martin first thing tomorrow morning.

By eleven o'clock, Dunn and I were headed west through Roadtown. The streets were crowded with Saturday-morning shoppers and tourists strolling through the market. Brightly patterned shirts and dresses hung from every available hook and billowed in the breeze. Delicately crafted wood sculptures and native dolls lined the tables.

Every few blocks someone would yell from the street or a doorway and Dunn would wave and honk his horn. As we worked our way through town, Dunn would periodically pull over to talk, reverting to the patois that I simply could not understand. I could never tell if the conversation was friendly, or if they were engaged in heated disagreement. It was always fast, hard, and loud. Then I'd catch a smile or a laugh and they'd part with a wave.

"My nephew," he'd explain, or "My wife's aunt, wants me to stop for mangoes at West End."

Once out of town, the road continued along the ocean, past harbors filled with sailboats and beaches with fishing boats pulled up on shore, fish traps stacked nearby. Names were etched carefully along the sides of the boats—*Lily, Big Mama, Rockin', Lucky Seven*. Like the clothes in the market, the boats radiated color, each one meticulously painted.

I wondered about the psychology of color. Why we avoided such vibrance in the States. From homes to clothing to boats, the islands were exploding in color. Maybe it was the warmth and the sun—people simply reflecting their environment. That would explain the muted tones of the American East Coast and Midwest, where winters were long and dreary. Maybe it was the difference between an African, slave culture and the staunch, New England heritage of the first East Coast settlers. There were places that radiated color in the U.S., like New Orleans. But a home painted yellow and pink in suburban Denver would have been considered gauche.

Dunn interrupted my aimless reverie. He had pulled Michael's phone records for the month before he died. I looked through them as he drove. There were calls to Lydia, to his parents in the States, to Environment and Fisheries, the dive shop, O'Brien. Nothing unusual. But the morning that he died there was a call—to the police department.

"What do you make of this?" I asked.

"Yes, I saw it. Lorna is usually in at that time of the morning. Otherwise the machine would have picked it up. Lorna writes the messages down and leaves them on my desk. I received nothing for that day from Michael."

"Any idea at all why he would be calling?"

"No, although he and I had had several conversations about Arthur Stewart. Michael was angry about Arthur's attempts to get him arrested or removed from the island with all the drug accusations. Said it was harassment. Of course, he didn't want to press charges against his girlfriend's father. But he wanted to make sure I understood what was happening. I reassured him that I did. That I had looked into Arthur's accusations, found them ludicrous, and that was that."

"This call was made at seven-oh-two. Would Michael have expected someone to be in that early?"

"Don't know. Might have."

I wondered why he would call that early and not leave a message if no one picked up, then head out in his boat and die. Just didn't compute.

By noon we were dropping down the hill into Soper's Hole. It was a beautiful little harbor of pink roofs, red shutters, and blue, green, and peach stucco buildings with balconies and turrets. The beach was scattered with umbrellas, Sunfish, and Windsurfers. Several rows of sailboats lined the docks, and tanks sat out on a boat ready for the next batch of underwater explorers.

"Back in the late sixteen-hundreds, this little harbor was a pirate's kingdom," Dunn explained. "It is well protected from the wind and sea and could be defended from the hills and ridges that ring the harbor. They could spot enemies or prey on ships carrying gold. The main harbor was deep enough for their big ships, and the mangrove lagoon was perfect for their shallow-draft attack boats. The nearby reef was rich in conch, lobster, fish, and turtles, the land loaded with fruit and wild pigs and goats. They lived the good life here."

I'd read the tales of pirates like the infamous Blackbeard, who had plundered ships heavy with treasures from the New World.

"One Danish pirate, Gustav Wilmerding, was considered the king of Soper's Hole," Dunn continued. "He settled on Little Thatch, that small island there." He pointed to a lump of land just west of the harbor. "Folks say he kept a harem dressed in silk, diamonds, and gold, and trained in exotic dance. Many say the place is haunted. They talk about seeing ghosts wandering the beaches and phantom ships floating near shore, and say they hear singing and piercing screams. Fishermen report mysterious lights that bob in the trees. Every year or so, some dreamer decides there's buried treasure to be found over there or on one of the other islands."

We pulled up to the ferry dock just as a boat was

unloading tourists coming in from Saint Thomas and
islanders coming back from a visit to the U.S. Virgins
or to work at the restaurants, hotels, and shops, or on
construction. A black man was supervising the unloading of boxes of Heineken and Carib, the locally
made brew.

"Hey dere, Clarence, whatcha got goin' dis fine
day, mon?" Dunn smiled, shifting without thought
from his perfect King's English. I was beginning to see
a pattern. When outsiders were around and an islander didn't want to be rude by excluding them from
the conversation, he would revert to this half step into
carefree island slang instead of launching into patois.

"Ah, Chief, good ta see ya, mon; ya lookin' good!
Marie be feeding ya jus' fine, I sees."

"This here be Hannah Sampson," Dunn said,
"lookin' inta that boy's death over by the *Chikuzen*."

"Oh, yeah, mon, I be hearin' bot you, miss. Nice ta
meet ya," he said, shaking my hand and trying to examine my face without being rude. So maybe half the
island did know I was here. I'd figured Dunn had
been exaggerating.

"Wondering if you can tell us if you got a ferryboat
driver name of Billy," Dunn said. "Maid over at the
Treasure Chest said he was hanging out over at da
hotel on Thursday, thought he be workin' for da
ferry."

"Well, we got a Billy, seems like dere always be a
Billy or two about. Why ya be askin'?"

"Big guy, over six feet, heavy?" Dunn asked, ignoring Clarence's question.

"That'd be Billy Reardon," Clarence said.

"He have the run through the islands that day?"
Dunn asked.

"Naw, Billy done got hisself fired coupla weeks ago. He be drinkin' on da job. Fool, he gots a pack a kids, nice missus. Don't know how dem folks is eatin' now. S'pose he down by Roadtown whoring 'round, 'scuse me, miss. Hope he ain't done sometin' real stupid wid dat family and all dependin' on him."

"It's probably nothin', but we need to talk with him. Any idea where we can find him?" Dunn asked.

"Lives up in the hills above Carrot Bay. Ya know, Chief, dat bit of a town up dere. Anyone up that way can point ya da way ta Billy's."

"What do you think about this Billy?" I asked Dunn as we got in the car.

"Probably just out of work and hanging around the hotel looking for some action."

"Well, I'd love to see more of the island," I said.

We headed inland and started up into the hills. At the top, Dunn stopped at the side of the road and we walked down a short path to look out to the sea. "Cross the way there is Jost Van Dyke. Home to Foxy's. Written up in one of those newsmagazines as one of the three places to be on New Year's Eve. The others being Times Square and Trafalgar Square. Amazin', isn't it? This tiny little spot in the BVI? You shoulda seen it for the 2000 celebration. None of the sensible yachters would have been within miles of the place, but the harbor was crammed with sailboats, bow to stern, and ferries running all night between Cane Garden Bay and Little Harbor. Some folks died that night, boats overloaded, folks overboard and drunk. Crazy, crazy scene."

"You'd never know it now," I said. The vista that spread before me was serene.

"To the left down there is Long Bay, then Apple

Bay. Carrot's the next one down," he said, pointing. "We'll take the road down along the waterfront, then head back into the hills there."

We found Reardon's house, which was really more like a shack, nestled in among the trees. The place looked like it would collapse if a stiff breeze came up. There was a small, well-tended garden at the side and a rusted old bicycle propped against the fence. A woman hung laundry on a line, an infant fast asleep in a sling around her chest. Two kids, around two and three years old, played in the dirt nearby—naked from the waist down, black little tummies protruding beneath their shirts. A look of expectation turned to fear as she heard our car, then recognized the police emblem on the door.

"Miz Reardon, I'm Chief Dunn. This is Hannah Sampson, a police officer from the States."

"What's happened?" she said, voice trembling. "It's Billy. What has happened to Billy?"

"Nothing, ma'am. As far as we know, he's fine," Dunn reassured her. "Just here to ask him a couple of questions. I take it he's not here?"

"No, he been gone now for a couple of days," she said.

"Let's go inside, Miz Reardon, outta this sun and heat," Dunn said gently.

Walking into her home, we stepped into poverty. There was no electricity, no running water. The floors were dirt, the walls just wooden slats. A small gas stove was perched on sawhorses in the corner.

"I'm sorry to be rude. My name's Clara, Clara Reardon." She graciously offered us coffee, which we both declined. It was pretty clear how dear a cup of coffee would be to this woman.

"Bethy," she said, "go out and watch the little ones, honey." A child of five or six appeared from a room in back. She was clearly undernourished, her clothes patched but spotless.

"You're a good girl, Bethy," she said.

"Is she your oldest?" I asked.

"Lord, no. The three boys is off. I jus' hope they doin' more than foolin' around. They suppose ta be catchin' us some supper."

So that made seven. I figured Clara Reardon had been pretty much pregnant for the last eight or nine years. She was just beginning to show now, and the baby in her arms couldn't have been more than six or seven months. I was shocked to see a big TV in the corner.

"Billy brought it home," she said, seeing my dismay. "Won it playin' cards. Dat man is so proud of dat television. Says he gonna get us a generator so's he can watch his soccer games, have his friends from the bar over. He a proud man, Billy."

Right, I thought. *Proud* would not have been the word I would have used. The guy should have sold that TV to put some groceries in the cupboard.

"When was Billy home last?" Dunn asked.

"He be gone for three nights now. I be gettin' worried. Billy don' never stay gone more dan one night. Comes home draggin' in da afternoon."

"Do you know where he spends his time?" Dunn's tone was soothing.

"He goes down to da bars in Road Harbor," she said. "Billy got a pain down deep. He think he can cut it out with drink and women but dat pain, it only gets worse. I keeps hopin' he gonna figure dat out one day and come home ta stay."

"Did he say anything about where he was going or for how long?" I asked.

"Naw, Billy don' do no answering ta me. But he did seem more happier dan usual. Said he be comin' home wid some money, had some kinda big plan. Thing is, Billy always have some kinda big plan. But he be sayin' this time is different, and he promised the kids he be bringin' them each a present. Askin' 'em what they wanted. Promised to bring me a blue silk dress. Lord knows what I'd do with it. He had them kids so excited. They ben watchin' for him ta come back every day."

"Do you know how he was getting this money?" I asked.

"No, I was hopin' he found hisself a new job," she said. "He got hisself in some kinda trouble with the police? Billy's not a bad man; he jus' got dat pain."

"We're just checking people who were seen in the area of a break-in Thursday night. Talking to lots of folks," Dunn said.

"Gad almighty, tell me Billy not a part of dat. You see him you tell him to come home to his children. He don' needs to bring no presents," she said.

On the way out, I stopped to admire a photo in a beautiful gilt frame, a gift from her mother, Clara Reardon explained. It was their wedding portrait, a radiant Clara, face alive with expectation, and Billy handsome and protective, holding her hand. Though ten years younger, I recognized him at once. Billy Reardon was the man who had tried to kill me.

# Chapter 18

❧

The next morning I called the Duvalls. Caroline answered. She got George on the other phone and I gave them both a rundown of what I'd found so far. "What's the bottom line?" Duvall pressed. "Was Michael murdered?"

"Yes, I'm fairly certain he was," I admitted.

"Find out who did it. I don't care what it costs," Duvall whispered, and hung up.

I headed down to the marina and found O'Brien scrambling around on the front of a boat, pulling on ropes, checking sails, looking in compartments. He looked like a kid with a new toy.

We would spend the day diving, then sail down to Saint Martin at dusk. I planned to meet with Vanderpool at the Saint Martin Port Authority. It was time I found out why Michael had gone down there and what he had discovered. Besides, I couldn't accomplish much more on Tortola. Dunn would continue to look for Reardon, and he had a deputy checking around about the pipe. I didn't think he'd find much. That piece of steel could have come from anywhere.

"Good morning," O'Brien called when he saw me

watching him, "Step aboard." He held out his hand and I leaped from the dock onto the back of the boat.

"Nice," I said. The boat was perfect, not a scratch on her, beautifully painted to mimic clouds and sea.

"She's just out of the factory," O'Brien said. "She's a thirty-eight-foot Beneteau, one of the smaller boats in the fleet. Two cabins, two heads, sleeps six in a pinch, but two people can handle her. She's small enough that the lines are manageable and in easy reach for tacking or adjusting sails.

"A lot of charterers want the big boats, the fifty-footers or the catamarans. The cats are notorious party boats because there's so much deck space to socialize. Seasoned sailors know better than to anchor anywhere near a big cat, unless of course they want to go join the party until dawn."

Down below, a dockhand was organizing the kitchen. She was storing groceries in a space about five by seven feet.

"Everything's designed for efficiency on these boats," he said, showing me around the galley. "It's kind of a one-man operation unless you are intimate with the cook." A smile washed across his face.

In the middle section nestled along one wall was a dining table, teak polished to a fine hue. Along the other wall was a bench and the chart table with an instrument panel above it, a radio, switches for pumps, water, lights, GPS, autopilot, and a stereo system.

O'Brien showed me to the cabin in the forward section, where a built-in bed narrowed and came to a point, molded to the shape of the boat. A door inside opened to a tiny bathroom.

"The head," O'Brien explained. "To shower just close the door and turn on the water. The drain's in the floor. Toilets are pumped with seawater, but when we are under way, valves have to be closed; otherwise we end up with a boat filled with water. Come on," he said. "Let's go sailing. Get situated and we'll head out."

Dock crew were throwing lines into the boat as Peter maneuvered her out of the slip and into the harbor. Sailboats were coming in and out, and a cruise ship was docked at the ship terminal. At least a hundred people were getting off to spend the morning in Roadtown.

I caught sight of a black disk floating in the water just below the surface. Suddenly a tiny head poked out of the water, then disappeared.

"A hawksbill turtle," O'Brien explained.

Once beyond the jetty he turned the boat, and before I could object he gave me the wheel.

"Just keep her pointed into the wind," he said. Right, easy for him to say.

He hauled the mainsail up, took the wheel, and killed the engine as the huge expanse of white canvas filled. He pulled on another line that he identified as the jib sheet, and the sail in front billowed, filling in the wind. When he tightened it, the boat picked up speed, tilting on its side.

"This is great!" I shouted over the wind.

"Yeah, there's nothing like that moment when the wind fills the sails. It's still a thrill for me even after all these years. It'll take us a couple of hours to get to Ginger Island. Want some lessons?"

He was a good teacher. "Sailing is half know-how, half instinct," he said. "After a while it becomes automatic. You don't have to think about the position of the wheel; you just feel it."

He explained point of sail, the interaction of wind and water, and how the boat was able to move through the water even when the wind was coming toward the boat. It was all complicated physics and I was following about half of it, picking up the terminology as he talked.

"You've got to stay aware," he said. "Watch the water, the wind, the weather moving in. Things can change in an instant. You might spend thirty minutes slipping through the water, sails perfectly trimmed, when you have to come about because the wind suddenly shifts. It is a maneuver that must happen quickly or the boat will lose speed and become difficult to control."

He gave me the wheel and I was amazed at the power. I could feel the pressure of the wind in the sails and the water on the keel. The boat felt solid and responsive. O'Brien kept telling me not to fall off the wind and to keep the sails full.

"You're luffing," he'd say. I assumed that must be a bad thing.

Finally I began to get a feel for how to keep the wind in the sails. Both the jib and the mainsail had a nice bow to them, and the boat sliced quickly through the waves. The only trouble was that we weren't headed even remotely in the direction of the island O'Brien had identified as our destination. I was about to point that out to him when he said it was time to come about. All I had to do was check my compass reading and turn the boat about ninety degrees when he gave the command.

"Ready about? Helms alee," O'Brien shouted.

I decided this must mean turn, so I turned. When I did, sails started flapping like crazy as the boat crossed through the wind. O'Brien started pulling in on the jib line and cranking the wench like mad. Everything shifted as the wind came over the other side and we kept moving swiftly through the water.

By eleven o'clock O'Brien was easing the boat up to a dive mooring at Alice's Wonderland, a dive site off of Ginger Island. My job was to stand on the bow of the boat with the boat hook, a tubelike telescoping device with a hook on the end. With this device I was to hook the rope that floated from the mooring, pull it out of the water, and attach it to the cleat on the front of the boat.

My first attempt was an embarrassing failure, and O'Brien circled around to make another pass. I concentrated every fiber of my being on that rope and managed to hook it. That turned out to be the easy part. But O'Brien was good. He managed to give the boat just enough power to keep it directly over the mooring ball, so that the rope was not ripped from my hand.

I fumbled to get the rope under the side rail and onto the cleat, while at the same time struggling to untangle the damn hook, which I had somehow managed to catch in the jib sheet. All this while trying to keep from falling overboard in what seemed like extremely rough water. I felt like a klutz.

"Kind of tricky," O'Brien said. "This site can be bumpy. It's exposed to the northeast trades, but the reef is one of the most magnificent in the BVI. It's worth the discomfort."

*Discomfort* hardly seemed the right adjective. I'd had plenty of experience donning dive gear in the back of the speeding Denver Dive and Rescue vehicle.

But this damned boat was rocking and rolling without any rhythm.

I got into my wet suit and then my vest and tank and managed to get to the back of the boat without falling on my ass. No easy task with fifty pounds of compressed air on my back and another sixteen pounds belted around my waist, weight necessary to get me to the bottom. Attached to the inflatable vest were the tangle of hoses that dangled around my knees.

I climbed onto the back platform and pulled on my fins and mask as the boat reared up the side of a swell and then plunged down the other side. I could hardly wait to get off the boat and below the choppy surface.

O'Brien followed me in and we descended the mooring line, clearing our ears as we went, to release the pressure. At the bottom I found myself in the midst of huge mushroom-shaped star coral that rose ten to fifteen feet, white sandy valleys running between them. We were dwarfed by the towering structures. I could see why the site was named Alice's Wonderland. I wouldn't have been surprised to see the caterpillar smoking his pipe and lounging on top of one of these massive coral heads. Huge purple and green sea fans, pillar coral, and brilliantly colored sponges nestled among the boulder and brain coral.

We checked our gauges—depth eighty feet, 3,200 psi in each tank. Then we took a minute to get neutrally buoyant, which involves adding air to the vest. Too much air and you end up drifting back to the surface; too little and you sink to the bottom. Just enough and you hover effortlessly just above the bottom, never brushing up against the delicate sea life.

We swam along the sandy canyons, then up to explore the coral ridges at about fifty feet, releasing air from our vests as we went. O'Brien pointed out a lone Elkhorn coral jutting out of the sand. It was at least ten feet tall, but instead of its typical golden fuzzy appearance, it was gray and smooth.

We frightened a peacock flounder disguised in the sand, only its eyes protruding. When he saw us, he darted off, changing hue to match his surroundings, from tan to a brilliantly spotted blue.

Since my dive at the *Chikuzen*, I'd picked up a couple of books about the reef. I wanted to know what the hell I was swimming with. A robust community of parrot fish, queen, stoplight and blue, nibbled on the coral, then swam past me. I'd read that they can change sex from female to male. Though why they'd want to do so was beyond my understanding, especially since it seemed they couldn't go back again. These fish use their powerful beaks to extract algae from the porous skeletons of dead coral. In the process they consume huge amounts of the reef's structure, calcium carbonate, which gets ground up in their system. It has nowhere to go but out. Every once in a while I observed the process in action as they deposited plumes of sandy waste. Just one parrot fish can make hundreds of pounds of sand in its lifetime. Thanks to the parrot fish, gorgeous expanses of white sandy beaches abound in the Caribbean.

The place was crowded with life—squid, Christmas tree and feather-duster worms, and giant anemones, their long tentacles tipped by lavender and chartreuse. I was surrounded by blue chromis, yellow-headed wrasse, and banded butterfly fish. A pair of French angelfish swam around a big green sponge. A ray drifted by in the distance and disappeared.

I swam in to get a closer look at a purple sea fan that swayed in the current. Attached to its brittle surface, O'Brien pointed out, was a tiny snail covered with orange spots outlined in black—a flamingo tongue. Suddenly I found myself under attack. I'd wandered too close to a damselfish's personal piece of reef. I suppose he was to be admired. No bigger than my palm, he will chase away anything that invades his territory, even divers. A brilliant orange washed from the fish's snout halfway down his dorsal fin, iridescent blue flecks dotted his head and back, and a dark spot ringed in light blue marked the back of his dorsal fin.

I was so distracted by the beauty that if O'Brien hadn't grabbed me, I would have run right into a colony of fire coral. It had a distinctive bladelike shape, white tips, and a mustard-colored smooth surface. While I knew it wouldn't kill me, it would inflict a nasty sting that would stay inflamed and painful for days. I was learning to be wary of some of the most innocuous-looking sea creatures. Forget sharks and sea snakes. Watch out for anything labeled fire: fire coral, fire sponges, fire worms.

It was all about protection, though. I mean, how could you blame the sting ray for whipping its barbed tail into your calf if you stepped on it? Brush up against an anemone, it will sting, maybe leave a welt. Touch a black, spiny urchin and it will pierce your skin with a venomous spine. Most of these injuries just hurt like hell for a couple of days. Clearly the key is to watch where you're going and to keep your hands to yourself.

I was beginning to understand what Michael had been talking about when he'd written that the reef was one of the most complex animal and plant communities on earth, rivaled only by that in the tropical rain forest. I was surprised when O'Brien took my arm and tapped on his gauge. I'd been so mesmerized by this underwater fantasy that I'd lost track of the time. I checked my pressure gauge—500 psi.

Reluctantly we started back up, emerging right where we had started behind the boat. O'Brien got out first and took my tanks. After we'd stowed our gear, he started the engine and moved up on the mooring ball. This time my job was to remove the line from around the cleat in the bow, setting the boat free. I accomplished my responsibilities in fine fashion; that is, without plunging over the side in the rough seas.

I made my way back to the cockpit, holding on to anything in my grasp, mostly flexible wire lines attached to the mast, the boom, along the side of the boat, all of which provided just enough support to keep me upright but not enough to make it look graceful. I decided that there was probably no way to look graceful on a sailboat in these conditions and gave up.

O'Brien motored around the point, where we found a calm little cove where the water was like glass. Amazing how the water conditions could vary so drastically.

While I lounged in the sun watching pelicans dive, O'Brien went below and brought up the lunch. We sat in the cockpit, eating and talking about the dive.

"Did you see that Elkhorn coral I was pointing to?" O'Brien asked.

"I did. It looked like it was dead," I said.

"It was. Last year it was majestic—flourishing. It had to be over a hundred years old. I don't know why it died. Perhaps too much stress on the environment—one too many anchor lines or diving fins brushing against it."

After lunch we headed to Gorda Sound. The only boats we saw were other sailboats, many with the Sea-Sail logo. Peter O'Brien was obviously engaged in a booming business here in the islands. I was admiring a beautiful boat coming toward us flying a French flag. It took me a minute to realize that the captain stood at the wheel, buck naked. The rest of his crew were the same, though a couple of them sported caps and sunglasses.

"Those French." O'Brien smiled. "They know how to sail!"

# Chapter 19

❧

We spent the next four hours sailing up to Virgin Gorda, the fat virgin, named by Columbus for the island's silhouette. At the far end we made our way into the narrow entrance that opened into Gorda Sound. Just ten feet off our starboard side, a man was standing in the rocks that jutted into the water, collecting mussels. Gorda Sound was like a big, deep lake, surrounded on three sides by land and reefs. O'Brien sailed around the shoreline, pointing out the sights. The Bitter End Yacht Club sat at the water's edge at the far end. Behind it, fuchsia-colored flowers blanketed the hillside. Along the water's edge were colorful sailboards in front of ritzy hotel rooms. The harbor was filled with sailboats, some in slips and about seventy-five tied to moorings. We sailed back to the other end of the bay and dropped anchor in a quiet spot just off a place called Drake's Landing.

O'Brien pulled a grill out of a locker and attached it to the side rail. When the coals were hot, he cooked steaks while we sipped cabernet and watched for turtles. Pelican fished nearby and goats cried from the hillside.

"I keep thinking it can't get any nicer," I said. "This is exquisite."

"Isn't it? I could never leave these islands."

"Really? You plan to grow old here?"

"Yes, someday I'd like to marry, have children, pass my parents' business on to them."

"What about Lydia?" The cop in me still questioned O'Brien's motives. If he were romantically involved with Lydia, he'd have one more good reason to want Michael out of his way. Unfortunately, my own motives for asking went beyond the investigation. I was falling for O'Brien.

"Lydia? Absolutely not," he said, amazed that I was even suggesting it. "Michael was a good friend. Lydia still is. Since Michael's death I've tried to be there for her, but never as more than a friend."

"She is a beautiful woman. No one would condemn you for stepping in."

"Not going to happen. I've never thought of Lydia in that way. Are you asking because you're a cop or do you have some other interest?"

"Just curious."

"What about you, Hannah? Is there someone back in Denver that you care about? Or are you consumed only by your work?"

"I was in a relationship once."

"Once?"

"Yes, it ended." I really didn't want to talk about Jake.

"You don't let many people know you, do you? What are you so afraid of?"

"Afraid? Don't be silly."

"I think you were hurt and now you're protecting yourself."

"He died, okay?" I was trying to stay matter-of-fact. O'Brien was right. I was afraid of my emotions and afraid of what opening up to him might mean.

"I'm sorry. What happened?"

"Jake was my dive partner on the Denver team. In fact, he's the one who got me into diving. We'd been called to do an underwater investigation up at one of the alpine lakes. A car had gone in the water—a Mercedes, with a woman inside. It didn't look like an accident. The local sheriff roped off the area and called us. Diving at altitude is always a little tricky, and the water was freezing, the lake deep. We'd already done a couple of preliminary dives. On the third, Jake was right next to me one moment, and in the next he was gone. He just disappeared. They recovered his body the next day."

"How did he die?"

"It seemed likely that he'd blacked out. It can happen. His dive partner should have been aware enough to help him."

"So you blame yourself."

"Yeah."

O'Brien remained silent. At some point he had put his arm around me.

"Dance?" he asked.

"Here?" There was about a foot of open area to move around in the cockpit.

"Why not?" He pulled me up and wrapped his arms around me, his embrace firm but at the same time gentle. We shuffled around the cockpit table, our bodies pressed together. A sea breeze brushed against our faces; then a lone goat gave a final cry and was silent. O'Brien leaned down, kissed my neck. I was losing myself—in the scent of the sea and in O'Brien's

embrace. It felt good—too good. For the moment I forgot that O'Brien was still a suspect.

We were swaying to Rod Stewart's "For the First
Time" when a dingy pulled up alongside, two men
aboard.

"Ahoy, Peter!" a voice called.

"Louis, come on aboard." Louis threw a duffel bag
over the rail and then stepped aboard. He thanked the
driver of the boat, who gave us a quick wave and took
off.

"Hannah, this is Louis Capriot. Louis, Hannah
Sampson. Louis and I will spell each other for the passage over to Saint Martin."

So much for dancing in the moonlight. I was relieved and at the same time disappointed to learn that
O'Brien and I would not be making this trip alone.

"Louis has been a captain at SeaSail for, what?"
O'Brien was asking.

"Jeez, gotta be coming up ta twenty-five years.
Since Peter here was 'bot diz tall," he said, holding a
hand up to his waist. Louis, a sinewy five-eleven with
skin the color of eggplant, was close to sixty-five.

"For a long time it was just my parents running
things with Louis's help," O'Brien said. "He is the
best sailor in the islands and knows every rock and
shallow. He can practically sail the islands blind-
folded."

They went over the chart, discussed compass readings and GPS settings. We'd be sailing in the Anegada
Passage, against the wind. The weather looked good
but there were predictions of squalls from the south. It
was possible we could pass through a storm. The
fourteen-hour trip, O'Brien explained, was best done
overnight so that we would arrive at Saint Martin at

dawn, when it was light enough to safely enter the harbor there.

O'Brien and Louis spent an hour preparing the boat, rigging the lifelines, stringing a radar reflector in the mast. The reflector would make the little sailboat a more obvious blip on any large boat's radar screen.

"We don't want to be rammed by some freighter or cruise ship out there," Peter explained. "Amazing how it can happen with so much ocean. We also have radar so that we know what boats are in the vicinity."

I could just see it: a wall of steel bearing down on our little vessel and crushing us like a toy boat under its massive bow.

Louis had brought an EPIRB, a device that would send an emergency signal to a satellite in the event that the boat sank. It was important that someone be able to locate us if we were floating out in the open sea without a boat, they explained.

Christ! I was beginning to think our chances of survival would be thin. If we didn't get rammed by some huge freighter, we'd get caught in a storm and sink.

"And the rule is, if you're up top, you wear a life jacket attached to a lifeline," O'Brien said. "If you go over the side in the dark, it would be hard, maybe impossible, to find you. With the lifeline, you're attached."

Wonderful. If I fell overboard, I'd be dragged through the sea for miles gulping salt water, bait for every big game fish in the area. I should have opted for air travel to Saint Martin.

We headed out of the sound and into open water. O'Brien went below for a couple of hours of sleep, and Louis took the first turn at the wheel. He set the heading and switched on the autopilot. We watched the last rays of light bounce off the clouds. The sky turned a glowing pink that shifted to purple and then black. By the time the sun sank into the water, Virgin Gorda was just a dark outline in the distance. It would be several hours before there would be any moonlight. It became painfully clear why they had taken so many precautions. We were enveloped in a purple void, a speck being tossed in water hundreds of feet deep.

Our running lights reflected on the water that chopped and swirled around the boat. The only other light was the soft glimmer from the cabin below and the light on the compass. We seemed utterly alone in an abyss.

"I can't imagine how anyone could spend months at a time out here. Those sailors who circumnavigate the globe must go a bit mad in this vast emptiness," I said. "It would have to get very lonely."

"I did it," Louis said. "Was about thirty-five years old, just lost my wife and only child to meningitis. I was hurtin' real bad. Took to the only comfort I knew—the sea. Was gone more'n a year. Went from the BVI around Cape Horn, up the other side of South America, came through the Panama Canal, found jobs on the docks when I ran outta money along the way, did some heavy drinkin'. Guess you could say I worked my way into oblivion and back. Finally made it back to the islands with nothin' but the boat, no money, no family left."

"How did you end up working for SeaSail?"

"Met the O'Briens down at the marina," he continued. "I was livin' on the boat. They was jus' startin' up back then, had two boats, knew I needed work and offered me a job. Been there ever since. They got to be the family I lost. After they died, I kinda took up the slack, helped Peter run things till he could get his feet under him. He took their deaths real hard, but he was bound and determined to keep the business going. It was their love. Now it's his. And it's not just the boats. It's the islands and the people here. The O'Briens loved these islands, really became part of them. They respected the way of life and the beauty. They passed all that on to Peter."

"You think the people who were born here can accept someone like him, an outsider?" I asked.

"Peter isn't considered an outsider. He is well liked and respected. Folks think of him as a native islander. He's doing a lot for the territory. That goes a long way with the people here. He feels real strongly about raising the standard of living and getting kids educated. Established a fund for education, getting kids to school, keeping them going, helping them go to college if they want."

"Seems like all of that would be a good public relations ploy and good for his business," I said.

"That's not it at all," Louis said, angry that I'd suggest it. "Peter is concerned about growth. Says that a well-educated population will be able to find ways to control it and still maintain a good standard of living. Lots of people get real mad at him. Say he's threatening their livelihood. Say it's easy for him to talk about controlling growth and tourism; he's already got all the money he needs. But he supports the programs that he promotes with his own money."

"Sounds like you admire his efforts," I said. Louis seemed sincere enough. Maybe O'Brien was the kind of man who cared more about people than money.

"Peter is a good man. Guess you could say that I love him like he was my own son. Hey," he said, looking at his watch. "You ought to go below, get thirty winks."

"You'll be okay up here by yourself?" I asked.

"I've spent half my life alone up top," he said. "I'll be calling Peter in a couple of hours to take his turn at watch."

O'Brien was still awake when I went below. He was sitting at the table with his feet propped up, shirtless, reading *Moby Dick*. The cover was tattered, the spine broken.

"It's old," O'Brien said, handing me the book. "It was in my grandfather's library. I'm fascinated by the story of Ahab's obsession to kill the whale whatever the cost. Did you know that Melville based it on an actual event—the ramming of the *Essex* by an enraged sperm whale? There were all sorts of tales back in the late nineteenth century about whales turning on the huge square-rigged ships that preyed on them."

I sat next to him and fingered through the book. It was one of those old hardbound copies that felt good to the touch, the pages yellowing and fragile.

"Think you'll be able to sleep down here?" O'Brien asked. The boat was heeled to the side and waves crashed over the bow.

"I'll be fine," I said. "What about you? Thought you were already asleep."

"I decided I'd wait for you. Make sure you got settled in okay," he said, mischief in his eyes.

"Awfully considerate."

He took the book from my hands and gently placed it on the table. I knew where this was going. He brushed a stray hair off my cheek, pulled me toward him, and kissed me with that same tenderness I'd felt while we danced. I found myself kissing him back.

There was something about O'Brien that I didn't want to resist.

When he raised my tank top over my head, then ran his fingers lightly over my breasts, I didn't stop him. It felt too good. I moved into him, pressing my bare chest against his, skin on skin.

We stood and he moved up behind me, his hands moving along my neck, fingers exploring my collarbone and then skittering over my belly. My breath came hard; heat radiated from deep inside my chest all the way into my fingertips. Without a word we went into the cabin and dropped onto the bunk, where he carefully removed my left shoe, then the right. He smiled playfully and actually started nibbling on my toes. Then he slid his hand up my calves, thighs, hips, and pulled off my shorts.

I fumbled with his, always awkward when it came to removing men's pants, afraid I'd damage something. He laughed, did the unzipping for me, and threw the shorts on the floor. He smelled of sunscreen and tasted like coconut.

"Hannah," he said, "you are an amazingly gorgeous woman. You don't know how beautiful."

"You look good too, O'Brien."

I hadn't felt this way in bed since Jake. It was more than just the sex.

O'Brien rolled over on me and we pressed together, chest thumping against chest, and got lost in each other.

I awoke once, aware that O'Brien was gone, the boat still rocking and splashing ahead. Then it was light and the smell of coffee brought me back to consciousness. I stretched and opened my eyes to find O'Brien standing beside me, a mug of coffee in hand.

Still naked, I sat up with the sheet wrapped around me and sipped the rich brew.

"We're about an hour out of Marigot Harbor," he said. "How did you sleep?"

"Like being rocked in a cradle," I said, the warmth of coffee and the heat of the night's passion hitting me at the same time.

"Any regrets?" he asked.

"Are you kidding?" I smiled, pulling him toward me. "You said an hour?"

He laughed, took my mug, climbed back in bed, and pulled the sheets over our heads.

# Chapter 20

❦

O'Brien dropped me off at the main dock in Marigot. Louis gave me a knowing smile and wink as I threw him the line and helped them push off. They were taking the boat to the marina at the east end of the island, to a harbor called Oyster Pond, where they would get her settled in the SeaSail fleet. O'Brien planned to spend the day going over the operations and financial records with his base manager while Louis looked over the condition of the fleet. We agreed to meet at a place called Enoch's on the waterfront for dinner before taking one of the puddle jumpers back to Tortola.

I found Derrick Vanderpool sitting behind his desk at the port authority, smoking and fanning himself with a notebook. He was at least fifty pounds overweight, and though it was only ten-thirty, his shirt was already drenched with sweat and his hair stuck to his forehead. I'd been right about the badge. Once Vanderpool saw it, we were buddies.

"Please pull up a chair. Coffee?" he asked, lighting a cigarette off the end of the other. He gestured to a cracked vinyl chair that looked like it had been sitting there since 1952.

"No, thanks." I sat across from him and tried to avoid breathing in all the secondhand smoke that infused the small office.

"When did Michael Duvall contact you?" I asked. I wanted to get straight to the point and out of there before some renegade cell in my lungs started replicating itself.

"He was down here sometime around the end of the year asking a lot of questions about the *Chikuzen*. I've only been in the job since June, but I knew a little about the ship. An old Korean refrigeration vessel, used for storage, pulled out of port before Hurricane Henry hit, drifted up to the BVI. Duvall wanted to know what was stored on her, whether there were records of use, who worked on the ship. That kind of thing. Said he was doing research, testing the water around the wreck. Found a bunch of dead fish lying inside the hull.

"I pulled the old records for him. The file on the *Chikuzen* was pretty thin. Just the ship's papers, a couple of inventory sheets, a diagram."

"Can I see the file?" I asked.

"Yeah, it's in the back. Don't know why we need to keep the old stuff. Got a whole file of records on ships no longer around." He came back and handed me the file labeled *Chikuzen*.

I thumbed through it. No diagram.

"Damn, he must have taken it," Vanderpool said.

"He?"

"Duvall. He asked if anyone was still around who knew about the *Chikuzen*. I'd told him he should talk with Bert Wilson, old guy was working down here when the ship was in port. Then he came back later in the day asking to see that file again."

"Did he say why?"

"Something about wantin' to check the diagram and inventory again. I left him standing at the counter in front and went back to answer the phone. When I came out five minutes later, he was gone. File lying there on the counter. Never checked the contents. I just put it back in the file drawer."

"Could someone else have taken the material?" I asked.

"Naw, I haven't pulled that file since the day he was here, and no one else has access to the back."

Something that Michael had discovered after he left the port authority office had brought him back for the diagram. But what?

"Can you tell me where I can find Bert Wilson?" I asked.

"Runs the little grocery over on Main Street—the Marigot Hamper."

At the store, the clerk pointed to a set of stairs that led up to the Wilsons' apartment. Bert Wilson was a grizzled old gentleman who lived above the store with his wife, Rose. The place was small and worn. The kitchen was vintage sixties, with an old wooden table, a brown electric range, and red Formica countertops. In the living room, two overstuffed chairs, the cushions indented and frayed, were situated for prime television viewing. A drab green sofa and an imitation Queen Anne coffee table took up the remainder of the room. Every available surface held photographs, the sagas of children growing up, marrying, having children of their own.

The Wilsons were the kind of people who loved

company and loved to talk. I told them I was a cop doing some checking about a man from the States, but you'd have thought I was their long-lost daughter or something. Rose was just putting lunch on the table, a huge pile of fried chicken and mounds of mashed potatoes, corn bread, beans. It reminded me of Sunday dinner on my aunt's farm back in Illinois, rose china and all. They insisted I join them.

"Sit yourself down, honey; you can use a bit a fat on them bones," Rose said. "You an' Bert can talk after we eat."

It was a one-way conversation over lunch. By the time we were finished, I knew how many kids and grandkids they had, about the son-in-law who had cheated on their daughter, and the grandson who was studying at MIT.

"You and Bert go on into the parlor," Rose commanded. "I'll bring you some rhubarb pie and coffee."

"Wait till you taste Rose's pie," he said. "She's famous all over the island for her pies, even sells 'em in the store. Bought up the minute she puts 'em out."

The pie was delicious, crust so light and flaky I knew she'd used lard, straight animal fat, same as my mother. I swear I could feel my arteries clogging.

"Mr. Wilson, did Michael Duvall come to see you a couple of months ago, sometime in December?" I asked.

"Well, let's see, my memory ain't too good. Rose, you remember that boy come see us by the name of Michael a while back? That in December?"

"Sure. Sweet boy, he ate with us, stayed and talked a long time. He was some kind of scientist, remember, testing ocean water or something, livin' over on Tortola."

"Oh, yeah. He was askin' about the *Chikuzen*—that old refrigeration ship. Said he was doin' some research out there, had been diving the wreck. Don't know why the cargo woulda been something he'd be interested in, but heck, that science is like a foreign language to me. I worked down on the docks when the *Chikuzen* was tied up there. Told the young fella that the ship was just an old hulk, only used for storage."

"Was it possible that hazardous material was stored on her?" I asked. "Michael mentioned finding dead fish in the hold."

"Wouldn't be surprised," he said. "But most everything should have been offloaded before the ship was towed out to sea. The foreman of that operation kept records of all the stuff on the ship and where it was stored. That ship was a maze of companionways and compartments, all filled with something. The foreman was the only one who knew what was on her or where anything was."

"Would he have kept records of any toxic material on board?" I asked.

"If he did, they wouldn't have been for public viewing," Wilson said. "He wasn't the most honorable guy. For a price, he would take stuff off people's hands that they couldn't dispose of. Seen that skull and crossbones on more than one can he'd carried on board. Could have been other chemicals in there, maybe cleaning supplies and preservatives for fish. The big refrigeration units were used to hold the catches brought in till they could be shipped to market."

"I'd like to talk with the foreman," I said. "Is he still living on Saint Martin?"

"Hell, no. He got himself killed by the police," Wilson said. "Robbed the big jewelry store over in the ritzy shopping district. Rose, we still have those newspaper articles?"

"I think so." Rose went to a desk and worked her way through a stack of junk, and finally retrieved a couple of yellowing papers.

"Here they are," she said, triumphant, and handed them to me.

The first paper was dated August 2, the same date Michael had written in his diving guide next to the description of the *Chikuzen*. The article described a robbery on the Rue de La Republique in Marigot, an area renowned for its precious stones and jewelry. I remembered now seeing a reference to the robbery when I'd been at the library.

"Guess Demitri and Alvin Getz had it all planned out," Burt said. "Went into that store right around lunchtime. Too hot to be out on the street. Most folks staying cool inside. The emporium had just gotten in a big shipment of precious gems—diamonds and emeralds, worth something like $11 million. Can you imagine that? Demitri and ol' Al forced their way into the store just when the manager was locking up for the noon break. Guess he kept a gun behind the counter. Nobody knows who fired the first shot, but that manager ended up dead. I'd of never thought those two would do anything like that. Police found the getaway car when a woman reported a man lying in a car in front of her house."

They found Alvin in the front seat soaked in blood, dead. A couple of hours later a police cruiser spotted Demitri boarding the ferry to Saint Barts. They cornered him on the upper deck. "Damned if he didn't start shooting at the police. He tried to jump off the ferry onto the docks. Got shot and ended up floating in the bay. Police sent some divers in there to search the bottom for the jewels."

On the front page of the other paper that Rose had given me was a picture of a pile of debris on the dock, the caption, "Only treasures found so far—an old alligator shoe, a lobster trap, and a pair of women's panties!"

"Did they ever recover anything?" I asked.

"Naw. Divers looked for a couple of days. The police questioned me and Rose, other folks that knew him and Alvin. Don't think anyone could tell them much. We were all shocked."

"So the foreman of the *Chikuzen* was a Demitri Stepanopolis?"

"That's right."

"Who was this Alvin?"

"One of the dockhands that worked for Demitri, kind of a loner, no family. Police say it was Demitri who killed him and left him bleeding in that car."

"Did Michael know about the robbery?" I asked.

"Not till Rose got to gabbing. That Michael was a nice boy. Was helping Rose clean up the kitchen, wash the dishes. Rose got to talking, like she does, goin' on about people we knew back when the *Chikuzen* was in port. Came up about the robbery. Rose was pretty upset when it happened. Men and their families that worked on the docks back then were tight, wives socialized, kids played together."

"So the jewels never turned up?" I asked.

"Not that I heard," he said. "Hurricane moved in pretty soon after, and with all the scrambling to get ready for it and the bad damage after, folks kind of lost interest in that robbery. People figured those jewels got washed away in the storm. High winds, waves three stories, not much that was in the water or around the shore survived too good. Those jewels probably ended up in some fish's belly."

"I was shocked," Rose interjected. "Bert worked with Demitri. We had them here for meals, our kids played together; me and Lorraine, Demitri's wife, and some of the other wives used to play cards every Thursday night."

"What kind of family were they?" I asked.

"Well, I don't like to speak poorly of the dead, but Demitri was a hard man," Rose said. "Hard as he was, though, Lorraine ruled. She say jump, he asked how high. Same with the boy. Strong-willed woman could be mean as nails if someone crossed her."

"Come on, Rose," Bert said, "just because she took her cards seriously."

"*Serious* is hardly the word," Rose said. "I still say you gets to know a person real well over a card game. Lorraine did not like to lose. She'd cheat. Can you imagine? Over a penny-ante game? She was a woman thought the world owed her and hers. Both of 'em unhappy about their lives down here, always talkin' about makin' good, gettin' rich. We used to kid them about it. How they goin' to get rich on a dockhand's pay? Guess we found out after he robbed that store."

"What happened to her?" I asked.

"Police questioned her a long time," Bert said. "If she knew anything, she never told them. She stayed down here less than a year. She worked as a waitress, other odd jobs. Finally moved away. Too many people knew what happened. Too many questions. No one could believe that she didn't know what Demitri was up to."

"Probably put him up to it," Rose said. "She just up and left one day, never said boo, was just gone."

"You said there was a son?" I asked.

"Yeah. Junior. He was already gone. Away at college when all this was goin' on," Bert said.

"Did you talk about this with Michael?" I asked.

"Sure, he was real interested. I mean, who wouldn't be? Huge bag of jewels never found. Rose, get that photo album you showed Michael."

Rose pulled out an album, opening it to the first page. "Look at Bert there; can you believe he was ever that handsome? That's our oldest, Sam, eight then, and June, five. Oh, there's our old house before we got the store."

"Rose! Show her the pictures of the picnic for the dockhands that Michael was so interested in. She don't want to see our life history," Bert said.

Rose flipped through the book to shots of people sitting at picnic tables and running three-legged races. "This here is all the guys that worked on the docks back then. There's Bert; that there is Demitri on the end."

He was a burly guy, short and stocky, dark hair, dark-skinned. Something about him was vaguely familiar. Around his neck he wore a chain with a religious medal on it. It looked like one of those Saint Christopher medals. I was sure I had seen it before. There was an empty place on the page where another photo had been.

"Michael asked to take it," Rose explained. "It was a picture of Demitri with Bert and another dockhand. He promised he'd send it back but never did. Guess I know why now. It's a cryin' shame. That was a good boy. Too much life ahead of him. Would of been a fine husband and father. Makes me just sick to know he's gone."

"Did he say why he wanted the photo?" I asked.

"No, but I think he could have recognized Demitri," Bert said. "How would he know him though?"

I was asking myself the same question. I remembered the photo stuck in one of Michael's books. I'd looked at it briefly, wondered about it. It had seemed odd for him to have it, an old picture of three guys. I'd placed it back between the pages and forgotten it till now.

"Kinda makes you wonder, don't it?" Bert said, walking me to the door. "That robbery, the *Chikuzen* hauled out to sea about the same time, Michael comin' around askin' questions about the ship, takin' that photo, endin' up dead."

"Yeah, makes you wonder," I said.

With an hour to kill before meeting Peter and Louis, I decided to take a walk around town and work off the five thousand calories I had just consumed at the Wilsons'. Saint Martin was cosmopolitan and filled with tourists, a world apart from the islands of the BVI. There were casinos, condominiums, scores of hotels, and hundreds of duty-free shops, basically just one big shopping mall. I passed stores filled with exclusive watches, handcrafted eighteen-carat gold jewelry, silver, crystal, emeralds, diamonds. No wonder Demitri Stepanopolis had been lured by the riches on these streets.

# Chapter 21

❧

I found the photo where I had left it, stuck in the back of the diving guide. The three men stood, shirtless and smiling, beers in hand. Bert Wilson, another man, bald with a beer belly hanging over his pants, and Demitri Stepanopolis. I could clearly see the religious medal, a cross with intricate engraving on it, hanging from a long chain around his neck.

I was sitting out on the balcony off my hotel room, still wrapped in a bedsheet, feeling satiated and smug. O'Brien had just left. He'd ordered breakfast—eggs Benedict and fresh fruit. We'd lingered over coffee, watching wisps of clouds drift in the deep blue sky. Sailboats were heading out of the marina, sails lifting and flapping in the breeze. The wind was blowing gently, about fifteen knots, O'Brien had informed me.

I was learning about O'Brien. His psyche was oriented to the sea. He paid attention to weather—temperature, wind speed and direction, clouds and rain—and he analyzed it in terms of its effect on the water. I couldn't imagine him being happy living more than a heartbeat from the water's edge.

After O'Brien had gone, I'd spread Michael's research notes, books, the photo, and my notes out on the patio table. Missing was that damned diagram.

Times like this always reminded me of when I was a kid. A rainy Saturday, cartoons over, my sister and I bored, we'd dump a thousand-piece puzzle on the kitchen table and begin. It was all a confusion of shapes and colors. She would start with random pieces, trying to fit them together, while I would start analyzing, putting colors together, all the pieces that looked like trees in one corner, red barns in another.

That's what I was trying to do now. I had a bunch of random shapes and colors spread out all over the table. Somehow I knew they were all connected. I found myself resorting to my sister's technique—aimlessly moving pieces around. Stepanopolis, foreman of the *Chikuzen*, the robbery in Saint Martin, the photo of the three men, Michael's death at the *Chikuzen*, his research.

The fact that Michael had borrowed the photo was too much of a coincidence. There had to be a connection to Stepanopolis. How could Michael have known him? He would have been in graduate school in the States when Stepanopolis was killed. Yet Bert Wilson was sure Michael had recognized Stepanopolis. Did that mean that Michael's death was connected to the robbery? Maybe, maybe not.

Maybe the Stepanopolis connection tied to the research. Had Michael found pollutants at the wreck site? Were toxins being stored on that ship? And the wife? Where had she disappeared to? What had happened to the jewels? Washed out to sea? Or hidden somewhere in the maze of a ship for which only Stepanopolis knew the layout, a ship with an unscheduled date with the deep blue? It all seemed a bit fantastic.

What about Arthur Stewart? Harry Acuff? Billy Reardon? Were they stray pieces of another puzzle? Was Acuff a local no-account, just as he appeared, Reardon an opportunist preying on tourists, Stewart a caring father incapable of murder? What about Michael's call to Dunn's office? Why hadn't he left a message? There were too many pieces still missing.

I thumbed through the photos I'd taken during my dive at the *Chikuzen*, studying them for at least the fourth time. There was something about the marks on the compressor that didn't fit. On one side it looked more like scrapes than like a bar had been wedged underneath it. Almost like it had been pushed off the ledge rather than pried loose. Would Michael deliberately have pushed the compressor down to get a look at what was behind it? If he had, it would have been pretty difficult for him to end up underneath it. Had someone pushed it onto him? It was possible that the marks had occurred when they'd recovered the body, but I didn't think so. Carr had said they had tumbled the compressor off the body with a crowbar, which made sense.

I opened the notebook that I'd found on the *Lucky Lady*. I'd picked it up from the evidence room after Dunn had had the boat and its content dusted for prints.

Michael had made hundreds of entries in the notebook at sites all over the BVI. It looked like he would survey an area and move on to the next until the entire region was tested. Then he went back to retest, noting carefully the weather conditions, air temperature, wind direction and speed, water temperature,

water visibility, currents. He also included information on the number of sailboats, dive boats, and
motorboats.

I guessed that he was looking at any short-term
changes that might have correlated with the change in
activities as well as gathering data for the long view,
correlating how water quality looked now as compared to last year and making predictions about the
years to come.

Michael had done the same testing at the *Chikuzen*.
None of the data meant anything to me. Next to the
most recent entries at the *Chikuzen* were notes about
the dead fish, mostly parrot fish, some squirrel fish,
sergeant majors.

*Nothing unusual in water samples. Try testing for other
substances. Talk to Maynard,* it read.

I'd pay another visit to Maynard. He'd never mentioned any discussion with Michael about his
*Chikuzen* data. Maybe it had not been significant.
Maybe Michael had never had the chance to talk with
him. But then, maybe Maynard had something to
hide.

I was on my way out the door when Dunn called.
A body has been found out at Steele Point. From the
description, Dunn said it sounded like Billy Reardon.
He was on his way out there and figured I'd want to
come along.

Ten minutes later he pulled up at the hotel. He
filled me in on the way out to the site. The body lay at
the bottom of a steep, jagged rock formation that
dropped straight into the ocean in places. Evidently
some tourists in a motorboat, trying to get a closer
view of an exotic-looking house that nestled in the
rocks out at the point, had ignored the no-trespassing

signs on the pier and stumbled on the body. They'd thought it was a pile of clothing in the rocks until they had gotten close enough to see the blood.

Steele Point was at the western tip of Tortola not far from Soper's Hole. The house was perched on the tip of the point, with spectacular views from several strategically placed verandas. Wooden steps connected each of the levels of the house and ran to a swimming pool up above.

"Christ, this place must be worth millions," I said.

"Yeah, owned by some famous sculptor." Dunn pointed to where the steps led up the hill. "Up there is his workshop."

Some workshop. It was balanced out over the hill, its windows and verandas providing more expansive ocean views. Surrounding gardens and terraces were filled with frangipani, oleander, hibiscus, and stone sculptures.

"I could handle living here for a while," I said.

"It's sometimes available for rent. For about nine or ten thousand dollars, you could probably stay for a week."

"Right. And maybe I'll win the lottery."

We made our way down the long winding steps that led to a private jetty and swimming deck. The tourists were down the beach, complaining about the fact that they were being detained.

"You Dunn?" one of them asked, cocky and belligerent.

"Yes, I am Chief Dunn."

"Well, Chief," he said sarcastically, "we've been here for two hours waiting for you."

"And you are, sir?" Dunn was really keeping his

cool with this asshole. I had to admire his restraint. I would have been threatening arrest by now.

"Gordon, Gordon Green," the guy said. "Why the hell are we being detained?"

"It's routine, Mr. Green. You did find a body. Don't you think that warrants a bit of your time?"

"Hey, we didn't see anything," Green said. "We were just minding our own business."

"You were trespassing, Mr. Green. If you hadn't gone where you shouldn't have, you wouldn't be standing here now. Just a few questions and you can be on your way."

Green and his cohorts couldn't provide much. They had been fascinated by the house, decided to take a closer look, tied up to the pier, found the body, called the police.

Before letting them go, Dunn gave them a good lecture about privacy and respecting the folks who live in the islands. By the time Green and his friends left, they were duly contrite.

The body was wedged in the rocks, twisted and broken. One leg was bent backward at the hip and under the torso. The head was battered, face bloody, neck clearly broken. It was Reardon.

Next to him, lying in the sand, was my backpack. Dunn picked it up by the strap. It was empty. Scattered nearby were my passport, airline tickets, and empty wallet. We searched the area. The diagram of the *Chikuzen* was simply not there.

"S'pose he could have been drunk, stumbled over the edge," Dunn speculated. "Take someone with some muscle to force a man this size off that cliff."

"Yeah, or he was dead when he went over and dumped here," I said.

Reardon would have been expendable, a local drunk hired to do a job. Maybe they'd argued about his failure to complete his end. Maybe he'd demanded more money.

"Whoever was at the bottom of this would have known that Reardon would be a threat, cause trouble sooner or later," I said. "One good drunk and he'd be bragging about his deed or he'd come back for more money, threaten exposure. If those tourists hadn't been trespassing on the beach, it might have been months before he was found."

We headed back up to the house. It was empty. According to the groundskeeper, who had just arrived from Soper's Hole, no one else had been there for several months.

"Place was pretty well locked up when I left. That front gate was padlocked. It's been forced open," he said. We'd seen the broken lock when we'd driven in. The driveway was about four hundred feet, gravel, and now covered with fresh tire tracks from police vehicles.

"I was up here last week to check on things," he said. "Everything was fine. Haven't been up since. No one using it till next month."

We walked along the edge of the cliff. The terrain was rocky but still managed to be thick with vegetation and trees. It offered plenty of cover yet was too rocky to provide much in the way of footprints. There were some scuff marks in the rock where Reardon must have gone over. Some of the rocks had been dislodged. It looked like there had been a struggle or that Reardon had been dragged to the edge and pushed over.

"My men will be looking for anyone who might

have seen something, but this is a pretty isolated place," Dunn said. "I'll have the medical examiner do the autopsy this afternoon. Should have something by tomorrow."

Before I left, I filled Dunn in on my visit to Saint Martin, my talk with the Wilsons, the jewel heist.

"Jewels?" he asked, incredulous.

Dunn was still processing the information when I left. I caught a ride back into Tortola with one of the deputies as they were hauling Reardon's body up the side of the cliff. He dropped me off at the Environment and Fisheries office. Based on my reception the last time I saw him, I figured Maynard would be pissed when I walked through his door. I wasn't disappointed.

He was on the phone. "Ms. Sampson," he said, covering the receiver. "What brings you here?" I could hear the animosity seething beneath the surface.

"Hoped you could shed some light on some of Michael's data," I said, pulling the notebook out.

"I'll call you later," he said into the phone. "Just get it fixed."

He placed the phone back in its cradle. "These part-timers," he said. "Don't want to expend any effort. Damn boat's been out of commission for days." I wondered why he was explaining all this to me.

"I'm sure there is nothing else I can help you with," he said.

"What about these notes?" I asked. "Is there anything in this data that indicates a problem at the *Chikuzen*? High levels of toxins, that kind of thing?"

He took the notebook and studied the entries for several minutes. "Nothing here too unusual. The levels are pretty much what we would expect for that region."

"Did Michael ever talk to you at all about any concerns at the *Chikuzen*?"

"Mike was studying the reef life. He was concerned about pollution, which, based on these numbers, was not a problem. Just what are you getting at?"

"He's got a note here about talking to you about dead fish," I said, pointing to the entry.

"Yeah, Mike mentioned that to me," he said. "I told him that it was just an aberration. Probably an old battery in the ship that leaked. The data does not indicate a problem with the water quality around the ship."

"Did you conduct your own tests out there?"

"No. Mike actually wanted my office to help him do a complete search of the ship," he said. "I told him it was a waste of time and resources. He decided to go down to Saint Martin to check on the cargo records. I told him it was a wild-goose chase, but what the hell; I guess he could afford it. Parents had all that money."

"I went down there too," I said. "Talked to a guy named Bert Wilson, wife Rose. Michael had talked to them about the *Chikuzen* right before he died. You know them?"

"Now how would I know some old geezers from Saint Martin?" he asked.

"What makes you think they are old?"

He hesitated for a split second. "It's just an expression," he said.

"Michael never mentioned them to you?"

"Look, why would he? We worked on water-quality stuff, not his half-assed notions about some plot to pollute the ocean."

"What do you mean?" I asked.

"Look, he was one of those guys who was always looking for someone to blame when it came to the environment. Fish die, a few fish, some parrot fish, sergeant majors. Christ, ocean's full of 'em. You'd think they were an endangered species or something. Typical academic. Didn't matter whether it was relevant." Maynard's voice had risen an octave and his face grew tighter.

"Isn't it your job? To investigate any environmental concerns?"

"Sure, if it's well-founded. But the department is on a tight budget and my boss looks at expenditures very carefully. This is a government-subsidized operation, after all."

"Why would it bother you that Michael was so insistent about the environment?" I asked. I couldn't understand his attitude. Michael's activities didn't take any funds out of his pocket.

"I got tired of hearing about it," he said, face reddening in anger. "Sticking his nose in where it didn't belong. Just in the damned way."

"In the way? What do you mean?" I could not understand why Maynard was so upset by the fact that Michael had wanted to examine the *Chikuzen* more carefully. "Seems to me that Michael was just pursuing an element of his research. Finding dead fish would be a part of that."

"Just shouldn'ta been going in that wreck," he said. "Guess you can see why."

"Did you know Billy Reardon?" I asked, shifting gears.

"Reardon? Can't say I ever heard of him," he said. "Why?"

"Dunn just found him lying at the bottom of a cliff

near Soper's Hole," I said. "Turns out he was the guy who broke into my room the other night." I was watching for some sort of reaction from Maynard. Surprise, guilt, something. He was either really good or totally uninvolved.

"Yeah, sorry to hear about that. Guess you're no worse for wear, though."

"Do you know if Michael knew Reardon?"

"I wouldn't know," he said. "I told you. I've never heard of this Reardon."

"You ever heard of a Demitri Stepanopolis?" I asked.

"No! Now I've got work," he said, getting up and ushering me to the door.

I was really beginning to feel unwanted. "Thanks, Mr. Maynard," I said sarcastically.

"Look, I'm sorry to be short with you, Ms. Sampson, but I've got other things to worry about besides your investigation."

I wondered just what was more important than a dead colleague.

When I got back to the hotel, I called Mack.

"Sampson. How's things in paradise?" he asked.

"More questions than answers," I said. I told him about being attacked in my room, about finding Reardon dead, and about what I'd discovered in Saint Martin. That I'd been following the same trail that Michael had followed.

"Jeez, Sampson. First you just about drown diving and then you're almost smothered? Maybe I should come down there. You okay?"

"I'll live. Just a few new battle scars."

"You've obviously got someone worried. Think this Reardon was after the diagram?"

"It was the only thing missing when we recovered my backpack at the scene. The question is, Why?"

"Got to be information on it someone wants."

"Yeah. Right now I've got plenty of people who might have wanted Michael dead, but no one who is connected to that diagram. I figure that Michael had it, and someone else wanted it. He took it from the file in Saint Martin, dove the *Chikuzen*, and was killed."

"That's got to be the connection to the break-in up here and Greta's murder. Whoever it was, was looking for that diagram."

"That's what I figure. What about the break-in at Duvall's office? Any leads?"

"Not much," he said. "Duvall's had his people going through all the material in the office. So far nothing appears to be missing. One set of prints doesn't match up with anyone who works in the office. If they belong to the killer, he or she doesn't have a record. The prints are not in the database."

"Anything else?"

"Yeah, guys collected some fibers and hair. Lab says the fibers are blue, synthetic, probably from a sweater. We're following up, but they could have come from anywhere, maybe not even the killer. The hairs are brownish black, about six to eight inches long, and chemically treated."

"Really? A woman?"

"That would be my guess, though a lot of men are coloring their hair these days."

"What about DNA?"

"Lab's pretty sure they will be able to get some from the hair. Be a while. With the hair and the fibers, we'd probably have a couple of good links to the murderer if we had any suspects at all, which we don't."

"Anything on the guy the janitor saw leaving the scene or the bag lady?" I asked.

"The guy checked out," Mack said. "Just one of the employees in a hurry to get to happy hour. No sign of our bag lady. Checked the shelters, been keeping an eye out in the parks, other places the homeless hang out. She's pretty much disappeared. Maybe the murder scared her off."

Before I hung up, I asked him to run a check on Demitri Stepanopolis.

# Chapter 22

❧

"Hannah. I have the autopsy results," Dunn said when I walked into his office the next day. "Looks like Billy Reardon was dead when he went over that cliff. Coroner found a deep puncture wound to his femoral artery that bled out. He was stabbed. Coroner said the wound was small in diameter. Could have been an ice pick. All the other bruises and cuts were postmortem. None of the bleeding that would have occurred had he gone over still alive. Guess he didn't slip, but he did have a high blood-alcohol content."

"Do you think Reardon had any connection to Arthur Stewart?" I asked. It was possible that Stewart was the one who hired Reardon. Maybe he thought I was getting too close to the truth. If he'd had Michael killed, I'd make sure he was exposed, and he knew it.

"No obvious connection," Dunn said, "though if Arthur had hired Reardon, he would have made sure that he would never be connected back to it. Arthur is no dummy. He knows how to protect himself."

"What about Ralph Maynard?" I asked.

"Maynard? Why Maynard?"

"Just a hunch," I said. "He practically booted me out of his office yesterday afternoon."

"Ever think he might just resent the questions?"

"Yeah, maybe."

"I'll be checking on Reardon's associates," Dunn said. "Figured I go up to talk to Clara this afternoon. Not something I'm looking forward to. Want to come along?"

"Yeah," I said, resigned to the fact that I needed to go. "Anything on that piece of pipe?"

"We got lucky. Turns out there is only one shipyard on the island that uses that particular type. Place called Tortola Yacht Repairs. They think it's the best made, tempered steel or something. Thought we could stop there on the way back from Reardon's."

I showed Dunn the photo that the Wilsons had given Michael.

"Michael must have recognized someone in the picture," I said. "Anyone here familiar to you? You ever heard of Stepanopolis?"

We were talking about the jewel theft when Lorna walked in with the final autopsy results and Dunn's lunch.

"Here you go, Chief. Coroner says to tell you there's not much in the report that he didn't already go over with you on the phone. Got you a turkey on whole wheat," she said.

"Lorna, you do take good care of me," he said. "Don't know what I'd do without this woman. She not only runs this office single-handedly, but she keeps me fed!"

"Someone's got to watch out for you when you're not at home." Lorna set the report and lunch on

Dunn's desk. "You ever notice, Ms. Sampson, how helpless some men are?"

I refrained from comment. The only thing worse than a helpless man was a woman who encouraged it, and Lorna encouraged it. She'd obviously made herself indispensable in the office. Good way to ensure a job, I guess.

"I don't recognize anyone here," Dunn said, passing the photo to Lorna. "You recognize anyone, Lorna?"

"No, sir," she said, hardly glancing at the photo and handing it back to Dunn.

"What connection could this photo or Stepanopolis have to Duvall's death?" Dunn asked.

"I don't know, maybe none," I said. "But it seems pretty coincidental that Michael ends up dead in the hold of a ship that he had developed such an intense interest in and that he was carrying around a photo of the man who was once the ship's foreman. A guy who also just happened to have robbed a jewelry store and gotten killed."

"You mind if I take my lunch now, Chief?" Lorna said, interrupting our discussion.

"Course not, Lorna, you go ahead."

I walked out with Lorna, planning on a quick lunch before meeting Dunn back at the office for the trip to the Reardons'. I was not looking forward to seeing Clara Reardon.

"Like to join me for a bite?" she asked.

"Sure," I said. Why not. I figured Lorna knew everything that went on in the islands. No telling what valuable little tidbit she'd pass on.

She suggested a restaurant in an alley off the main street, a hole-in-the-wall crowded with local folks.

Lorna talked nonstop as we stood in line for lunch. She was one of those women who carried on stream-of-consciousness conversations, barely stopping to take a breath. Indicating three women sitting in the corner, she told me about one whose husband had died just last month.

"Already found herself another man!" she said. "How come I'm not that lucky?"

I didn't suggest that it might have something to do with the fact that the woman at the table was drop-dead gorgeous, five-four, a perfect size six, and looked a bit like Halle Berry. Lorna, on the other hand, was a pear-shaped size sixteen, her dark hair in desperate need of a touch-up. Yes, I am a cynic. I believe that most men want drop-dead gorgeous.

By the time we made it to the end of the line, Lorna's tray was overflowing, a half a chicken, heaps of rice, some kind of yellow stuff I couldn't identify, Jell-O, chocolate cake. I opted for a chicken breast and the cake. I've never been known to pass up chocolate.

"Were you ever married?" I asked as we settled at a table in the corner.

"Oh, yes. A no-account man. I left him years ago," she said. "Truth is, I like it just fine not having a man around. I like my freedom, no one around to bother me 'cause dinner's not on the table or 'cause he has no clean underwear. You married?"

"No," I said without explanation. I had no compulsion to tell her my life history.

"Smart. I bet your job keeps you plenty busy too. How is your case going?" she asked.

"It's going."

"You thinking the Duvall boy didn't just drown?"

"Hard to say." I was there to get information, not

give it. And I certainly wasn't about to confide in Lorna. I figured half of Tortola would know the essence of the conversation by the end of the day. I could just envision her picking up the phone the minute she walked back in the office and calling all her friends, swearing them to secrecy, of course.

She kept after it, though, failing to pick up on the fact that I wasn't interested in talking about it.

"Who is this Stepanopolis fella?" she asked.

"Just a name and a face in a photo. I'm sure it's nothing."

"Yeah, I bet you have to follow all kinds of false leads," she said. "Most of the time things are just what they seem. I think that boy just drowned. And I'd bet that Reardon was plain drunk and looking for a good time when he broke into your room. He was always whoring around. Oh, Ms. Sampson, not that he should have thought you were a prospect," she added quickly, blushing.

"How do you know Reardon?"

"Didn't really know him. Just heard things."

"What kind of things?"

"Guy was a bastard. Excuse my French, but he treated his family like dirt. Guess he got what he deserved. I wouldn't be surprised if some jealous boyfriend or husband did him in. He was askin' for it."

"Do you remember talking to Michael Duvall, or a message being on the machine the morning he disappeared?"

"No. I already tole the chief."

"What time did you get into the office?"

"I was in on time that day, just like always. There

weren't no calls." She obviously didn't like my questioning her work ethic.

"Can you think of anyone who would want Michael Duvall dead?" I asked.

"Only one I heard of was Arthur Stewart. I knew what was going on. All those nasty phone messages he left for the chief and trying to get Michael thrown out of the islands. But you ask me, I say the boy drowned. Everybody says so."

"Like who?"

"Well, the chief for one," she said. "And the divers that brought up the body."

"You talked to the divers?"

"Well, sure. I mean 'cause I took down their statements for the file."

"Neither said anything about having doubts that the drowning was accidental?" I remembered Carr saying he wondered how Michael could have gotten trapped under that compressor.

"Naw. They said he was caught in the wreck and he run out of air. Typed it just like they told it."

"Did you tape their statements?"

"No. Don't need to do that. Like I said, I typed it just like they said it. Look at the time," she said, checking her watch. "I'd better get on back to work."

So much for slow-paced island time. Lorna was suddenly in a hurry. She'd managed to inhale her entire meal while we had been talking. Only a bit of chocolate icing remained. She scooped it up with her fingers as she got up and left me sitting with a plateful of food.

"Sorry to rush off and leave you. You should take the rest of the day off," she said. "Go to the beach, relax in the sun. Leave all this nonsense about Michael

Duvall alone and enjoy these beautiful islands." She smiled. "Pretty thing like you should be out showing off that figure in your bikini."

Right, I thought. Anything but stirring up trouble in paradise.

I finished the chocolate cake and went back to Dunn's office for the trip to the Reardons'. Lorna wasn't back yet.

"She gets distracted," Dunn explained, a twinkle in his eye. "Sometimes ends up taking a couple hours for lunch. I've spotted her coming back from the marina. I'm sure it's some fella working down there. Haven't figure out who yet. I don't say much. She does a good job here, and we all be deservin' a bit of afternoon delight. Got to admit to taking a long lunch at home myself once in a while," he said, smiling.

Yeah, I thought, I could handle a little afternoon delight. I wondered what O'Brien was doing at the moment. God, I'd better watch it. I didn't need any complications in my life right now. Complications could be fatal.

# Chapter 23

❧

A big man, shirtless under denim coveralls, was up on the roof tacking new tar paper over the cracks when we pulled up in front of the Reardons'. A stack of shingles lay nearby. He waved and smiled as we walked up to the door where Clara stood, a child in her arms.

"My sister's husband," Clara Reardon explained, inviting us inside. The house had been transformed since our last visit. The kitchen counters were piled with food, and an overstuffed blue sofa and matching chair had been added to the living space. Bethy hid behind her mother, covering her face with Clara's skirt.

"Hello, sweetheart," I said, coaxing her out. "Don't you look pretty."

Her hair was braided close to her head and held in place with pink barrettes. She wore a crisp new purple satin dress with a big bow at the waist. She smiled shyly and twirled, the dress flaring out around her.

"Now that Billy is gone, the family can step in," Dunn whispered as Clara made coffee. "While he was alive, it was considered his responsibility and improper to intrude. Clara and the kids will be a lot better off without him."

But the expectation was gone. They weren't waiting for their father any longer, and the hope that had been in Clara's eyes had been replaced with a kind of dullness.

I couldn't understand it. From all accounts, Reardon had been a terrible husband and father. You'd think she'd be glad to have him gone. Clara Reardon was a nice woman. Maybe that was the problem. Or maybe there was something in Reardon that only she understood.

Clara set the coffee and a plate of oatmeal cookies in the middle of the kitchen table and sat down with us. Out of nowhere, two young boys appeared like bloodhounds and waited quietly behind their mother.

"You can each take one," she said. They each grabbed a cookie and ran out into the yard.

"They're good boys," she said sadly. "Don't know what they will do without their father teaching them about things."

The boys were amazingly polite. Most likely Clara's doing. I wondered if their uncle, the big man on the roof, would step in. He'd be a whole lot better father figure than Reardon had been.

I sat across from Clara, sipping the deep, rich brew and letting Dunn take the lead. Who were Billy's friends, had Arthur Stewart ever come to their house, was Billy upset or worried about anything?

Clara could tell us little more than she had when we first spoke to her. She didn't know Billy's friends—just a bunch of guys who hung out at the bars.

"Was there any place in particular where Billy spent his time?" Dunn asked.

"Place called the Gold Doubloon," Clara said. "Somewhere just outside of Roadtown."

"I know it," he said, getting up. He almost grabbed a cookie on our way out, then held back. I knew what he was thinking—save them for the kids.

When we left, Clara was out hanging laundry, just as she had been doing the first day we'd gone up there. I wondered how much life would change for her. How she'd manage raising seven, soon to be eight, children without a father.

Dunn and I headed back into town and parked out in front of the Gold Doubloon.

"We break up at least one fight here every Saturday night," Dunn said, opening the door.

The place had seen better days. It was dark and smelled of stale beer and cigarettes. The pirate theme had probably once been lavish. Now it was faded. Sabers, a cannon, a battered crow's nest were muted in a layer of dust. An old treasure chest, overflowing with fake gold coins, sat in a prominent place behind the bar, surrounded by liquor bottles.

The bar was empty except for the bartender and a heavyset waitress. She looked as worn and frayed as the décor. Her makeup was layered on thick over a puffy face, mascara so heavy that her eyes sagged.

"Afternoon, Chief. What's your poison?" the bartender asked.

"Just a coupla of questions," Dunn replied.

"Always business, ain't it, Chief?" the woman said, flirting with Dunn.

"I'm afraid so, Mona," he said. "This is Hannah

Sampson, cop from the States. We're doing some checking about Billy Reardon."

"Yeah, I been hearing about you," Mona said. She wanted to know more but knew better than to ask.

"Did you know Reardon?" I asked.

"Sure. Everybody here knew Billy. He was in here most every night, whether he had money or not," she said. "Owes practically everyone comes in. Guess some be pretty upset he dead. Course, there be others glad to see him go."

"Like who?" I asked.

"Like anyone bring his girlfriend in here. Billy put the moves on anything in a skirt. More than one fight when Billy got too much whiskey in him and started up with another man's woman."

"What about in the last couple of days?"

"Last time Billy in here he was braggin' up a storm," she said. "Talkin' about gettin' hisself some money, buyin' everyone in the place drinks. Said he be takin' me upstairs and payin' me real good for my services. I'm a masseuse," she added quickly.

Right, I thought. "Anything else you remember about that night?"

"Well, yeah. I do remember Harry Acuff and Billy gettin' into it," Mona said. "Harry grabbed Billy real rough like. He was mad. He and Billy went out arguing."

"Any idea about what?" Dunn asked.

"Harry was tellin' Billy to keep his damn mouth shut," she said.

"You remember when that was?" I asked.

"Coupla nights ago. Night that steel band was playin'. Real noisy. Damn racket gives me a headache."

"Joe," she said, turning to the bartender. "What night that steel band play?"

"That woulda been Wednesday," he said.

Reardon had been in my hotel room jamming a pillow into my face on Thursday night. By Friday he was dead.

"Let's go talk with Acuff," I said to Dunn.

"Yes," he said. "Just so happens he works over at Tortola Yacht Repairs. Same place that uses that pipe."

Tortola Yacht Repairs was on Wickhams Cay II, just behind the marina. The place was surrounded by chain-link fence. Inside, boats from fifteen-foot speedboats to sixty-foot yachts were perched on trailers or scattered about the yard. Some were for sale; others were in storage or in various stages of repair. A few looked like they would never float again. We found the manager back in his office shuffling a stack of papers.

"Hey, Chief," the man said, getting up from his desk. "What brings you in?"

"Looking for Harry Acuff," Dunn said

"Harry? He didn't show up this mornin'," he said. "My guess, he's nursin' a hangover. Harry shows up when he feels like it, and more times than not he don't feel like it. Could be drinkin' over at the Doubloon, down shooting the shit with one of dem yachties, maybe out fishin'. He does what he damn well pleases. I'd fire him, but he's the best around when it comes to doing the underwater repairs."

Dunn asked him about the pipe.

"Like I told your deputy, we're the only ones that use that particular kind, mostly on the propeller shaft. More expensive but we save in the long run. Nobody coming back to complain or have the job redone."

"Guess Acuff uses that piping all the time when he's working on one of your boats?" I said.

"Sure," he said. "Acuff's the one doing most of the underwater repairs."

It wasn't hard to locate Acuff. He was down the street at the marina. We spotted him as he was climbing out of the water and onto a Department of Fisheries boat.

"Well, if it ain't the chief and Ms. Sampson," he said as he slipped out of his dive gear. "Any more near-death experiences?"

I wondered if he was referring to our dive at the *Chikuzen* or if he had heard about the encounter with Reardon.

"Hello, Harry." Dunn said. "Are you working?"

"Yeah. Damned Maynard's been after me to get this thing fixed. About time they had this ol' girl completely overhauled," he said.

It had probably been Acuff whom Maynard had been chewing out on the phone about getting the boat fixed when I'd been in his office earlier in the day.

"Can you can tell us anything about Billy Reardon?" Dunn asked. "Mona, the waitress down at the Gold Doubloon, said you two had some words the other night. Want to tell me what that was all about?"

"That no-account owed me money and he was in there buying everybody in the place drinks, talking big. I wanted what he owed me before he had it all spent," Acuff said.

"Mona thought you were upset about all his talk," I said.

"Hell, I don't care what he was saying, just about what he was doing. Spending my money."

"You know he's dead," I said.

"Yeah, I heard. Not surprising. Him falling off that cliff."

"Why do you say that?" I asked.

"Hell, he was always drunk," Acuff said, "and a couple of guys at the Doubloon didn't like him much, fooling with their women."

"When did you see him last?" Dunn asked.

"Not since that night at the bar," he said. "Hey, I hope you're not thinking I had anything to do with it. I had no reason. Besides, now I'll never get my money. If there's nothin' else, I need to get back to work."

"Actually, there is something else," I said, fed up with Acuff's attitude. "Remember that piece of pipe I recovered when we dove the wreck a few days ago? Turns out the only place on the entire island that uses that particular piping is the same place you work. Kind of a coincidence, don't you think?"

"Yeah, well, coincidence it were, matey," Acuff said, sneering.

"You want to explain that?" Dunn asked.

"I was out at the *Chikuzen* first part of last month," Acuff said. "We got a radio call from a boat out there having trouble. Said their prop fell off. Couldn't figure out why the boat wouldn't move when they put it in gear. Captain jumped in with his snorkeling gear and saw that the prop was plain gone. Funny, huh? Damn thing was laying in the sand on the bottom. Boss sent me out."

"That doesn't explain how the pipe got in the wreck," I said.

"I probably dropped one when I was working," he said. "Some diver probably picked it up, carried it into the wreck for one thing or another. Hell, it could have been Duvall."

"A lot of probablys and could-haves," I said.

"Yeah, well, shit happens."

Yeah, I thought, especially when Acuff's around. I was thinking about the faulty hose on my regulator that had almost gotten me killed.

"You get the name of the captain of the boat?" I asked.

"Christ, I've fixed a lot of boats between then and now. You expect me to remember the name?" He was starting to get pissed.

"No, Harry, I wouldn't expect you to remember much of anything most of the time," I said.

When Dunn and I left, Acuff was sitting on the side of the boat, lighting up a cigarette. God, he was cocky. I was sure he was up to his ears in Michael Duvall's death.

We headed straight back to Tortola Yacht Repairs. They had to keep records of repairs that had been done, copies of receipts, something. When we got to the office, the manager was still sitting at his desk pushing papers around.

"Man, how am I going to find a receipt without a name?" he asked.

"Don't you keep records by month? Try checking through last month's billings," I suggested.

"This will take some time," he complained. "I'll have to look through every damn bill. Owners are too cheap to fork out for a computer."

"We'll wait," Dunn said, leaning against the wall and crossing his arms.

I took a nearby chair and picked up the only magazine in the office—some sort of "how-to" for boat repairs. Forty-five minutes later, I'd been through the thing three times and pretty much knew how to dismantle the bilge pump on a Hunter 410. Dunn was still leaning against the wall, arms crossed, the epitome of stoicism.

The manager had gone back six months without finding any record of a repair done out at the *Chikuzen*.

"Are your records accurate?" Dunn asked. "Is it possible the paperwork was misplaced or misfiled?"

"Not a chance," he said, clearly insulted.

"So much for coincidence," I said to Dunn as we rode back to my hotel.

"Yes. Looks like Harry's got something to hide. Question is what? I'll check around, let you know."

I didn't like the idea of Acuff running around out there. If he'd been responsible for my faulty equipment and for Reardon's attack on me, he'd be determined to get it right next time.

# Chapter 24

❦

I called Mack when I got back to my room. Damned if I was going to sit around twiddling my thumbs while Dunn tracked down leads on Acuff. Mack should have something by now.

"Hey, Sampson," Mack said as he chewed on some cholesterol-filled tidbit.

"Hi, Mack. Anything else on the break-in at Duvall's office?"

"Nothing since we talked last," he said. "Did come across some interesting stuff on this Stepanopolis you asked me about. He was in the States for a while. He was being investigated for a mob hit in L.A. when he dropped out of sight. Turns out he was connected to a guy named Skip Driscoll. Driscoll was heavily involved in the drug trade and prostitution in L.A."

I could hear Mack shuffling through paper and chewing. "That was ten years ago. No record of Stepanopolis since. Guess he got lost in the islands just long enough to get himself killed stealing $11 million worth of jewels."

"How did he and Driscoll get hooked up?" I asked.

"Let's see. Okay, here it is. Seems Driscoll and

Stepanopolis were related. Wives were sisters name of Maynard, Lorraine and Sandy Maynard."

"Maynard?" I said. "Anything at all about the sisters?"

"Looks like Stepanopolis and his wife disappeared together," Mack said. "Guess the sister is serving time. Caught in a big drug bust. Driscoll was killed."

"Any kids?"

"Driscoll didn't have kids. Looks like Stepanopolis had one son, Ralph Stepanopolis."

"Christ," I said. "I'll call you back."

"He's out," Lorna informed me when I called Dunn's office. "Had business over on the other side of the island near Cane Garden Bay. Said he'd be talking to some people about Harry Acuff while he was over there. Said to tell you he would call you if he found anything important. He'll be back in the office early in the morning, by seven o'clock at the latest. He's got to catch up on all the paperwork that's scattered all over his desk."

"Would you ask him to call me if you talk to him?"

"Sure will," she said, and hung up.

I planned to spend the rest of the day keeping an eye on Maynard. He had to be involved in Michael Duvall's death, he and Acuff. Maynard had to be Stepanopolis's son. He'd probably taken his mother's maiden name to avoid any association with his father.

But there wasn't anything Dunn could do. No real proof. Just because Maynard was the son of the *Chikuzen* foreman, the man who got away with millions in jewelry in a Saint Martin robbery, did not mean Maynard was a murderer. Right. Those jewels had to be hidden on the *Chikuzen*, and Maynard knew it.

Michael Duvall had stumbled across the robbery

when he'd decided to do some background research on the *Chikuzen*, because of the dead fish he'd found there. He'd been spending a lot of time out at the wreck, trying to figure out what had killed the fish. He'd probably run into Maynard and Acuff out there searching for the jewels, queried them about what they were doing. That's what Maynard had meant when he'd said Michael was always sticking his nose in where it didn't belong. Even before Michael went to Saint Martin, Maynard would have been concerned that Michael was suspicious of their activity.

When Michael talked with the Wilsons, he'd recognized something in that photo that tied Demitri Stepanopolis to Ralph Maynard. That's when he'd made the connection to the jewelry heist. He'd stolen the diagram from Vanderpool's office and dived the *Chikuzen* the next morning. But why had he gone out there alone? I had trouble believing he was after the jewels for himself. He just didn't fit the profile. His phone records showed he'd called Dunn that morning. Maybe he intended to let Dunn know what he'd discovered. Why hadn't he left a message? And how had Maynard and Acuff known he'd found that diagram and would be out there diving the site?

Outside the hotel, I found Robert parked in his usual spot at the curb.

"Afternoon," he said. "Where you be wantin' to go? You finally be ready for a tour of the islands? I knows dis place like da back a my hand. I take ya ta Sage Mountain, da botanic gardens, shoppin' downtown, maybe the Bomba Shack? That be one rockin' place. 'Specially during the full-moon party. Guy walks around dere sellin' psilocybin mushrooms, servin' psilocybin tea in the parkin' lot. Course, I be thinkin' dat tea be made mostly of mushrooms dat come right off da supermarket shelf!"

He was disappointed when I told him I couldn't do the tour, but captivated by the idea of a stakeout. Nothing like getting an innocent cabdriver involved. But what the hell. Robert had a car and was available. He got right into the spirit of the thing, finding a place to park where we could see the door to Maynard's office and still be discreet. We sat for an hour, listening to reggae.

At five, Maynard came out and locked the door. We followed him to a little bungalow, where he parked in the dirt drive and went in. Lights went on.

"Diz here detectin' kinda borin', ain't it," Robert said several hours later. "We gonna sit out here all night?"

"Let's give it till midnight, then call it," I said.

An hour later we were harmonizing with Jimmy Cliff, "You can get it if you really want, try and try, try and try, try and try." We were trying to stay awake when a car pulled up. It was Harry Acuff in the blue Honda with the broken headlight.

He got out, stumbled to Maynard's door, and knocked. Maynard was settled in, wearing a robe when he opened the door.

I headed across the lawn for a closer look, trying to move quickly and stay out of sight. The night was warm and scented with blossoms. Crickets chirped in the brush, and I could hear music down the street from one of the roadside shacks that were called bars.

I found an open window that was right above a tangle of bushes loaded with flowers. It was also loaded with thorns. I was definitely not dressed for the occasion, still in shorts and a tank top. By the time

I'd maneuvered to a spot under the window, I was covered in scratches and the bugs were attacking. Desperate, I swatted at one.

"What the hell was that?" Maynard said, moving to the open window. He gazed out, his hands perched on the sill just inches from my head. It seemed like he stood there forever. He was so close I could smell his aftershave—Brut. Figured.

"You're too nervous," Acuff said as a bird flew out from beneath the bush.

"Yeah, well, I've got reason to be." Maynard moved away from the window. "What the hell were you thinking, bringing Reardon in on this? Just luck you were able to pull Sampson into the water before he told her everything. Damned amazing that you got the diagram off of him before you pushed him over that cliff. Did you bring it?"

"I got it in a safe place, Juunioorr," Acuff said, dragging out the *Junior* in long, mocking syllables. "Kind of considering it my insurance policy."

"Cut with the Junior crap. You should have found that diagram after you killed Duvall. You searched his boat. Why the hell didn't you find it then?"

"Who woulda thought he'd stash it in the damned boat cushion?" Acuff said.

"Well, if you had thought, we'd of had those jewels a month ago. We wouldn't have followed those damned boxes to Denver, and for nothin'. Wouldn't have Sampson breathing down our necks now. Couldn't even run her down in the street. And trying to scare her off with that damn stunt diving with her and Constantine just made her more suspicious. Now she's got Dunn checking you out, too. You didn't drink so damn much you'd be able to think straight.

It's been one screw-up after another with you. Leavin' Duvall's body right in the ship, for chrissake."

"I tole you. No way I'm dragging a body out of the water and inta my boat," Acuff said. "No telling who woulda spotted me. 'Sides, I didn't leave no evidence. After I threw that net over him, alls I had to do was wait. Think it was a stroke a genius, prying that compressor loose and pushing it down on him. Looked just like an accident. Everybody knew he was spending a lot of time out there. No reason to suspect anything 'cepting he was diving and got careless."

"Well, Sampson's been back asking me questions," Maynard was saying. "Knows Duvall was snooping around down at Saint Martin. Knows about Demitri. Won't be long she'll be puttin' two and two together. We've got to finish this first thing in the morning. Did you get the boat fixed?"

"Yeah, she's ready. I worked on it all day. Was just finishing up when Sampson and Dunn showed up to give me grief."

"Good. Meet me at the docks at seven o'clock. Be there on time, and lay off the sauce. And bring the fucking diagram."

"I'll bring it, but looks like a buncha nothing on the damned thing. Don't see no X marking the spot. You sure that ol' dad a yours knew what he was doing?"

"He knew."

After Harry left, Maynard made a call. "We're set for the morning. No, he didn't bring the diagram. Christ, you know there's no damned way anyone could figure it out, especially Acuff. I saw the schematic for about a minute when Sampson brought it into my office. It's a jumble of notations in a maze of passageways and compartments. You have to know what to look for. Once we have five minutes to study it, we'll find the jewels. Yes, I know that," he said, irritated. "Don't worry about Acuff. I'll do what I need to do."

God knows who was on the other end of that conversation. I waited under the window, getting eaten alive, until the lights went out. No more phone conversations. Robert and I watched the place for a while longer. Nothing.

I dropped into bed around three in the morning, hoping for a few hours of sleep. Robert promised to be outside my hotel by six A.M. We'd be waiting down at the docks before Maynard got there.

At six-thirty the next morning, Robert and I were hunkered down in his car guzzling coffee and waiting for Maynard. We didn't wait long. He showed up at the dock, followed by Harry Acuff, beer in hand. Acuff looked like he had slept in his clothes.

Before I'd left the hotel, I'd called Dunn's office and left a message on his machine. I'd asked him to meet me down at the docks with a boat and backup. I knew where Maynard and Acuff were headed. Once Dunn arrived, we would go straight to the *Chikuzen*, wait for them to retrieve the jewels, and intercept them when they surfaced.

I called again from a phone booth down the street. The machine picked up again. It was past seven. It seemed Lorna was slacking off.

I asked Robert to stick with the car and keep an eye out for Dunn. I wanted to get a better look at what we would be up against out at the *Chikuzen*.

I slid out of the car and crept around the back of the marine supply store. Off on the left side was a rock jetty, made to protect the harbor from waves. It was basically a pile of rocks about six feet high. They were covered with barnacles and algae, and I slipped several times. By the time I had worked my way out to a place from which I could see Maynard's boat, my shoes were soaked and I'd managed to cut my ankles on the jagged rocks. This jaunt in paradise was really taking its toll. Denver had never been this hazardous.

Just the two of them were on the dock. I could hear Maynard swearing at Acuff as he grabbed a beer can out of his hand and threw it into the water. Not cool. Could have at least put it in the trash.

Maynard carried what looked like a Browning 9mm tucked into his pants. I could see no other weapons. It was just the two of them. They were loading their dive gear and tanks into the boat. Then Acuff started the engine and moved the boat around to the gas pumps, where he began filling it up.

I headed back the way I came, shoes squishing, to wait for Dunn. When he arrived, we'd wait just long enough before going to the wreck to give Maynard and Acuff time to locate the jewels.

Good plan. Too bad it never worked out. I was rounding the corner of the marina store when I caught a blur of green out of the corner of my eye. An instant later something hard crashed into my skull.

# Chapter 25

Black, curious eyes surrounded by white fluff starred down at me. For the second time in a matter of days, my head felt like it was filled with soggy cotton. When I moved, the eyes vanished in a flurry of feathers—a seagull. I was lying in the bottom of a boat on top of a pile of life vests and ropes. I could hear people arguing nearby. When I tried to sit up, pain shot from the top of my head all the way into my chest and I puked all over the deck. This was getting old. I really had to change careers before my brains turned to scrambled eggs.

"Goddammit!" Maynard yelled. "Acuff, throw some water on the deck."

"Let's just shoot the bitch," Acuff said as he drenched me with a bucketful of salt water. "Shoulda shot her back at the marina."

"You're just that stupid. Gunfire would have brought all the yachties in the harbor down on us." There was someone else on the boat. I recognized the voice.

"You two get down there and locate those jewels. I'll be having a little conversation with Ms. Sampson."

As my vision cleared I realized that Dunn probably wasn't going to make it out here.

"That's right, Hannah," the woman said. "Dunn didn't get the message. I did."

Lorna Simms was sitting in the cockpit, dressed in that god-awful lime-green running suit. She held a gun—a .38. It was pointed at my face. We were tied to the mooring at the *Chikuzen*, and Maynard and Acuff were preparing to dive. The diagram of the ship was spread out on a bench.

"Folks used to call me Lorraine Stepanopolis. Simms seems a little less ethnic, don't ya think? Junior here's my boy."

Ralph shot her a look but didn't say anything. I could see that he was afraid of her. It looked like Lorna had not been enjoying quickies down at the marina after all. Too bad. It would have taken the edge off the mean streak. Instead she'd probably been spending her time away from the office plotting with Maynard to recover the jewels.

"So, Junior, is it?" I taunted. "Should have known you didn't have the balls to carry something like this off yourself."

He kicked me hard in the ribs. I doubled over, writhing in pain and trying to protect myself as he prepared to again insert his shoe into my belly. Lorna interceded.

"Just get in the water and bring up those jewels. I'll take care of Ms. Sampson."

Maynard took a final look at the diagram. He had drawn a route on it in red; from the opening in the refrigeration hold it wound through the interior, to a place circled in the galley. Then he and Acuff got in the water and headed down the mooring line to the wreck.

Lorna pulled me up to the seat. I could see that she wanted to talk. I tried to listen to her in spite of all the static emanating from my bruised body.

"He's a lot like his father," Lorna said. "Needs lots of direction. Can't get anything accomplished without me."

"How did Michael end up in the middle of this?" I asked, hoping to forestall the inevitable. She was still pointing the gun at me.

"Duvall called the police department same as you. Chief wasn't in yet. I took the call. He told me everything. What he'd found out in Saint Martin about Junior and the jewel theft. Said he had the diagram. I couldn't believe he'd found it. He wanted the chief to meet him out there. I told him I'd get in touch with Dunn right away. Course, I didn't. Junior was up at Jost Van Dyke, so I sent Acuff," she said. "I got your message this morning, too. It's been real handy being Dunn's little gal Friday.

"Got so he depends on me for everything. I know everything that's going on. It was convenient having Acuff on the recovery team and me in the office writing up the reports for the file. I made sure Carr's suspicions never went anywhere. Course, Acuff knew exactly where to find the body and that there was nothing for Carr to find."

"Were you involved in the jewel robbery with Demitri?"

"Involved?" she said. "Hell, I was the brains. Helped him plan the robbery and made sure he hid those jewels where no one would ever find them. That diagram mapped out every nook and cranny on the ship, and Demitri had labeled every item stored there. It was easy to mark the place he hid those jewels without anyone noticing. You'd have to know the jewels were there and what to look for. Damned if Duvall didn't figure it out." Lorna pointed at the place that Maynard had circled. "Looks like just one more notation, doesn't it?"

"Yeah." It was a tiny outline of a diamond ring, for chrissake. Cute. Michael would have realized what it was only after learning about the jewel robbery at the Wilsons' and then studying the diagram carefully. Just like a good scientist.

"Why didn't you get the diagram?" I asked.

Lorna was dying to tell me how hard things had been. It was easy to keep her talking. I kept scanning the horizon, hoping someone would show up. No one. It was one empty ocean.

"I thought that Demitri had the diagram on him when he was killed. When the cops never found it, I was sure it had ended up in the water. I still don't know when he hid it in the file at the port authority. Damn Demitri. He never told me he'd be putting it there. You'd think he didn't trust me or something."

"Yeah, you'd think." Obviously Demitri was well acquainted with his wife's ruthless tendencies.

"No one ever gave that file a second look after the ship was hauled out of port until Michael Duvall," she said.

"How did you expect to find the jewels without the diagram?"

"After Demitri was killed, I figured I'd wait for things to cool down. Then I'd search that ship every night until I found them. He'd told me he would find a place in the galley or crew's quarters somewhere.

But I never had the chance to even step foot on the ship. That hurricane headed toward us and they towed the ship out before I even knew what was happening. Just my luck. Not a damn thing I could do."

"Until now?"

"That's right. When I heard where she'd sunk, I moved up here. Got the job with the chief when his secretary came down real sick all of a sudden," she said, smirking.

I didn't give her the satisfaction of asking for details.

"I tried to find the jewels before Ralph got here," she said. "Brought in a fellow who could dive. Had to kill him when he decided he could find them and keep them all for himself. Funny how folks underestimate a woman like me. Would never think I could get the best of him or put a bullet through him. Guy actually laughed in my face. I shot him in the leg first so's he could see it coming. Then I walked right up to him and put that gun between his eyes and watched that smirk turn to pure terror before I pulled the trigger. Demitri always said to keep it in the family. Well, after that I decided he was right.

"If those batteries hadn't started leaking, Duvall wouldn't have gotten on to us. Demitri put anything on that ship that he damned well pleased. Always trying to make a buck, taking old batteries, huge cans of hazardous waste. Anything anyone wanted off their hands, he'd store on the ship for a price. Just about ruined everything. Duvall was always out at the wreck, testing, trying to figure out why those fish died. Started to get suspicious about Junior and Acuff diving out there all the time. Then he goes to Saint Martin and talks to Rose. Damn Rose. Once she started talking, it was all over. That photo, though. Don't know what he saw in that picture."

"It was the medal," I said. I'd noticed it as Maynard was suiting up to dive. "Probably not another one like it. Michael would have seen it every time he and Ralph dove together."

"Course," she said. "Ralph never takes that thing off. Says it's his good-luck charm. Only thing left of his daddy's. Guess it's not so lucky after all. But that Duvall boy did find the diagram for us. Without it, we'd probably never have found those jewels. Junior and Acuff have been combing that damned ship, but it's huge and turned all topsy-turvy now."

"Why didn't Acuff wait for Michael to find the jewels before he killed him?"

"Acuff's not real creative. I'd told him Duvall would be out at the *Chikuzen* waiting for Dunn. He was supposed to go out there, kill Duvall, and get the diagram. But when he got there, Duvall wasn't on his boat. He was in the water diving the wreck. Acuff panicked and went in after him. When Duvall spotted him, Acuff killed him. Unfortunately, Duvall had not yet found the jewels."

"And then Acuff couldn't find the diagram."

"That's right. When Acuff didn't find it on Duvall's boat, we were sure it had been shipped back to the States in Duvall's effects. I couldn't believe it. First the ship ends up here; then the diagram ends up in the States."

"You arranged the break-in at Duvall's father's office?"

"I went myself. Only way to get it done right. Told Dunn my sister was real sick, had to go up to Denver to see her. Damn secretary nearly scared me to death coming out of that file room. Thought everyone was gone for the weekend. She saw me, thought I was some old bag lady wandered into the wrong office."

Of course, Lorna was the homeless woman who had been sitting outside George Duvall's office. Not panhandling but waiting for the boxes to be delivered. So much for sick sisters.

"I tore those boxes apart and grabbed a couple of the files to check more carefully later. The diagram wasn't there. I froze my ass off in front of that office for nothin'," she said, dismayed by her continued bad luck. "Then you came down here and found it for us. Probably woulda been hidden in that cushion for years. We really appreciated your help. About time things turned my way after going so wrong for so long."

I could tell Lorna was winding down. She was through talking, and damned if I could come up with another inane question. I should have asked her how she'd poisoned the secretary.

"You know I hate to kill you, Hannah. I kind of like you. Remind me of myself when I was young. You don't take any grief from anybody. Thing is, you're real persistent. And Acuff—too stupid to run you down, or drown you, or even get Reardon to kill you. I knew you were trouble the minute you walked into Dunn's office."

God knows how I was going to get out of this. I was on a boat in the middle of the ocean with a woman who had just admitted to killing two people pointing a .38 at my chest. Had Robert thought anything about my failure to return? I clung to the hope that he had notified Dunn. But there was still no sign of any boats.

Just then Ralph surfaced. Acuff didn't follow.

"Did you get them?" Lorna asked.

"Yeah!" he said, lifting the bag up to her and climbing into the boat.

"Finally! Guess it was worth the wait," she said, never once taking the gun or her eyes off of me as she dumped the contents of the bag on the deck. A fortune in diamonds and emeralds lay glistening in the sun.

"Now, that there is a beautiful sight," she said. "You took care of Acuff?"

"Sure did. He never saw it coming. Got him as we came up the mooring line. Left him dead and bloody on the bottom. Sharks and fish will take care of him," he said, removing his gear. "Why haven't you taken care of her?"

"Just a bit of fun and company till you got back," she said. "Guess that's about it, though, Hannah. Want to take it in the face or in the back of the head?"

"Very considerate," I said. I was running out of options.

"Least I can do," she said. "You finding that diagram for us and all."

I raised my hands, moved to the side of the boat, and turned slowly to take one last look at the sun-drenched sea.

# Chapter 26

⌇

I had one choice. I jumped. Bullets streaked by me as I dove beneath the surface. Lorna was reloading when I came up behind the mooring ball. I was a sitting duck.

"Ain't got nowhere to go, Hannah. I'm sorry I've got to shoot you," she yelled, taking aim.

A bullet plunged into the mooring ball, a sickening thud into hard foam just inches from my skull. Maynard was maneuvering the boat around for a better shot. I kept the mooring ball in front of me as he swung the boat around, grasping the line that held it to the bottom and treading water. Another thud and a chunk of hard Styrofoam stung my cheek. I tasted blood. A couple more well-placed bullets and the ball would be reduced to shreds. Lorna was right: I had no place to go. I was alone in the middle of the ocean, not another boat in sight, and in a few minutes my only protection would be floating in pieces around me. I took in as much air as my lungs could hold and dived.

Acuff's body had to be right below me, at the bottom of the mooring line. How far down? At least fifty feet, more like sixty or seventy. My only chance was to get to his air tanks. I was pretty sure I could make fifty, but seventy? I would have to be good.

I grabbed the mooring rope and pulled myself down hard, hand over hand, eyes closed against the sting of salty brine, clearing my ears quickly between pulls. I developed a rhythm—pull, pull, clear; pull, pull, clear. I tried not to think, not to panic. Something big brushed against me. Shark? Barracuda? Had Harry's blood already drawn a host of predators? I kept my eyes closed and kept going, down, down. I'd done plenty of dives in dark, murky water. I could do this. God knows it was all I could do, my only chance to survive. Definitely a long shot.

I was beginning to lose my sense of time and space. I had no idea how deep I was or how far it was to the bottom. My lungs were bursting, and the deeper I got the more my body craved oxygen. It took every ounce of will to keep pulling on the line.

Suddenly I hit bottom. I opened my eyes. No body. Where was he? I was beginning to feel panic take over. I shut my eyes against the stinging salt, and forced myself to take control. I felt around me and touched something soft. Acuff. Lying right behind me.

I ran my hands across his body, locating the air hose. I followed it up to his head and ripped the regulator out of his mouth, jammed it into my mouth, and sucked in. The remnants of panic subsided as the relief of that breath filled my lungs. I would live a little while longer.

I sat on the sandy bottom breathing, trying to regain my equilibrium. Then I slipped off Acuff's face mask, snugged it on my face, tipped my head back, and blew air into the mask to clear the water out of it.

Next I retrieved his vest and tank and snapped them around my body.

Acuff had several gaping wounds in his chest, and the water around him was tinged pink. Three or four sharks were darting around the periphery. I pulled on his fins, grabbed the knife he had strapped to his ankle, and got out of there. When I looked back the sharks were tearing him apart. A couple of them were fighting over the torso. Another was swimming away with an arm hanging from its mouth. I felt my throat constrict and I stifled a sob. Acuff had been a nasty human being, but he had been human. Now he was reduced to a meal. I pulled my mind away from the horror. I had to figure out what to do next.

I could see Maynard's boat circling above, waiting for me to surface. By now they would have seen my bubbles and realized I'd gotten to Acuff. They weren't about to let me go. They knew I could survive in these warm Caribbean waters for hours, and that a fisherman or recreational craft would come by eventually. And they knew I would track them down.

I wasn't surprised when Maynard jumped in. He would have put on a fresh tank and have more air than I had.

Maynard carried a spear gun, and he would also have a knife. He definitely had the advantage. He hadn't been injured and he knew his way around down here.

I swam for the wreck, the only place that offered any protection at all on this otherwise sandy and barren bottom. When I looked behind me, Maynard was just a few feet back, spear gun in one hand, knife in the other. He was on top of me before I knew it. He grabbed my ankle and yanked me into him, grasping me hard around the waist. It felt as though a stake had been plunged into my damaged rib cage. I fought to ignore it. If I didn't, I knew I'd end up bleeding in the sand. Maynard was in the process of lifting the knife for the final deadly plunge into my chest. Before he had the chance, I wrenched the regulator from his mouth. He immediately released his grip, but recovered his regulator and was coming at me again before I had a chance to do anything but retreat. I got the hell away, swimming hard.

When I glanced back, he was behind me, spear gun raised. I turned and the instant he fired, I darted into the nearby refrigeration hold.

Big mistake. I knew it the minute I got inside. I thought about swimming back into the bowels of the ship, but quickly ruled it out. No doubt Maynard knew his way around the wreck as well as Acuff had. After all, he had spent hours inside over the past months, looking for the lost jewels. He'd trap me back in the wreck and then all he'd need to do was wait until I ran out of air. I was backed into a dead end. He'd be coming in right behind me, and I'd be easy to find. Even in the dim light, he'd be able to locate my bubbles.

I had to do something and do it fast. One utterly reckless plan emerged. I removed my gear, took one last gulp of air, and left the tank with the regulator gushing air in the dark corner of the hold. Then I swam back to the opening, crouched against the wall, and waited, Acuff's knife in hand.

Maynard came through the opening just seconds later. He stopped, got his bearings, and cleared his mask. Damn, was he coming in or not? I figured I could hold my breath for another minute, minute and a half max. Then I'd have to make a dash for the surface. I knew I'd never make it past him.

Finally he saw the bubbles and swam past me toward them. I moved quickly through the space between us, a prayer to the sea gods running through my brain—Don't let him turn around; don't let him turn around. He didn't.

By the time he realized what I'd done, I was on him. I knew I had one chance. Frantic, I grasped his regulator hose and sliced through it with one desperate stroke. I figured that without air, he would head straight to the surface, but Maynard was enraged. I could see murder in his eyes. Killing me was his only objective.

He came at me like a maniac. Right before he grabbed me, I managed to snatch air from one of the huge bubbles that were breaking right into my face from his cut hose. It bought me some time. Neither one of us could last much longer without our air supply. But Maynard was relentless. He held me down on the bottom, all his weight pressed into my chest. It had been several minutes since I had abandoned my tank, and the brief gulp from the air bubble was diminishing rapidly. I felt smothered. Terror was about to take over. Christ, I was about to die in this steel tomb.

I still had the knife in my hand, but my arm was wedged beneath him. I could see him smiling behind his mask, watching me weaken, the struggle ebbing from my body. He knew it would be over soon. Convinced that he had won the battle and air-starved himself, he made a mistake. He shifted his weight. In that instant, I managed to free my arm, and in a last-ditch effort to survive, I pushed the knife into his belly. For a moment he hung on, confused. Then he released his grip and sank to the bottom of the hold.

I somehow managed to grope my way back to my regulator and fumbled the mouthpiece between my lips. I gasped into it, pulling hard. Rasping, choking on the dry air, I couldn't breathe fast enough. Relief flooded every cell along with the precious oxygen. I leaned back against the steel hull, exhausted, too drained, both physically and mentally, to move.

I could see Maynard lying in water a few feet away. If he was still alive, he wouldn't last long. I took a few long, slow breaths and forced myself up.

I grabbed the handle on the back of Maynard's vest and pulled him out of the hold. In the open water, I released his weight belt, filled his vest with air, and sent him to the surface. I figured that once Lorna saw him, she'd haul him into the boat.

I would try to wait it out on bottom, now the safest place to be. Lorna was no diver. She couldn't come in after me herself, and with Maynard hurt or dead, I hoped she'd get her ass out of there. Besides, she had what she'd come for—a sack full of diamonds and emeralds.

I settled on the sandy bottom, sitting Indian fashion, trying to conserve my air. My gauge was in the red zone. Maybe five minutes of air left. Maybe less. The sharks had disappeared into the deep, off digesting Acuff somewhere more private. I heard Lorna start the boat, but before she could put it in gear, another boat came alongside.

Slowly I made my way back up the line to the mooring ball. When I surfaced, I could see the chief, Rasta Robert, and O'Brien on the police boat anxiously scanning the water. Lorna was in the back leaning over Maynard.

Robert saw me first. He started jumping up and down, pointing and yelling. Recognition, then relief, spread across their faces. O'Brien leaned against the rail and smiled. I waved, tried to smile back, but damn, I was tired.

# Chapter 27

Dunn, O'Brien, and I sat at a table at the Treasure Chest watching the sun flame into the water. We had just finished eating—Mai Mai, accompanied by Heinekens. Dunn's treat.

He'd been a good loser. But then, I hadn't rubbed it in—much. Dunn had been shocked at Lorna's involvement and a little embarrassed that he hadn't picked up on it. Never questioned her background, her long lunches, or her sudden trip to the States.

But Lorna had been good. She'd set herself up as the sweet motherly type, and made herself invaluable to Dunn. There was no reason to suspect her. She'd been rude when I'd first encountered her on the plane, but then she'd probably been a bit out of sorts. After all, she'd just flown all the way to Denver, had to hang out on the street in the snow waiting for those boxes to arrive, killed someone, and been on her way back without the diagram. No wonder she'd been cranky.

She'd be in jail for a long time, maybe the rest of her life. She'd be convicted of at least one murder—Greta's. Her fingerprints matched the unidentified prints in Duvall's office, the results of the DNA test indicated the hair found at the scene was hers, and her gun matched the bullet recovered from Greta's body. As far as the guy she had brought on to help her recover the jewels and then killed and dumped in the ocean, little proof existed to connect her, and there was no body.

Acuff had killed both Michael and Billy Reardon. Lorna and Maynard would be tried as accessories in those deaths as well as for Acuff's murder and the attempt on my life. Maynard had managed to survive and was recuperating in the local hospital. He'd be out in time to stand trial.

I'd helped with the cleanup out at the *Chikuzen*. Edmund Carr, other members of the BVI Search and Rescue team, James Constantine, a couple of other concerned divers, and O'Brien had all teamed up to remove the poisonous waste that Stepanopolis had hidden in the ship.

Maynard had actually been right about the corroded batteries. The cadmium that had leaked out had killed the fish swimming in the area, then dissolved quickly to become harmless. There were about two hundred more on the verge of doing the same thing. And that was the least of it. Hundreds of cans and fifty-gallon barrels of hazardous waste were packed in the deepest compartments of the ship. Their contents ranged from DDT to what was finally determined to be waste from a chemical plant.

Stepanopolis had found a way to provide a steady supply of cash, until he got more ambitious and robbed that store. If Michael hadn't noticed the dead fish, the pollutants would have gone undetected until it was too late, and Maynard and Lorna would have gotten away with millions in jewels. I'd explained it all to George and Caroline Duvall. I don't think it was much comfort. A high price to pay—their son's life.

The toxic spill would have been minor compared to what occurs in the ocean every day, thousands of gallons of oil from freighters, DDT washed into rivers and out to sea from agriculture, human waste running from sewers untreated into the sea.

But I was glad to help. Somewhere along the way I had gotten hooked. It had taken only a week of diving in this spectacular environment. The cacophony of color, the richness of life was so overwhelming that it was difficult to comprehend. I was only beginning to see it. Worms that looked like soft, flowering featherdusters; sea slugs that resembled blue-, yellow-, and red-tinged pieces of leaf lettuce with antennae; moon jellies, their blue and pink domes fringed with delicate tentacles; crabs only an inch long that looked like tiny sticks perched on soft coral. The fact that these creatures could be destroyed gave me just one more reason to be angry. Not that I needed one.

Before I headed back to Denver, I went to see Lydia. There was still something I didn't understand.

"Why do you think that Michael dived the wreck alone that morning instead of waiting for Dunn?" Lydia and I were on her patio, sipping iced tea.

"You had to know Michael," she said. "He'd have waited about ten minutes and then decided to go down into the *Chikuzen*, retrieve the jewels, and be lounging on the *Lucky Lady* when Dunn arrived. I told you—Michael was driven with the need to solve difficult problems, to be the one to find answers. And he was fearless. He thought he'd live forever."

I remembered feeling the same way once. Even now, I take risks that I shouldn't. I could understand how Michael thought. I left Lydia sitting on the veranda and headed to the airport.

I planned to be in Denver only long enough to get my dog and put in for an extended leave at the police department. Then I'd return to the islands. Dunn had actually offered me a job. With the growth in tourism and the inevitable increase in crime, he needed someone with solid investigative and diving experience. I was considering it. Besides, I needed more time with O'Brien to figure out whether the relationship was going to go anywhere at all.

I called Mack from the airport to let him know when I'd be in and that I was going to come back down to the islands for a while.

"Jeez, Sampson, you mean to tell me you've started worrying about snails and sea slugs, for chrissake?"

"Well, come on, Mack. It's paradise—no snow, unbelievable diving, hardly any concrete, and almost no TV reception. People actually take the time to stop and talk when they meet you on the sidewalk, and almost nobody has a cell phone stuck to their ear." I didn't mention O'Brien and great sex under moonlit sails. Neither did I admit that it might be a place to reflect, maybe forgive myself and move on.

# AUTHOR'S NOTE

For information about coral reefs and how to protect them, go to:

The Association of Reef Keepers:
http://www.arkbvi.org/frames_ie.htm

The Coral Reef Alliance:
http://www.coralreefalliance.org

Green Reef:
http://www.greenreefbelize.com

ReefGuardian International:
http://www.reefguardian.org

Reef Relief:
http://www.reefrelief.org/main.html

～

To the best of my knowledge, the facts surrounding the sinking of the *Chikuzen* are accurate except for the date. The ship went down in 1981.

SIGNET

# COMING IN NOVEMBER 2003
# FROM SIGNET MYSTERY

### THE DEVIL'S HIGHWAY
### *A Mystery of Georgian England*
by Hannah March                    0-451-21071-9

Traveling to his new employer's country home, private
tutor Robert Fairfax discovers a tipped stagecoach—and
the dead bodies within it. But this is more than a
robbery. And the victims are not who they appear to be.

### MURDER OF A BARBIE AND KEN
### *A Scumble River Mystery*
by Denise Swanson                  0-451-21072-7

Skye joins Scumble River's social club and ends up
at a party at the home of socialites Barbie and Ken
Addison. But not long after, Skye gets caught up in a
murder mystery when she finds the perfect couple,
perfectly dead.

**Available wherever books are sold, or
to order call: 1-800-788-6262**